CW01209632

# DAYBREAK

TSEZAR BRATVA DUET (BOOK TWO)

NICOLE FOX

Copyright © 2019 by Nicole Fox

All rights reserved.

No part of this book may be reproduced in any form or by any electronic or mechanical means, including information storage and retrieval systems, without written permission from the author, except for the use of brief quotations in a book review.

Created with Vellum

# MAILING LIST

Sign up to my mailing list!
New subscribers receive a FREE steamy bad boy romance novel.

**Click the link below to join.**
https://readerlinks.com/l/1057996

## ALSO BY NICOLE FOX

**De Maggio Mafia Duet**

Devil in a Suit (Book 1)

Devil at the Altar (Book 2)

**Kornilov Bratva Duet**

Married to the Don (Book 1)

Til Death Do Us Part (Book 2)

**Volkov Bratva**

Broken Vows (Book 1)

Broken Hope (Book 2)

Broken Sins *(standalone)*

**Heirs to the Bratva Empire**

**Can be read in any order*

Kostya

Maksim

Andrei

**Tsezar Bratva**

Nightfall (Book 1)

Daybreak (Book 2)

**Russian Crime Brotherhood**

**Can be read in any order*

Owned by the Mob Boss

Unprotected with the Mob Boss

Knocked Up by the Mob Boss

Sold to the Mob Boss

Stolen by the Mob Boss

Trapped with the Mob Boss

**Other Standalones**

Vin: A Mafia Romance

**Box Sets**

Bratva Mob Bosses (Russian Crime Brotherhood Books 1-6)

Tsezar Bratva (Tsezar Bratva Duet Books 1-2)

## DAYBREAK

TSEZAR BRATVA

**He gave me a chance at happily ever after. And then he snatched it all away.**

COURTNEY

Did the man of my dreams sell me to the monster of my nightmares?

I don't want to believe it.

But no matter how hard I pinch myself, the horrors won't go away.

The facts are this:

I'm locked on a ship with my daughters, bound for a slave auction half a world away.

I'm surrounded by killers. Imprisoned by a psychopath.

And Dmitry is nowhere to be found.

All I have left is one desperate hope:

Will my husband come to save us?

Or was our love a lie all along?

# 1

# DMITRY

I feel the pain in my hip before I can even open my eyes.

The pain may be what woke me up in the first place.

It is a throbbing, piercing kind of pain that radiates from my hip into my chest and down my thigh. I groan as I shift my leg out from underneath me. My foot prickles like a thousand needles being poked into my skin as blood finally rushes to it.

Where am I?

My vision is blurred, my eyes heavy as I blink against the dim light coming through the window. It's too dark to be daylight outside, so it must be the glare from the security light above the garage.

Which means ...

It takes me several seconds to realize I'm in Olivia's nursery ... on the floor.

Then, several seconds more to remember what happened.

The room is empty now except for me, but as the memories resurface, I can see Devon sitting in the rocking chair holding Olivia in the same way I always hold her to rock her to sleep. I turn to the crib. I can still see the curled indentation of where Tati lay in her sister's bed, put there by Devon or one of his Yakuza minions, no doubt.

And Courtney.

She was battered and lying on the floor only a few feet away.

Devon had knocked her unconscious.

How hard did she fight to protect her girls? Our girls?

Did she wonder why I left? Why I wasn't there to help?

I push myself upright and try to walk, but I have to stumble forward and grip the doorframe to keep from falling.

"Hello?" My voice is little more than a rasp, and I cough to try and clear it.

Whatever drug they injected me with, the effects are slow to fade. The hallway tilts and whirls with every blink. I feel like I'm walking through a fun house, though there is nothing at all fun about this experience.

"Hello?" I call again, my voice stronger this time.

For years, I was accustomed to no one answering my calls. When I'd stub my toe and curse or drop the bottle of shampoo in the shower, no one would hear the noise and come to check on me. But then Courtney came into my life and there was someone to care.

Someone to respond.

Courtney brought companionship into my life in a way I never knew I needed it. Our relationship began as nothing more than sex to cover her father's debts, but she slowly became more important to me. Vital. Essential to my happiness.

She adopted Tati as her own daughter and then gave me another.

And with Courtney, Tati, and Olivia in my life, I felt needed. I felt cared for.

And in this moment—calling for them and hearing nothing in return—I realize I've taken them all for granted.

Tati's ballet shoes are piled in the corner of the hallway, and Olivia's favorite teething ring is sitting in the middle of the floor where she likely dropped it while Courtney carried her to bed. I can still smell the vanilla scent of Courtney's bodywash coming from under the bathroom door.

Evidence of them is everywhere, yet I'm met with silence. Unending silence.

"Hello!" I scream, pushing my voice to the extreme until it breaks.

When I'm met with nothing but echoes, my strength gives out, and I fall to the floor.

My knees crack against the floor, and I press my hands into the carpet and take deep breaths. Slowly, the desperate pain shifts into rage. Achingly slowly, I find the strength to stand up and move forward, walking through my now empty house. Knowing my family has been taken.

Since no one responded to my shouts for help, I'm not surprised when I make it to the guard room downstairs and discover they're dead.

The guards were probably dead before my car even left the driveway. My family was no doubt being attacked while I sat in Elena's living room, attempting to offer her money she neither needed nor deserved. And for what?

Honor?

Fuck honor.

What good is honor when my family is gone?

I wish I'd killed them all. I wish that after finishing Rurik, I'd tracked down his family and murdered them all. That's what you do with a diseased plant—pull it up, root and stem.

Instead, I took the merciful approach. I allowed Elena to carry on living, and then I allowed myself to be lured into a false sense of security. Since it had been over a year, I assumed my worries were over. I assumed all was well.

I'm a fucking idiot.

I slam the door shut on the guard room and then slam my fist into the wall.

Pain erupts in my knuckles, and I curse, the word echoing off the high ceiling. It does nothing to make me feel better.

Emotion is what got me into this mess in the first place.

Compassion, guilt, shame—all of it weakened my ability to care for my family in the way I needed to. So, if emotion got me into this mess, it won't get me out.

I shake my hand out, slightly easing the pulsating pain in my knuckles, and take a deep breath.

My family is gone.

I push away the stab of emotion that threatens to split me open and focus on the fact.

My guards are dead.

Rage flares my nostrils, but I breathe it away.

I'm alone in my house with no idea where anyone is.

After acknowledging that fact, there is no emotion, but there is a path forward. It's a problem I can solve.

I spin away from the guard room and jog into the kitchen. It looks shockingly ordinary compared to the bloody scene in the guard room only feet away. I sit down and pull my phone out of my pocket.

One by one, I call my lieutenants—the men I can trust. I tell them to get to my house now.

~

My men are angry.

Many of them are not my blood family, but they love Courtney and Tati and Olivia as their own. They have sworn to protect me and my family, and like me, they are frustrated to have failed them.

The guards in the guard room are removed, but nothing is cleaned. Every inch of the house is searched and inspected.

Devon clearly got in through the sliding glass door that opens onto the large deck. The lock is broken and the door is halfway open. After that, his Yakuza lackeys took out the guards and attacked my family.

As the events are laid out before me, rage thrashes against the wall I've built around my heart, like a wild animal desperate to escape and kill. But I keep it in.

I've failed my family. I've failed to protect my family in full view of my men, and if they see me lose my wits, I will have lost all of my dignity. There will be no coming back from it.

So, I keep it in. For my girls more than for myself. I will need the help of my men if I want any chance of getting them back.

The realization that there is a possibility I won't get them back awakens the beast in my chest again, and I have to close my eyes and breathe deeply to keep from kicking through a wall. I stand in the dining room, eyes closed and breathing, until Pasha finds me.

"We found this in Tati's room," he says.

I open my eyes, and he is holding an envelope out to me, his hand shaking slightly.

I recognize it as the money I left for Elena. It's the reason I was away from my family in the first place, and now it's in my house.

I snatch it out of his hand and tear it open as though Elena might be hiding inside.

All of the money is still there. I don't need to count it to know. She returned every penny that I gave her. But why? Why bother? The money is a small enough amount to make no difference to me, and she clearly doesn't need it. Why not just throw it away? Or use it. That would be adding insult to injury. Kidnap my family and use the money I generously and idiotically gave her.

Then, I see it. Tucked in the back of the envelope between a few of the bills is a small picture.

It's me and Courtney and our girls out on the beach. We are smiling and playing. Tati is throwing sand in the air like confetti, and Courtney is shielding the baby's head and laughing. I'm rushing towards Tati, arms wide to scoop her up and throw her in the air.

Every face but mine is crossed through with a red 'X.'

It's a childish thing to do. A move so simple and mocking as to be almost stereotypical, and yet ... it shakes me. Seeing my beautiful girls' faces slashed through brings a wave of panic down over me so strong my vision blurs at the edges.

"Do you recognize the picture?" Pasha asks, pulling me from the breakdown just in time.

I narrow my eyes, trying to see beyond the violent red scratches in the picture. I recognize the red swimsuit Courtney is wearing. Later that afternoon, when the girls went down for a nap, I peeled it off her with my teeth. We made love in the walk-in shower until the floor was covered with sand and the water ran cold. It was a beautiful day.

But we didn't take any pictures.

The photograph is taken from further up the beach and we are blurry, as though the photographer zoomed in a good deal before snapping the shot.

"We were watched." I throw the picture on the floor, letting it slide across the tile and land under the table. "They were watching my house—my family—and I didn't know."

"None of us did," Pasha says, laying a hand on my shoulder. "We all failed them."

The emotion I've locked deep inside bubbles to the surface again, but this time it's gratitude.

Still, like the rage, I push it away. Letting anything through puts me at risk of letting it all through.

I step away from Pasha's comfort, and he lets his arm fall.

"We need to go back to Elena's."

Pasha nods and turns to deliver my message to the other men.

I know she won't be there. Taking my family there to hide would be the dumbest, most obvious move, and as much as I wish it wasn't true, Elena is smart. She and Rurik arranged all of this. They kept their son a secret for years so he could be used as a pawn against me. Even with Rurik no longer at the reins, I know Elena would never take my family back to the house where she first laid bare the plans she had for me.

Still, I'm disappointed when I pull up out front, parking in the same space I parked only hours before, and see the house is dark.

The windows are blank and gaping like black holes. No movement inside.

I kick down the door and the alarm system doesn't even trigger.

There are no security measures put into place. No guards. No effort taken to keep anyone outside, which means there is nothing important inside.

The furniture is there. Art is on the walls. There is even a pair of shoes next to the door.

But no Elena.

No Devon.

No Courtney, Tati, or Olivia.

My men search the house the way they did mine, investigating every possible hiding place to ensure there are no traps, no tricks, no stones left unturned.

When they return, someone hands me a baby sock. It's white with pink on the toes and heel. Olivia's.

She was here.

At one point, my family was here, and now they're gone.

Something bubbles up inside of me again, but this time, it isn't emotion. It's nausea.

I turn and walk out of the house, the sock pinched between my fingers, and stumble back to my car.

I shut the door, throw the seat back, and take deep breaths as I stare up at the roof.

I'm too many steps behind. Elena and Devon are moving quickly. My family is in their control right now, and I have no idea where they have been taken. No idea how to find them. No idea what to do next.

The list of things I don't know crushes down on me until I can't inhale a whole breath. I'm so focused on breathing and getting oxygen to my brain that I don't hear the passenger door open. I don't even know anyone is there until someone's throat clears.

I look over and see Yorik.

He is only in his mid-forties, but there are thick patches of gray at his temples and throughout his beard. Laugh lines crinkle around his eyes, and I realize this is the first time in a long time I've seen him without a smile on his face.

Usually, his unfailing happiness annoys me. Now, the absence of it spills dread in my chest.

"You don't have to run away from us," he says gently, his eyes on my face.

I turn away and stare out the window, hoping he'll do the same, but he doesn't.

"You lost your family, and we all understand. We all want to help."

Yorik has a wife and two sons. He has been married since he was nineteen. If anyone can understand what I'm going through right now, it is him.

"I know you are losing your shit right now," he continues. "I know this is the shittiest thing that has ever happened to you. We all understand that, and we want to help."

"You keep saying that," I bark.

"Because it's true." His voice is calm and even. It would be soothing, if only his words could penetrate the wall around my heart. "Emotion does not make you weak. Your father believed that, but I know you don't. We all know how much you love your family, and when that kind of love can be channeled into action, nothing in the world is stronger."

I consider his words; consider my desire to bring vengeance down on the heads of anyone responsible for taking my family. I know he is right. The rage I feel is not separate from my love; it is fueled by it. Without anyone to give my love to, the wasted emotion is being channeled towards other, more useful emotions. It is spurring me on, and every second, more of it is being created. Every second, rage builds inside of me, desperate to escape, and I know that if I don't find Elena and Devon, if I don't get my family back, it will kill me.

"No one thinks you are weak," Yorik says.

The word triggers something inside of me. *Weak.*

I know Yorik is right. I can feel the truth of it in the burning of my chest, but I still turn towards him, lip curled back in distaste.

"I don't know why you think you can talk to me so candidly, but if you do it again, I'll slice your balls off."

Yorik is not surprised or angry. He looks sad. His eyes turn down at the corners, and then he nods and leaves.

I sit in the car for a few more minutes before stuffing the baby sock into my glove compartment and going back into Elena's house.

No other signs of my family have been found in the house, so I order my lieutenants to begin reaching out to our rivals.

"Cut whatever deal you have to cut," I say. "Give up whatever you have to give up to get information, but don't let them know my family is gone. Make it seem like we're simply looking for stolen merchandise."

If my missing family can make me look vulnerable to my own men, it will make me look pathetic to our rivals. It will be an opening for another family to exploit my weakness and take advantage of our distraction.

I can't let anyone see that I'm hurting, that I've been mortally wounded.

Even as my heart bleeds, I have to pretend I'm fine.

I have to *be* fine.

# 2

## COURTNEY

My arms are tied behind my back, feet bound together at the ankles so tightly my feet tingle, and I don't realize I've woken up because someone entered the room until the blurry shape in front of me takes the shape of a large, red-haired man.

*Devon.*

The little bundle in his arms is Olivia, and I instinctively try to reach towards her, pulling at the bindings on my wrists.

"She's fine," Devon says, rolling his eyes as though I'm being ridiculous. "Sleeping like a ... well, like a baby, I guess."

He laughs at his own joke, but the rumble of his laughter feels like an earthquake. Like the walls will come crashing down at any second. It sends a sharp jolt of dread through me.

"You ought to be taking care of the other daughter. She isn't looking so hot."

I turn and see Tati curled against the wall. She isn't bound like I am, but she is shivering, wearing nothing but her thin cotton nightgown in this cell.

"You're a fucking monster," I spit. "Why are you doing this?"

"Language," he warns before tipping his head to the side, considering. "Actually, I guess since little Deafy here can't hear us, we can say whatever we want."

I'm grateful at the moment that Tati is deaf. She didn't wake when Devon came into the room, so although she is cold, at least she is sleeping. Hopefully dreaming of being somewhere far, far away from here.

"Why are you doing this?" I repeat. "Is it for revenge?"

Before he drugged me earlier, Devon told me that Dmitry killed Rurik, which I already knew. But what I didn't know was that Rurik was Devon's secret father. Knowing that, revenge is the only motive that makes sense.

Devon grins, and like his laughter, it fills me with sickening dread. "Fun."

"Is this about money?" I ask, trying to get to the root cause here. As Dmitry's wife, I can barter and trade with other families just as he can. "Dmitry tried to give your mother money. If you wanted money, you should have just asked for it. You still can. I can authorize anything you want."

"It's not about money for me," he says, still smiling. "It was for Dmitry, though. He wanted a hefty price for the three of you."

It feels like a fist is gripping my heart. I can't move or breathe. Everything in the room seems to still. "What?"

"Dmitry *sold* you," he says plainly.

I'm shaking my head before the words even fully sink in. "No, he didn't."

Devon shifts Olivia in his arms, and I sit up, desperate to hold her and touch her and see her tiny face. Then, he pulls something from his pocket.

Immediately, Dmitry's voice fills the air.

It's too grainy for me to think he's actually in the room, but the deep, familiar timbre of it still makes me inhale sharply.

*"I want territory and weapons. Whatever you can offer in exchange. Three of them, all female. The merchandise is worth the price, believe me."*

The words are stilted and staggered, nothing like the smooth-talking man I know and love, but it is Dmitry's voice nonetheless.

"He called around and offered you to anyone who would listen," Devon says. "I just happened to offer the highest price."

"I don't believe you." I clench my jaw and inhale through my nose, pushing aside my desperation to hear the recording again. To analyze it.

I trust Dmitry, and I can't allow one ten-second recording to change that.

He wouldn't sell me or the girls. He'd never do such a thing. I know that, regardless of what the recording says. It could have been taken from any of his business transactions. Or several conversations could have been spliced together.

Devon shrugs. "Believe what you want, but I'm not lying. I bought you and no one is coming to save you."

Tati stirs in her sleep, and Devon looks down at her, his eyes sparking. He steps forward and presses the toe of his shoe into her back, shaking her awake.

I slide across the floor like a seal, no arms or legs, and position myself between them. "Don't you ever touch her."

He snorts. "What are you going to do about it?"

Tati groans behind me, and then I hear her gasp.

I turn, and her eyes are wide and red-rimmed from crying. She is staring past me at Devon, horror written into every line of her face.

I don't have my hands, so I can't sign to her. Instead, I speak slowly so she can read my lips. "Everything is fine. I'm here. Don't worry."

"Don't lie to the girl, Courtney," Devon says with a laugh. Then, he waves. "Hi, Tati. Your dad is gone. I'll take care of you now."

Her eyes go even wider, and I spin around and hiss at Devon to leave. Even though I know he'll leave with my baby, I tell him to get out.

I can't protect them both. As much as it kills me, I can't take care of them both, and Tati is the one who needs me right now. Olivia is sleeping and clearly being cared for by *someone*, so Tati has to be my priority.

Devon shrugs and turns to leave, and I actually feel my heart split inside my chest. Half of it wants to jump out of my body and follow Olivia to wherever she is being taken.

Then, the door slams shut with one last grinning leer from Devon as a parting gift, and I swallow my sob and turn back to Tati.

"We're going to be okay," I say to her as tears begin to fill her eyes again. I shift closer to her so she is pressed against my side. Her skinny arms wrap around my waist, and I can feel the cool of her skin through my shirt. She needs a blanket.

After a few minutes, she pulls away and asks where her dad is.

"I don't know," I admit. "But he's coming for us. I know he is."

Tati's chest rises and falls rapidly, and then she squeezes her eyes shut and rubs her palms against her temples.

Her headaches have been getting worse. The doctors we've taken her to have hinted that it could be a response to the trauma she has endured—her own parents being killed (by Rurik, we've since learned) and me being kidnapped. Tati's life has been anything but simple, and her fragile body doesn't know how to handle it. So, the confusion manifests itself as headaches.

She lays her head in my lap, and I desperately want to reach out and stroke her hair, to offer her any kind of comfort I can. So, I lean forward and lay my cheek against hers. The position is painful and uncomfortable, but I can't worry about myself. Not when my girls are suffering.

Tati and I lie like that until she falls back asleep.

While she sleeps, I replay the recording in my head, praying it's all a lie. Praying that I didn't just lie to Tati.

*Please let Dmitry be coming for us.*

I don't realize I've fallen asleep until the door bangs open, and I startle awake. Tati jumps up, surprised by my movement, and we huddle together as a guard backs into the room dragging another prisoner.

The Yakuza guards have been cruel, and I think this man is one of them—seeing only his inky black hair from the back. But when he turns, I see he's a white man. With incredibly blue eyes.

Then, I see the woman he's pulling into the room.

"Sadie?" I gasp.

I don't want Sadie to be here. I don't want anyone to be locked in this cell, but I'm still momentarily relieved when I see her familiar face.

As soon as she sees me, the same emotions cross her face. "Courtney?"

The guard lets her go, and Sadie hurls herself away from him, cowering on the floor next to me.

The dark-haired man follows her, but rather than going for Sadie, he grabs me.

"Don't touch me," I growl, pulling away from him. The man ignores my command and hauls me to my feet.

"Hold still before you fall," he says coldly.

I almost throw my head back to hit him in the nose, but then my ankles are freed. Blood rushes down to my feet and toes, and I sigh with relief. Then, he unties my hands.

I roll my wrists and my ankles, and almost say thank you before I realize I'd be thanking my captor. I haven't been here long enough to succumb to Stockholm syndrome just yet.

"Do you need to use the restroom?" he asks.

I want to spit at him and refuse, but then I think of Tati. I kneel down in front of her and repeat the question, grateful to have my hands to sign to her.

Tati eyes the man at the door and then looks to me. Nods.

The man lets me stay with Tati as he walks her across the hall to a small bathroom and then back into the room. He doesn't say anything or smile or show any human emotion, but he is gentler than the other guards.

When we get back into the cell, Sadie is still shivering in the corner, and the man ducks into the hallway for another second before returning with three blankets. He throws them in a heap on the floor the way you'd toss treats into a dog kennel at the pound. Then, he nods to Tati.

"Is she okay?"

Tati's face is pale, eyes squeezed in pain, and she is rubbing at her temples again.

"She gets migraines," I say harshly. "These conditions don't help."

He bends down, reaching towards her gently, and I jerk Tati away.

"I have medical training," he says flatly. "A little, at least."

I want to tell him to shove his medical training so far up his ass he chokes on it, but I also don't want Tati to be sick. What if she has a fever from being in here? What if she's truly ill?

Reluctantly, I nod, and the man reaches out and touches her pulse with two fingers. His blue eyes shift to the ceiling as he counts. Then, he lays his forearm over her forehead. Finally, he massages the lymph nodes under her jaw.

"She's fine for now," he says, lifting himself to standing. "Do you need anything else?"

*Water, beds, food, my baby back* ... The list goes on and on, but I don't want to ask this man for anything else. Not until I know his intentions.

He turns to Sadie. "Do you need anything?"

She whimpers and turns away from him. For the first time, an emotion flickers across his face, though it's gone so fast I can't register it. Then, he leaves.

The moment the door is shut, Sadie crawls to me, silent tears streaming down her face. Her words are jumbled and blubbery and snotty, but I gather the details.

She was taken from her bed in the middle of the night by strangers. They didn't tell her where she was being taken or why, and she thought it might have been because of her connection with the Italians, but all of the men she saw were Japanese.

"They wouldn't answer any of my questions and no one will tell me where Devon is," she says. "He might be dead for all I know."

Devon's name on my friend's lips cools me to my center. She doesn't know. Sadie has no idea she has been betrayed by her boyfriend. Her long-term, serious boyfriend

She and Devon *live* together. They have a shared bank account and were thinking about adopting a dog. They have a life together, and I'm about to bring it all crashing down.

"He isn't dead," I say softly, cradling Tati's head in my lap, smoothing down her blonde hair.

Sadie's eyes go wide, hope flaring inside of her. "You've seen him? Is he here?"

I nod to both questions. "He is here, but it isn't what you think, Sadie. He's working for them."

A line forms between her brows.

"Actually, I think he's leading them," I admit, shaking my head to try and deny the horror of it. "He came in here earlier and said that ... he said Dmitry sold us to him, but I know that isn't true."

"You're wrong," Sadie says quickly. "Devon wouldn't do this to me. Why would he do this?"

I try to explain to her that he's the secret child of the man who betrayed Dmitry, that Devon is doing this out of revenge, I think, for what Dmitry did to his father.

"Even if that were true," she bites back. "Why would Devon take me? He wouldn't. You're confused and upset and trying to find someone else to blame."

"I'm not trying to find someone else to blame. He's to blame, Sadie! He admitted it to me."

Sadie slides away from me, arms crossed over her chest. "You never liked Devon and now you're hallucinating or something. You're hungry and stressed. You aren't thinking straight. It makes way more sense that this would be Dmitry's fault. He's the one with powerful enemies who runs around killing people. He's the reason we are all here, I'm sure of it."

I want to argue and defend Dmitry, but I don't have the energy.

Sadie may not be right about a lot of things, but she's right when she says I'm hungry and stressed. I am overwhelmed and so far out of my depth, the pressure is crushing. I don't want to talk about why we're here. I just want to focus on getting out.

"We all need to sleep," I say softly, leaning down to press a kiss to Tati's cheek. "We need to rest if we are going to try and get out of here."

"I can't sleep," Sadie says.

I lean forward and grab a blanket to throw to her. "Try. They want us to be disoriented and weak. We have to stay strong."

Her chin is still set and determined, but Sadie takes the blanket and pulls it around her shoulders.

I cover Tati and myself and then gesture for Sadie to join our huddle. "We'll be warmer if we're together."

Tensions between us are still high, but she knows I'm right. And despite her claims about Dmitry, I know Sadie is not my enemy. The truth about Devon's role in all of this will come out soon enough, and when it does, Sadie will need a friend.

I lean my head back against the wall and fall asleep with Tati on my lap and Sadie leaning on my shoulder.

~

I awake again to a loud noise, but I don't jolt this time. Tati stays asleep in my lap, blissfully unaware of the loud voices in the hallway, but Sadie sits up and pushes her blanket to the side, ready for whatever is about to come through the door.

Then, I hear a baby crying.

My baby.

"Shut up, shut up!" a deep voice growls.

I sit taller. "Devon?"

"It's not Devon," Sadie says next to me.

"Stop crying," the voice begs again, sounding more and more frustrated.

"Devon," I call, ignoring Sadie's dismissal. "Give her to me. Let me help her. Give her here."

The crying grows louder, and I know Devon is waiting outside the door. Nothing can make a person more desperate than a baby who won't stop crying. I know. I've been there.

"Let me hold her," I say. "She needs me. Let me help."

The crying continues, but Devon doesn't say anything or more. There are no footsteps on the other side, and I wonder if this isn't some kind of torture in itself. Letting me sit five feet away from my screaming baby without letting me do anything to comfort her.

I can feel my chest opening, my heart breaking, and I want to kick down the door and gouge his eyes out for letting my baby girl suffer in any way.

"Let me help," I say again. "Please, Devon."

Sadie growls next to me. "It isn't Devon."

Her words, however, die on her lips when the door opens and Devon steps inside.

He doesn't even look at Sadie. His eyes are bloodshot and sagging. He has obviously been up for a while with Olivia.

"She won't stop," he says. "What's wrong with her?"

He hands her to me, and Tati sits up. She flinches away from Devon but then she sees Olivia and clings to me, offering a finger to her baby sister.

Olivia clutches Tati's finger and immediately stops crying.

Love fills my heart, warming me from the inside out, and I'm so relieved I want to cry.

"Devon," Sadie whispers next to me. Her voice is raw and broken and stunned.

Devon smiles at his girlfriend, and then turns back to me. "Put her to sleep."

I'm too wrapped up in the sight of Olivia to fully focus on Sadie's horrific realization. I stare into Olivia's blue eyes—the same shade as her father's—and sing her to sleep. The words are nonsense. Just random bits of different songs set to a soothing melody, but she falls asleep anyway. She's exhausted from her crying and it only takes a few minutes before she is blissfully, peacefully asleep.

The moment it happens, Devon steps forward and pulls her from my arms.

"I will kill you," I spit between clenched teeth. "If you harm my baby at all, I will—"

"What?" Devon laughs. "Good luck killing me from inside this cell."

Then, he turns and is gone.

I stare at the door, resolution solidifying inside of me.

The moment I have the opportunity, I'll kill Devon.

I will slaughter him for what he has done to my family.

Even if he is somehow telling the truth and Dmitry did sell us, I'll still kill Devon for buying us. For scarring Tati and letting Olivia cry. I'll murder him.

When I finally turn and take in the rest of the room, Sadie is blinking fast like she is having a seizure, her lips moving around silent words.

"Sadie?" I ask, reaching out.

The second my hand touches her, she collapses forward in a puddle of tears.

"I can't believe it," she moans. "Why? Why?"

I can't answer her questions, so I don't try. I just rub her back and sing the same song I just sang for Olivia, hoping it might help.

# 3

# DMITRY

Three days have passed since my family was taken. It feels like three years.

I tried to go back to the house once, but I didn't even make it through the front door.

It felt like crawling into a grave. Like curling up in a coffin.

Without Courtney, Tati, and Olivia, the house is dead. It's cold and lifeless, and the idea of sleeping there without them makes me physically ill.

So, I stay at Elena's house.

I could stay at a hotel or sleep in my office, but I like being in a place that, as wrong as it is, my family occupied. No matter how briefly.

Sleep doesn't come, though.

No matter how long I spend lying down, I end up getting up and wandering. I study the art on the walls, and when I get to Elena and Rurik's bedroom, I study the photographs.

Devon was hidden in plain sight.

His red head is in frames on the dresser and wedged between Rurik and Elena in photographs.

Even if I'd come into this room and seen the pictures, I would have thought he was a nephew. Or some other relative. Never their son.

Why would anyone keep a child a secret?

That question still plagues me. Why?

Or rather, how?

I can't imagine keeping Tati or Olivia a secret.

I didn't tell anyone Tati was in a coma for her own safety, but clearly, Elena wasn't lying to try and keep Devon separate from our dangerous world. She has thrown him into it headfirst now as a spy and a captor.

It doesn't make sense, but I still feel foolish for letting it pass unnoticed.

Sleep eventually comes in fits and starts until sunrise, and then I go back into detective mode.

Pasha has the rest of the men following leads all over town, and I've been calling as many allies as I can, but nothing has been resolved. In fact, our erratic movements have caught the attention of our rivals. Even if they don't know what is going on, they know *something* is going on, and they're exploiting it.

Pasha calls midmorning to warn me there are smaller rival families nipping at the edge of our territory.

I don't want to worry about it. I want to give all of my attention to finding Courtney and the girls, but if I allow what appears to be mercy, the problem will only grow.

"Kill them on sight," I say, pinching the bridge of my nose and sighing. "Anyone who is in our territory without authorization. Get rid of them."

There is a brief hesitation on the other end of the phone before Pasha agrees and hangs up.

I spent years trying to be better than my father. Trying to be an honorable, merciful man. Someone who killed only when it was the last resort.

That thinking has led to my family being taken from me, and now I'll burn the world to get them back.

No mercy. No prisoners.

By the afternoon, there is no one else to call. I have meetings scheduled, but until then, I can only wait. I'm restless.

So, I join one of the patrol teams on the border. Nothing happens for over an hour, but then we see a drug deal going down.

The group is small and poorly armed, so it feels almost wrong to take them out, but I can't be bothered with emotions as useless as pity. We fight.

I almost sigh with relief as I duck down behind the car to keep safe from the rain of bullets coming our way. It's action. It's physical. For the first time in days, I'm out of my own head. My body is flooded with adrenaline, and I'm focused on a single task, every other thought gone from my head.

When the last man is killed, I help the men clean up the bodies, not yet ready for the physical labor to be done. Then, I send them to continue their patrol without me. I have another meeting.

The Italians had connections in the police force, but so do I.

My father became close with Travis Knepp just before his death. Travis turned his head more than a few times when he saw our men on the streets, and he has proven to be a useful source of information, especially in regard to the movements of other organizations.

His car is parked in the back corner of a strip mall underneath a scraggly tree that looks half dead and ready to fall over. As I climb in the passenger seat, I notice the blood on my hands. It leaves a smear on his door handle.

"You need a towel?" he asks, motioning to the glove compartment. "I'd rather not have bloodstains inside my car. It doesn't look good."

I hold up my hands uselessly, and he reaches over to open the box for me. I grab a few fast food napkins and wipe the bit of blood from my fingers. "Sorry. I just came from work."

Travis breathes through his nose. "You should be more careful. I am still a cop, after all."

"What did you find out?" I ask, ignoring his weak threat. If Travis ever wanted to bring anything down on me, I have a box full of tapes and messages outlining his dirty deeds. He knows better than to mess with me.

"Nothing good," he sighs. His hands clench in his lap. "You sure you want to know?"

"Of course I fucking want to know. It's my family." Travis is the only person beyond the Bratva who knows with certainty my family is missing. He is a useful source of information, but he has to be persuaded. Dabbling in our world is a risk for him. So, I told him the truth and offered him a hefty sum.

He nods and holds out his hand. I give him the envelope with zero hesitation. I'd hand over my bank accounts, my house, and my entire empire. Take it all. As long as I can save my girls.

"You already know the Yakuza are involved," he says, staring straight ahead, his eyes watching cars pass on the road in front of us. "They do a lot of work over at the docks. See a lot of shipments coming and going."

"Of what?" I ask.

Travis turns and looks at me out of the corner of his eye. "What do you think?"

My stomach clenches. Fuck. *Human trafficking.*

He sees me put the pieces together and clenches his jaw. "I had a suspicion, but it was confirmed this morning. The girls are slated to head to eastern Europe next week. They'll be sold to criminal rings there."

My fist is clenched so tightly my fingernails are cutting into my palm. "You're sure about that timeline?"

"As sure as anything ever is," he shrugs. "I trust the person who gave me the information, if that is what you mean."

"Shit." I pound my fist on my thigh.

"Will you launch an attack at the docks?" he asks.

I'm not in the habit of offering my plans to anyone beyond my own Bratva, but my next move here is obvious. Either I attack the docks, or I say goodbye to my family forever. Only one of those is an acceptable option.

"I'll have to. My men are ready for a fight."

"With the Yakuza and the smaller families pushing in on your borders, it seems," he says, tipping his head to the bloody tissue in my lap. "They're probably tired. Are you sure you can handle it?"

I say nothing. No one needs to know how weak the Bratva is right now. No one needs to know the full extent of how completely everything has gone to shit. "If I couldn't handle it, you would not be the first person I'd tell, officer."

Travis holds up his hands in surrender. "Fair enough. But if you want my opinion, have your guys take out any rival they lay eyes on before focusing on the Yakuza. You don't want to be fighting on two fronts. Wipe them out and then focus your resources on the docks."

I'm prepared to tell Travis to take his opinion and choke on it. I've been in this business long enough to formulate my own battle strategies. However, as I turn towards him, I notice his hands drumming nervously on his steering wheel.

He is wearing a pair of leather gloves despite the mild weather, but that's not what I notice. As his fingers drum across the wheel, the tip of the glove covering his pinky bends backwards. As though the end is gone.

"Good advice," I say between gritted teeth, looking away from him. "I'll keep that in mind."

*Traitor.*

I shouldn't be surprised. Anyone willing to pledge an oath to protect people and then turn around and work with criminals isn't someone who can be trusted. Travis proved himself disloyal years ago. Yet, I never would have suspected he'd go all in with the Yakuza.

Every person who swears fealty to the Yakuza loses the tip of their pinky in a swearing-in ceremony. It is antiquated and bloody, but it marks them forever as having pledged themselves to the Yakuza.

For most officers, keeping themselves open and available to every family is the best way to bring in the cash. Everyone is bidding and vying for top-tier information. Whatever the Yakuza are paying him, it must be more than what I just handed him in the envelope.

"I think I can find the ship your family will be on if that would help," Travis offers. "It might cost a bit more money, but—"

"I can find it," I say.

He furrows his brow. "I'm not so sure you can. It would be a shame to show up to the wrong place and miss them, wouldn't it?"

"Then I won't show up to the wrong place," I say with a harsh smile.

Travis is here to lure me and my men into a trap. Every bit of information he has given me is leading me to my death.

I believe him that the girls are going to be on a ship and sold. But I also believe the Yakuza are going to be lying in wait for a full-scale attack. They are going to be armed and waiting for us, and like Travis said, my men are tired.

It has been days of searching and fighting, and they are spent. More days of searching and planning lie ahead of us, too. We need more information from untainted sources. By the time we get what we need, they'll be exhausted while the Yakuza are able to rest up and gather their strength.

It hits me, too, that of course Travis would want me to take out as many rival families as I can. Every rival family I take out is one less family who can stand against the Yakuza taking control of the entire city. Plus, it will expend the energy of my forces even further. I'm sure that particular command came from Akio himself, the leader of the Yakuza.

"Just let me write down what I might know for you," Travis says, reaching for a notepad in his console.

I wave him away. "I don't want it." His brow furrows, and I cover quickly. "You've done enough, and I won't pay you another dime today. I don't accept favors. It creates an imbalance."

"Come on, Dmitry. We've been friends a long time. Let me help."

I shake my head. "No. We're business associates. Not friends. I don't confuse the two and neither should you. Thanks for meeting me."

I need to get out of the car before I reach across the seat and strangle him.

There are Yakuza members around the parking lot, no doubt. Hidden, but present. If I show any signs of recognizing Travis has been sent to trap me, they'll move in. It won't be what they wanted, but the Yakuza will take whatever they can get.

Even if they can't kill all of my men, killing me will do the trick. The power vacuum it will create in combination with the chaos happening on our borders will be enough for them to step in and take over what I've built.

I have to play it cool, get out of here, and face this on my own. I can't rally my men because they'll see it coming a mile away.

There is only one thing that will ensure I can get to the ship and find my family:

I have to go in alone.

Travis sighs and runs a hand down his face. "I don't want to see you lose your family because of pride."

I give him a one-fingered salute and open the door. "Don't worry, I won't."

He is starting to say something else when the door closes, but I don't hear it. I get into my car as quickly as I can and leave before they decide not to take any chances and surround me right there.

I don't go back to Elena's house. It was stupid to set up camp there in the first place. I go to a safe house on the far edge of Bratva territory, telling no one except for Pasha where I am.

Nothing went the way I expected it to, but now I have a plan. And for the first time in days, I go to bed, and I sleep. I'll need the rest.

# 4

# COURTNEY

Three more women are thrown into the cell during the night.

They are dumped unceremoniously by a few of the guards with no explanation or introduction.

I hold Tati close and then feel guilty for being frightened of the other women. It's obvious they are scared out of their wits. One of the women sits in the corner for hours, staring and catatonic.

Still, I don't have the energy for guilt. There is only room for fear. Fear for Tati and her worsening condition. The guards gave her something back at the mansion to make her sleep, and she hasn't responded well to it. Her body is having a hard time shedding the medication. She was sleepy and confused for several days, but now she's sick. Nauseous, with headaches and muscle spasms.

And then there's my fear for Olivia.

Since the night when Devon became desperate and brought Olivia in to be calmed, I have only seen my daughter twice in passing. Devon allows small glimpses, but no touching.

I can't even be certain the baby he is holding is my daughter, which makes me feel like a horrible mother. What kind of mother doesn't recognize her own baby? Shouldn't I just innately know?

And the fear that is crowding out all of the others, the fear that seems to grow larger by the second is the thought that Dmitry might not be coming for us.

The moment we were captured, I told myself Dmitry would save us. Then, Devon claimed Dmitry was the one who sold us. I didn't believe it, but as days pass with no sign, no word ... it is getting harder to outright deny the claim.

"I can't believe Dmitry did this to us," Sadie says, pacing along the back wall like a tiger in a cage. "I can't believe Devon paid for us. Me, especially. His girlfriend."

Sadie's rants have been repetitive and nonstop for days. After her meltdown over Devon's betrayal, she wept and then quickly became indignant.

She believes Dmitry sold us, and no amount of arguing can shake the idea loose from her brain. So, I've given up. Sadie is too angry and emotional to listen to me. Our situation is far from normal, so I can understand it, but that doesn't make it easier to deal with.

"We have all been betrayed in some way to end up here," I remind her calmly. Not by Dmitry, of course, but I don't say that.

"My boyfriend got my ass thrown in here, too," one of the women says, her top lip pulled back in a snarl.

Sadie spins around. "Was his name Devon?"

The woman snorts. "I wasn't dating your boyfriend, girl. I ain't nobody's side chick. Though, I barely knew the guy. He might have been married."

Unbelievably, Sadie seems relieved by this. Devon has sold her into possible slavery and kept her locked in a tiny room for days, but if he was cheating on her as well? Unforgivable.

Sadie slumps down the wall and lays a hand on Tati's cheek. She is dozing on my lap, though I can tell she isn't really asleep. It's just easier to sleep than it is to be awake, and I don't want to begrudge Tati what tiny bit of comfort she can find in this place.

Suddenly, the door opens, and everyone tenses.

Will more women be thrown in with us? Are we being moved? Is a guard coming to separate us?

I grab Tati tightly. I already lost Olivia. I can't lose her, too.

Then, the guard with the food appears with three plastic trays. They are piled with various packaged foods in no particular arrangement. When he drops the trays on the floor, packages of chips and cookies scatter across the cement.

Sadie lunges for one of the trays and drags it towards us. She gives Tati a package of salted almonds and a granola bar—the healthiest things on the tray—and then we divide up the snack mix, chips, and cookie.

"The only thing they have here is a vending machine," Sadie complains, pinching off a bit of cookie and wincing as it hits her tongue. "An old one, too. This is stale."

"I didn't think vending machine food could go stale," I say.

We look at one another for a second, and then for the first time in days, I smile. Sadie lets out a small huff of laughter and shakes her head. "You learn something new every day, I guess. Even in captivity."

I'm about to eat a handful of my snack mix when two of the other women in the cell start to shout.

"You take every package of chips that come through this door," the blonde woman says, stabbing an accusatory finger at the frail, dark-haired woman across from her. "This one is mine."

"They're the only thing I like," the girl argues. Her hair falls in thin sheets around her gaunt face. It looks like she needs the chips more. She is scary thin.

"It doesn't look like you like much of anything," the blonde says. She shoves a finger in her mouth and pretends to hurl. "Do you actually eat anything or are you a fan of the binge and purge?"

The thin girl's cheeks go pink with embarrassment. "I don't throw up. Now, give it to me."

They each tug on the bag of chips between them hard enough I'm surprised the old bag doesn't rip right down the center.

Tati presses in closer to my side, her eyes locked on the two women, her lower lip trembling. And seeing her upset is the only reason I step in.

"Hey," I offer, holding my hands up in surrender before they even turn to look at me. "We have another bag of chips over here. If someone wants to trade it, we can make this work for everyone."

The blonde turns on me, eyes narrowed. "You three are a little unit. Don't pretend like you care about us."

"I do," I argue. "*We* do. We're all in here against our will. We aren't each other's enemies."

The girl lifts her chin, studying me. Then, she looks at our tray. "I'll give you half of my granola bar for the chips."

"Deal." I make the trade and watch as the two women retreat to their respective corners to eat their dinner of ancient chips and dirty water.

The third woman is still quiet and unmoving in the corner. She didn't move once during the entire fight, and I'm worried what will happen if she doesn't eat or drink anything. If she passes out, I'm not sure any medical help will be offered. If she starves, I'm not even confident the guards will remove her body.

It's that thought that propels me across the room with the half of the granola bar extended.

She stares through me and my food offering, but when I press it into her hand, her fingers close around it.

"You can have it," I whisper. "Please. We're all worried."

The blonde woman snorts. "I'm not worried about her. I'm worried about being sold to some man in eastern Europe who doesn't speak English."

Despite this, the silent girl lifts the bar to her mouth and takes the tiniest of bites. It is barely enough to even notice, but it is something. I spin around and grab her a glass of water, watching as she takes a sip of that, as well.

It isn't much, but it is something.

"Europe?" Sadie asks. "What do you mean?"

The girl continues to eat—slowly and sparingly, but still—and I move back over to sit next to Tati, distracting her so she won't read anyone's lips. I don't want her to know more about our situation than she needs to.

"That's where we're headed," the girl says. "I've heard about the operation a few times on the streets, but I didn't think I'd ever have to worry about it. Now look at me." She laughs grimly.

"The streets?" Sadie asks.

"I'm a prostitute," the woman says with one eyebrow raised, waiting for Sadie to blanch or reprimand her. "Or a 'sex worker,' as the politically correct among us like to say." She laughs, a dry, bitter sound.

"What's your name?" Sadie asks.

The woman casts her gaze to the ceiling like she's too good for the conversation, but she crosses her arms and answers. "Annika."

"I'm Sadie. And these are Courtney and Tati," Sadie says, introducing us. "What do you know about this operation, Annika?"

She shakes her head. "Not much. They send women to eastern Europe via ships, sell them, and then return for more. That's the nice thing about human cargo. It's always reproducing. Like fucking rabbits."

Suddenly, I can smell the salt in the air. And the rustle from outside that I'd written off as the wind in the trees is obviously waves.

We're near the water.

Near the docks.

My stomach clenches. We're going to be sold.

I push my packaged dinner to the side and lean back against the wall, no longer hungry.

It's good to know something about what is happening to us, I suppose. But then again, maybe I'd rather not know.

I close my eyes, trying to drown out the now obvious sound of waves lapping against the shore, and try to focus on Dmitry. I have to believe he is coming for us or I'll never survive. I have to believe he didn't betray me, or I'll die.

I fall asleep, wondering what Dmitry is doing right now.

~

*He is just a bump under the covers, sliding lower and lower down the mattress, and I swat playfully at what I suspect is his head.*

*"Tati will be up any minute," I argue, though I open my legs wider, letting Dmitry crouch between them.*

*He pulls back the blankets, smiling up at me with a lopsided grin. "Then we better hurry."*

*It should be illegal to feel this good first thing in the morning. I have bad breath and I know my hair is a mess, no doubt sticking up in every direction, but my body is liquid heat. Dmitry works my panties aside and swipes his finger down my center, and I roll my hips, moaning softly to encourage him.*

*He doesn't need any encouragement, though.*

*We've been married for six months, and Dmitry still treats every day like our honeymoon. Constant kisses and touching, letting me know he wants me, desires me.*

*Part of me worried after I had Olivia that he wouldn't look at me the same way, that he wouldn't desire me the way he did before. But if anything, his taste for me has grown, and I don't have a single complaint.*

*Dmitry lowers his head, and when his breath hits my center, I gasp. His hands are strong on my thighs, holding my legs apart, and I tense. Waiting for the moment when he'll finally touch me. Anticipating the moment when he'll put me out of my agony and kiss me in all the places I long to be kissed.*

*"You taste so good to me," he says just loud enough that I can hear it, though I'm way more focused on the warmth of his words against my sensitive skin.*

*I slip my hand under the covers and caress his stubbly cheek. "Prove it."*

*His lips are soft and gentle as they suck and massage, but it's like an electric bolt through my body. My thighs clench, and I grab a fistful of his silky hair. I hold him to me even though I know he isn't going anywhere. Even though I know he's going to stay there until I'm crying out his name, until my body is limp and spent beneath him.*

*Dmitry is a lot of things, but he is not a selfish lover. He gives and gives and gives.*

*His tongue flicks across me, and I tumble over the edge before I can stop myself. I'm gasping and shaking, and then I give in and it isn't falling at all. I'm flying.*

*Dmitry presses a kiss to me, peels my panties down my legs, and then crawls over me.*

*Then, he takes me.*

*I wrap my legs around his lower back, hooking my ankles, and he slides into me in one thrust.*

*Our bodies slap together at a crushing pace that still isn't enough. I roll my hips up to meet him halfway and arch my back, trying to give him more. To give him everything.*

*Then, his mouth is on my breast.*

*I don't even remember when he took off my shirt, but it's gone, and now that his warm mouth is over my nipple, his tongue flicking me, I don't want it back.*

*His hand snakes through my tangled hair and tugs, arching my back even further, and he bites my nipple until I'm on the verge of pain.*

*But this could never be pain.*

*The way our bodies come together is art. Pure and simple.*

*"More," I gasp. "Please."*

*Dmitry growls and slides out of me. In an instant, I'm lying on my stomach, and he is propping me up on my knees.*

*Taking and taking and taking.*

*But you don't need to take what is freely given.*

*I want this. I want him.*

*I can't imagine there was ever a time where I didn't burn for him this way. Where I didn't ache for him to fill me the way he does.*

*Dmitry digs his fingers into my hips and thrusts into me. I gasp and then roll with his pace, pushing against him as he meets me again and again.*

*I spread my arms out in front of me and bury my face in the mattress so I can scream his name as loud as I want.*

*Dmitry grabs my hair and lifts my face. "I want to hear you say my name."*

*"Dmitry," I moan, settling my hips back against him until our bodies are flush, and I'm filled with nothing but him and my love for him. My husband.*

*"Courtney," he whispers, caressing me with his words and his touch. His hand slips around my waist and finds my center, and I can't see straight. I squeeze my eyes closed and fight to keep in the scream of pleasure dying to break out of my chest.*

*His finger circles and flicks to the pace of his thrusts, and my body is his. He owns me entirely.*

*"Dmitry, yes," I whimper, my legs shaking with the impending orgasm. "Please. More."*

*He doesn't tease me. Dmitry grabs my hips again and sets to work to give me what I need. At the same time, he is finding his own bliss.*

*I feel his movements become more purposeful. He pauses with each thrust, moaning to the speed of our connection. When he jerks with release, I am already falling.*

*Our bodies find pleasure together, clenching and pulsing, entirely vulnerable in front of the other.*

*When we're both finished, Dmitry falls on top of me with a loud sigh, and I laugh, pretending the weight of him on my back isn't perfect. "You're crushing me."*

*"What a way to go, though, huh?" he teases. "Most people would love to be so lucky."*

*"You sure do have a high opinion of yourself."*

*He rolls to the side, kissing my shoulder blade, and then gives me a devastating smile. "Maybe I wouldn't if you didn't cry out my name so often. It's giving me a big head."*

*I press my thumb to his bottom lip. "Well, we can't have that now, can we? Maybe I should call someone else's name to keep you from getting too cocky."*

*His eyes spark with amusement. "You wouldn't dare."*

*I shrug and smirk. "Maybe I would. Who can say?"*

*He growls and crawls over me, and I can already feel he's ready again. "Maybe you already need another reminder of who you belong to."*

*I don't say anything because I'm incapable. I'm so happy and already so desperately, desperately ready for him. I bite my lip and nod, and Dmitry has kissed halfway down my midsection when I hear our doorknob rattle.*

*Tati walked in on us enough times that we finally installed a lock.*

*She knocks three times, and Dmitry groans. "This isn't fair."*

*I drag him back up to my face and kiss him. "There will be time later."*

*He's still pouting as he pulls on his pajama pants and opens the door. But the moment he sees Tati, he beams and scoops her up into a hug. They're still having a tickle fight when I hear Olivia start to stir through the monitor.*

*Within ten minutes, we've gone from one bliss to another with our girls lying in bed with us on a sleepy Saturday morning, and I can only look at Dmitry and smile. There are no words for this kind of happiness.*

*There is only love.*

~

I'm still smiling when the door bursts open and the other women begin to scream.

There are three guards in the room with us. One of them—a man with a large tiger tattoo inked down his forearm—yanks my arm and hauls me to my feet. I carry Tati with me, holding her to my chest so she won't be taken.

With no explanation, we're marched out of the room and down the hallway.

A door at the end of the hall is unlocked, and I can smell the ocean. I can hear the waves clearly. And when we get outside, I can see the water.

And a ship.

I instinctively jerk against the man's arm, and he squeezes me tighter until I wince.

"Where are you taking us?" Sadie asks.

I turn and see her guard is the man who offered us blankets and checked on Tati. I think of him as the "nice guard," but nice is a very relative term with this crew. He is nicer, but still a monster. Still loading women onto a ship like cargo.

"Shut up," the man holding me spits back at her. "You don't deserve to ask questions."

Just as he finishes, a woman at the back of the group screams, and I hear the guard scramble after her.

It's the catatonic woman. She never said a word in the cell, but now she is shrieking and running across the dock like a madwoman.

She's escaping.

At least, it certainly looks like she will escape. She's running too fast for anyone to catch and no one is chasing after her.

Only when the sound of gunfire cracks through the air do I realize why. No one was chasing her because they didn't have to. Because they have other means of making sure she can't escape.

Her body jerks with each shot, and then she collapses on the dock.

The man with the tiger tattoo jerks me forward, tearing my eyes from the woman's dead body on the ground. "Don't run, or you'll face the same fate."

Half of my mind is still trapped in my dream with Dmitry, so I can't understand that this is real. That this is happening.

Even as we are taken aboard a ship, walked below deck, and then locked in a small room behind a false wall, I don't recognize that there is no going back.

Dmitry isn't going to make it in time. He is not coming for me.

The thought tiptoes around the edge of my mind, but I don't allow myself to focus on it. I can't. If I do, I'll fall apart. And I can't do that. For Tati's sake, I need to stay present, stay ready.

She is trembling and crying at my side, and I hug her, whispering words she can't hear into her hair.

Sadie and I huddle around Tati and around one another, offering what little comfort can be had in such a cold, damp place.

I don't know how long we stay like that, but the next thing I know, the door opens and the tiger man is standing there with a little girl in his arms.

When he hands her to me, I can't even reach for her. Sadie has to do it for me.

Olivia.

Pink and perfect and asleep.

I don't grab her until the guard is gone, and Sadie lays her in my arms.

I know on some level that I don't want Olivia to be here. Not on this ship. Not headed for whatever horrors lie ahead.

But I can't deny myself the pleasure of looking at her perfect face and her beautiful round cheeks. When she opens her eyes and sees me, she smiles, and I'm struck with how much she looks like her dad.

I hug her and Tati to me, crying silently as I squeeze them, and I wonder how anyone could ever hurt them.

I don't believe Devon. I don't believe Dmitry would ever do anything to me or his girls, but even the thought of it feels like a dagger in my stomach.

And now, at my weakest, it's enough to kick me even lower than I already am. I don't believe it, but I also can't disprove it.

And now that we're on the ship headed for our destination, I doubt I will ever know the truth.

# 5

# DMITRY

My beard is longer than usual. I hate the sloppiness, but I try not to fuss at it as I sit in the park.

Birds peck at the cold ground and dry leaves rattle across the sidewalk. Otherwise, there is no movement. I'm alone.

It's too cold for children to be playing. Too late for a normal person to be out. So, the few people who have passed through in the last hour have avoided me.

I don't mind. I prefer it that way.

I stayed at the safe house for a day while I gathered my thoughts, but as soon as I had a plan, I left, and I've been moving ever since.

If I slow down, the Yakuza will catch up with me. They'll find me, capture me, and any chance of saving my family will be gone.

My ratty clothes and long beard are enough to fool the basic street criminals. They weren't suspicious at all of the man asking about the ship heading to Europe. Some of them knew nothing, some of them knew everything. They all had a price.

I paid for information on where the ship is docked, which ship it is, and where it's headed. Within a day, I knew exactly where my family was and it took everything inside of me not to storm the vessel and get them back.

Still, sitting in the park, it's a struggle not to move. Not to run towards where they are.

I can't.

I can't fight the Yakuza on my own, and I can't take my men with me.

This has to be covert, stealthy. I can't show up guns blazing and expect to walk away with my girls, no matter how badly I want to.

I check my watch—one of the few items I kept with me—and see that I only have a few hours left to wait.

A pimp downtown told me the ship would leave tonight. I didn't know whether I could trust him, but he assured me the information was legit. He'd just sent one of his girls there.

"She was washed up," he said coldly. "Stick-thin and half dead already, so I figured I'd sell her for whatever pennies the Yakuza would offer and move on. I doubt they'll make much off her, but what do I know about the taste of European men? You got someone on board, too?"

I wanted to strangle the man right then and there, but instead I just thanked him for the information and left before I could draw any more attention to myself.

I push my sleeve down and stretch out my legs in front of me. I'm about to stand up and leave when I hear laughing. I turn and see three men moving towards me.

They're gaunt with pockmarked faces and teeth so yellow I don't need daylight to see them. Clearly meth heads out looking for a fix.

"Nice watch," the man in the front says. He nods to my wrist as if I don't know where my watch is located.

I give him a one-fingered salute. The middle finger, to be exact. "Thanks."

He laughs, but his eyes narrow. "Mind if I see it? What did it set you back? A couple hundred?"

*More like a couple thousand.* "Something like that."

He steps forward and holds out his hand. "Let me see it. I'll be real careful."

"No thanks." I don't have time for this. Well, technically I do. But I don't have the patience for this. I have enough on my mind without dealing with three junkies looking to roll over a helpless hobo.

He steps in front of me and blocks my path, his two friends flanking him. "It wasn't a question."

Before the words are even out of his mouth, I jam my palm into his nose.

I hear the crack of it, and then he screams.

I wipe the blood on my jeans before pivoting towards the man standing stunned on his left and leveling him with a right hook. His head snaps back, and before he even hits the pavement, the last man standing gets a straight jab to the jaw.

"Fuck!" the first guy roars, clutching his nose. "What is wrong with you?"

I rear back and kick him in the stomach—not because I need to, but because I want to. "You have no idea."

I want to do worse to them. I want to leave them all dead and rotting on the pavement, but I don't want to deal with the cleanup or the attention. So, I shove my hands in my pockets and walk away, listening to the men groan and try to rally behind me.

To their credit, they don't follow after me to pick another fight. Maybe they aren't total idiots, after all.

I don't have enough mercy left in me to spare them a second time.

~

I use the last of my cash to buy a burner phone and take a taxi to another safe house within the city limits.

Pasha opens the door and grins when he sees me. "It's good to see you."

I hand him the phone and stalk past him into the house.

He closes the door and bites the corner of his lip nervously, his smile entirely gone. "Did you find what you needed to?"

I nod. "Keep that phone on you and charged. I'll call you when I need you."

He sighs but shoves the phone in his pocket. "Let me come with you. I can help. With just the two of us, we can keep a low profile and—"

I shake my head. "I go in alone. I need you here waiting for my call. You're the person I trust to help me when I need it."

I can tell Pasha doesn't agree, but he is honored by my admission. I mean it, too. I trust Pasha. He has always been loyal. Even when he was just a recruit, he was eager to learn and advance. Now, he is one of my most trusted lieutenants, and he earns that honor every day.

"Are you leaving tonight?" he asks.

"Right now," I say. "The ship leaves tonight."

He looks down at the floor and shakes his head. "I don't like you going in alone."

"You don't have to like it. You just have to respect it."

Pasha nods and crosses the room in a few steps. He lays his hand on my shoulder. "Be careful."

I can't make any promises. I'll do whatever I have to do to save my family. I'll throw myself in front of danger one hundred times over to save them.

"Wait for my call," I remind him. I shrug away from his touch and leave.

~

There is a lot of movement around the ship in the hours after midnight, but I never see any women being herded up the gangplank.

That's probably a good thing. I'm not sure I'd be able to control myself if I saw my family being dragged on board.

Around dawn, the movement begins to slow, with only a few crew members moving on and off the ship. Finally, when one lone crew member walks down the gangplank to grab a few suitcases on the dock, I make my move.

He doesn't see me coming as I approach from behind, so by the time he is fighting against me, my hand is over his mouth, keeping him from screaming for help.

I clamp one arm around his chest and hurl him to the side, smashing his head against the wooden railing. His body goes limp immediately, and I lower him to the ground.

The man is smaller than he looked from far away, and I'm worried I won't be able to fit into his uniform as I strip him of his black pants, T-shirt, and three-quarter zip jacket. However, the pants are elastic around the waist and the shirt is a stretchable cotton. The jacket is much tighter in the arms than I'd like, but I manage to pull it on fine enough.

I don't want to kill the man. He is mostly innocent—aside from the fact he's moving human cargo in the middle of the night—but I don't want to risk him waking up and alerting the ship to an unauthorized crew member. So, I slide him off the dock and into the water.

His body floats for only a second before sinking down into the inky darkness.

I walk calmly back towards the luggage the man was holding and walk it up the gangplank, looking as confident as I can, despite not knowing whose luggage it is or where to deliver it. Luckily, as soon as I make it to the main deck, there is a pile of luggage in the middle with people picking through it the way they do at the baggage claim of airports. I add the luggage in my hands to the pile and then walk down the left side of the ship. Port, maybe. Or starboard.

I make a note to learn the names of the sides of the boat as soon as possible.

There is a lot I should know about working on a ship that I don't. I've never been much for the water. I flew with my father often for business, but we never had a reason to be on the water. He owned a yacht that he liked to take out, but that was always a kid-free zone, and as I grew older, I didn't want to spend more time with him than necessary. So, I'm far out of my depth here—literally and figuratively.

"You lost?"

I stiffen at the deep voice and turn to see an old man with a thick white beard looking at me, eyes narrowed. He has on a suit, but the sleeves are slightly too long and his shoes are scuffed.

"Perhaps," I admit, trying to determine who the man could be. Considering he's in a suit—no matter how ill-fitted—I must assume he ranks higher than the man I killed and replaced.

"Kitchen is below deck," he says, one bushy eyebrow raised. "The boss wanted breakfast served immediately. If he sees you up here, you'll be overboard before we even set sail."

"It's a little early for breakfast," I say, looking up at the still-dark sky.

The old man pulls back in surprise and then cracks the smallest smile. "Be sure to tell him that if you want to be a eunuch."

"Let him fucking try." I should keep my mouth shut. I know that. But I also am not used to being ordered around. Clearly, I need to get used to it. Fast.

The man stares at me for a stunned second and then laughs. "Keep your sense of humor to yourself if you want to survive the voyage. The door you need is that way."

He points to a door halfway down the walkway I just came from, and I feel his gaze on me as I walk away. Two minutes on board and I'm already drawing eyes on me. I need to keep a much lower profile if I want to avoid detection.

I go through the door the man indicated and find myself in a maze of metal hallways. It takes me a few minutes of stumbling around and avoiding other crew members—none of whom stop to pay any attention to me—before I walk through the right door and into the kitchen.

*Galley*, I quickly learn, is the proper term.

One of the other cooks, a middle-aged man with a thick mustache looks me up and down and then shrugs as if he doesn't care if I belong there or not. Then, he points to a pot of oatmeal. "Stir that and then wash and chop that fruit," he says, pointing to a pile of strawberries in the sink.

I want to ask if he's the chef, but I suspect I should already know that. So, instead, I do what I am told.

If I'd ever cooked anything before, this would be easier. My entire life, I've had my own cook. I've watched her make enough meals that I can pretend, but I'm nowhere near the same level of skill as an actual cook. The strawberries I chop are misshapen and not uniform, but I throw them in the pot of oatmeal before anyone can notice.

The mustachioed man nods approvingly and begins dumping the oatmeal into bowls. "Enjoy the fruit. It will only last a few days and then we'll be using frozen."

"Is this food for us?" I ask.

He puts filled bowls on a silver tray and nods for a waitress to carry them out of the kitchen. "The scraps are for us. We cook the food, but we only eat what's left. Normally there is enough."

A tray of croissants and two coffee carafes follow a few moments later, and I wonder if any of it will make it to Courtney and the girls. What are they eating if even the cooks only get what's left?

I wash the giant stockpot used for the oatmeal and scrub the baking sheets in scalding water until my hands are red and raw. Then, when the trays come back, I eat a cold croissant with a bowl of overcooked, lukewarm oatmeal.

"So, are you the chef?" I finally ask the man with the mustache eating across from me.

He chuckles. "No. The chef is sleeping. You won't see him until lunch. I'm the sous chef, I guess you could say. Really, I'm just the idiot who gets paid less and wakes up earlier than the chef."

"If you're an idiot, what does that make me?" I ask. He has no idea I'm not getting paid at all.

"Poor," he says, wagging his eyebrows. "Don't worry, we can make it up tonight in poker."

"We can play poker?"

"Below deck," he explains. "You brought cash, right?"

I spent the last of my money on the burner phone and the taxi. I'm fresh out. "Shit."

"I'll spot you," he says with a dismissive wave. "Pay me back when you get your first paycheck. With interest."

"Thanks. What's your name?"

"Jake. You?"

I hesitate for a minute and can't believe I didn't come up with a fake name or try to figure out the name of the cook I killed before I killed him. Then, Jake points to my shirt. "Sorry, I guess I should try reading first."

I follow his finger and see "Andrew" written on a metal pin and stuck to the jacket I'm wearing. I laugh in both relief and surprise and nod. "That's me. Andrew."

"Well, Andrew," Jake says, handing me his empty oatmeal bowl to wash. "Hopefully you have a good poker face. Otherwise, I'll take you for everything you're worth."

I walk away from the poker game one hundred dollars richer than when I walked in, so I pay Jake back immediately and find my bunk.

It's a top bunk, which is something. I share the small room with an overweight pastry chef who doesn't speak a word of English. I honestly don't mind. That way, we don't even have to pretend to talk.

The ship pulls away from the shore just before sunrise, and I watch from a porthole as the city grows smaller and further away. My ability to back out of this absurd plan fades into the horizon.

Now, we are too far out for the city to be visible, and I'm feeling ever so slightly nauseous.

I wonder about Tati. Is she seasick? She sometimes gets motion sick in the car if she's reading a book while we drive. Does anyone have any medicine for her? Is Courtney able to help her?

I want to see them so badly. Knowing they are on the ship with me is harder than not knowing where they are. I want to search every crevice of the place until I find them.

I tried to bring up the topic casually during poker, but a man with a large tiger tattooed on his arm shut down the line of questioning, assuring me there was no illegal cargo aboard the ship. Everyone there knew the man was full of shit, but I backed down and feigned disinterest. "Just a rumor I heard. Doesn't matter to me either way as long as I get paid for my work."

Jake told me when we left not to mess with the man. "He's higher ranking than both of us. You don't want to get on his bad side."

Does his bad side look anything like mine? Is he willing to kill to get what he wants? If the man with the tiger tattoo really is the one in charge, I'm sure I'll find out answers to those questions soon enough.

I drift to sleep with thoughts of Courtney in my head, so it's no surprise when she finds me in my dreams.

*We're in our room, though our mattress has been replaced with a waterbed. Courtney shifts over me, her knees on either side of my hips, and we rock back and forth as though we're on a small boat in the middle of a storm.*

*Courtney drags her hands down my chest and dips her fingers beneath the waistband of my underwear. "Are you sure you don't feel well?"*

*"I'm fine," I say quickly, ignoring the lurch of my stomach. My attention has been suddenly shifted to another body part and the matter is very pressing. "I've never been better."*

*Her hand shifts lower, disappearing beneath the fabric and wrapping around my length. I groan.*

*"Never been better?" she whispers, stroking me. "Are you sure?"*

*I shake my head. "I'm getting better every second."*

*She smiles and licks her lower lip, tugging it between her teeth. "Let's set a new record."*

*Our clothes are gone in an instant, and she's on top of me, her hips circling in a delicious way that pulls sounds out of me I've never heard before. I grip her hips and hold her against me, thrusting upward.*

*"Courtney ..." I rasp.*

*She plants her hands on my chest and grinds down into me until I have to close my eyes. Until I tip my head back and let her have complete control.*

When I open them again, the ceiling is two feet from my face and the bed is shaking.

It takes me a moment to recognize where I am, and then I feel another kick to the underside of my bed.

My roommate is saying something I presume is "stop moaning in your sleep," but I can't be certain, since he's speaking Japanese.

"Sorry," I mumble, annoyed with him for pulling me away from Courtney. Even if it was only in my sleep, it was something. For a second, I could feel her body on mine. I could forget where she is and where I am, and we were together.

I roll onto my side and try to conjure the dream again, but it doesn't come. Sleep doesn't come, either. I lie there, thoughts of my family circling in my head, until I have to go back to the kitchen to start another day.

Hopefully, it will be a day that brings me closer to my family.

## 6

# COURTNEY

The food is barely edible.

Somehow, though, the rotten scraps and slimy leftovers are better than the endless bags of processed junk food they were giving us in the holding cell.

Sadie and I give as much as we can to Tati. Her headache has been unending since we got on board the ship, and her seasickness isn't helping things. The first night, she was up sick all night, dry heaving because there was nothing in her stomach.

Now, she's keeping things down, but she's too weak to sign more than a few words at a time. Not that I can see much of anything anyway. The shipping container is dark. During the day, there is a little light that leaks through the holes and cracks around the door, but at night, we have to use the flashlight the Tiger gave us, and we're doing our best to save the batteries, should we need it to escape.

Escape to where, I don't know. We're at sea, so there isn't anywhere to go, but thinking there is no way to escape is too bleak to consider.

He brings our food at least once a day, throwing it through the door like he's feeding a pack of wild dogs and doesn't want to get too close. The other guard—the quiet one with inky black hair—replaces the bucket we're all using as a restroom. That in and of itself is a small luxury. At least we're not forced to live with the constant odor of our own waste. I've tried to thank him, hoping he might be swayed to care about us and do something to assist us, but he's aggressively dismissive. He won't even look me in the eye when I try to speak to him.

I wish the Tiger would ignore us.

He ignores me, mostly, but Sadie receives the brunt of his backlash. I don't know if Devon told him who Sadie was, if there is some reason he zeroes in on her, but every time he comes into the shipping container, he torments her.

"Beg," he says, holding half of a sandwich in the air, dangling it like a carrot. "Beg for it."

Sadie crosses her arms and stares up at him. "No."

"Please," one of the other women says, falling on her knees. "I'll beg. I'll do it."

The Tiger shakes his head. "I want her to beg. Beg me."

Sadie shakes her head again. "I'm not hungry."

Before the words are even out of her mouth, the sandwich slaps her across the face. A streak of mayo splatters across her cheek and bread goes flying into the grimy corners of the container. If the entire situation wasn't so miserable, it would almost be funny, if only because of how ridiculous it was. Hitting someone with a sandwich.

"Bitch," the Tiger spits, following the sandwich slap with a kick in the leg. Sadie winces but tries to hide it, which only makes him angrier. He leans down, lip curled back to reveal yellowed teeth. "Starve for all I care."

As soon as he's gone, Annika scoots forward and hands Sadie half of an apple. "The core is soft, but you can have it."

Sadie tries to refuse, but Annika presses it into her hand. "We are all in this together, remember? Besides," she says, sliding over to pick up a piece of bread. "I've eaten worse things than a piece of bread from the floor. I don't mind."

Annika tears it in half and hands it back to a young girl only a few years older than Tati. We've figured out she's the daughter of the quiet woman who was shot on the docks. Like her mother, the girl is quiet, but she has told us the men kept her in a separate holding cell upstairs, next to a room with a baby.

*My* baby.

Larissa is the girl's name, and Annika has taken her under her wing.

"You dated a psychopath, so I know how you got here," Annika says, pointing to Sadie. Then, she turns to me. "But how did you end up in here?"

"Crazy boyfriend," Sadie explains before I can answer.

I glare at her. "Husband, actually. And he isn't crazy. He didn't lock me in here."

Sadie snorts her disagreement. "Either way, he's absolutely the reason you are here."

I want to argue with her, but I can't. Dmitry told me early on that his lifestyle was dangerous. I knew going in that there could be threats to my safety. Though, I never expected it would go this far.

I don't blame him, but his position within the Bratva must be at least partially to blame.

"What about you?" I ask, tired of considering my own situation. Tired of thinking about Dmitry when I might never see him again.

"Behind every tragic story is a man," Annika sighs. "I planned to leave this city and take off for California. I wanted to live somewhere warm, but then ... I met a man."

"Did he sell you?" Sadie asks.

"No," Annika says, but then she wavers. "Well, he didn't sell me to these blowholes. He was my pimp."

"You dated your pimp?" I try not to sound judgmental, but it's hard. Annika narrows her eyes at me.

"He wasn't always my pimp," she explains harshly. "We dated for a few months when he convinced me to—" she pauses to check that Larissa is asleep before she continues—"have a three-way. Then, he wanted to watch me with someone else. Next thing I know, I'm standing on a corner six nights a week and giving him the money."

Annika runs her tongue over her teeth and shakes her head. "It's a long, bullshit story. The son of a bitch beat me down, made me feel worthless, and then bought me pretty things when I brought in a lot of extra money. But even that stopped after a few months. Then, I was just another whore on the street to him. One of the many."

"How did you get here if he didn't sell you?" Sadie asks.

"He died," she says flatly. "I wish I could have been the one to kill him, but it was the head of the Tsezar Bratva who gunned him down. Cold bastard, that one. That's what they say, anyhow."

I feel Sadie look at me, and my heart clenches in my chest, tightening like a fist. But I try not to react.

"But yeah, he died. Got in a shoot-out a few days ago over some disputed territory. Right after his brother told me it happened, he got one last fuck out of me and then dropped me off at the docks. So, here I am, off to service men in Europe. My business is going intercontinental," she says sarcastically, the bitterness in her voice thick.

Sadie looks from Annika to me and back again, and I pray she won't say anything. Considering she believes Dmitry got us all into this situation, I know she wants to commiserate with Annika about how horrible he is, but for my sake, I hope she'll refrain.

Life inside this box is hard enough without everyone inside of it blaming me for their lot in life. Especially since I don't believe Dmitry did any of this on purpose. He didn't sell me and the girls, and he didn't mean for Annika to end up here.

Suddenly, the latch on the door shifts and light streams in, blinding us all.

I turn away from the sudden brightness until I feel a squirming warmth placed in my arms.

"I'll be back for her in a couple hours." It's the kind guard. Or rather, the guard who doesn't actively abuse any of us. And he has brought me Olivia.

She smells like the sea, but I can still catch a hint of the sweet cinnamon smell I've always associated with my baby. I nuzzle my face in her dark hair.

Devon must be getting tired of looking after a toddler because Olivia is being brought to me more and more frequently.

I wonder what his plan is for her. Then, as quickly as the thought comes, I push it away. I don't want to know.

I want to believe Dmitry will save us before that becomes relevant. I want to believe we will be back at home and in our house together again before I know it.

But if Annika is right, and I have no reason to believe she isn't, this operation is intercontinental. It reaches far beyond the bounds of a single city. Can Dmitry compete with something like that?

I don't see how the Bratva can go toe-to-toe with such a large operation, especially now that we're already out to sea.

Larissa wakes up from a dream crying, and Annika turns her attention from me to focus on the child. Sadie, too, turns away and curls up on the floor.

For the moment, the conversation is forgotten, and I do my best to focus on Olivia while I have her. She tugs at the ends of my hair and caresses my face with her tiny hands. Then she reaches over and hugs Tati's arm. Tati stirs and smiles, but I can see the pain in her eyes.

"Up. Out. Now!"

The Tiger is a man of few words, all of which are shouted in harsh barks of noise, waking us all from what little restless slumber we've managed to find.

"Where are we going?" Annika asks, hugging Larissa to her chest.

I gather Tati close to me. Instinctively, I look for Olivia as well, before I remember she's somewhere else on the ship.

"Doesn't matter. Just listen and go," he says, bending down to spit the words in Sadie's face, even though she didn't say anything.

We all file out of the container one by one, and despite the fear gripping my chest, I drink in the fresh, salty air.

We've gotten small waves of it when the door to the container opens and closes, but I'm usually too distracted by what the guards are doing or saying to enjoy it. This, however, is complete.

I tilt my head up and look into the midnight-blue sky dotted with stars, a thin layer of cloud cover the only thing obscuring the brightness. A damp wave of ocean air lifts my dirty hair, and I sigh.

"Move," the Tiger says, pushing me towards the railing. "You all have five minutes to air out before going back in."

I turn and see a few deckhands going into the container with mops and brooms.

"You're cleaning it," I say.

The Tiger turns to me, disgust written on his face. "It was beginning to smell. I couldn't stand it anymore."

*He* couldn't stand it.

We're the ones living in the container, but the smell bothered him. Poor little guy.

I want to tell him what a worthless piece of shit he is, but I also don't want to do anything to detract from the bliss of fresh air, so I encourage Tati to move closer to the railing and further from the Tiger, and try to enjoy the short window of relative freedom we have.

For the first time in days, Tati looks like a kid. Like a little girl. Her eyes are wide with wonder as she stares out at the water. We live on the beach, but I guess being out in the middle of the ocean just magnifies everything.

*It goes forever*, she signs, blinking in amazement.

*Not forever, but for a long way.*

She nods and then frowns. *Which way is Daddy?*

Tears well in my eyes, and I swallow them back as quickly as I can. I wish I could tell her. I wish I knew exactly where we are and where Dmitry is. I wish I could tell her he's coming for us, but I don't know. I have no idea where on the goddamn earth I am right now, and I hate that I can't offer her some form of comfort.

I try to gather the right words to comfort her without lying, but before I can, I hear the Tiger stomp across the deck.

For a second, I think he's coming for me, and I spin around, shielding Tati.

But then, I see a man standing ten feet to my right. I didn't even hear him approach, but he's stumbling towards the railing with his pants unzipped. Without warning, he pulls his dick out and begins to pee over the railing into the ocean.

"Hey, you drunk bastard," the Tiger complains loudly. "Get out of here."

The man mumbles something and gives himself a shake before zipping back up. "I needed a piss."

The Tiger grabs the man's sleeve and pushes him towards the side deck, but the man resists, turning for the first time to take in the sight of the half-dozen women standing in front of him.

"You let them out to play?" he slurs, obviously drunk.

"Not for you," the Tiger growls. "Get going, before I throw you overboard."

The drunk man digs in his heels and lifts a finger to point directly at Sadie. She's standing a few feet away from me, arms crossed over her chest to fend off the chilly ocean breeze. She's in a low-cut, long-sleeved pajama top with no bra, and the cold air is making that obvious.

"How much for her?"

"Not for you," the Tiger repeats. "Get out."

"For the night," the man says quickly. "Just for a night. Or an hour. I have cash."

The Tiger is quick to anger, so I expect him to deck the man and throw him overboard for insubordination, but instead, he releases his hold on him and steps back, looking from the man to Sadie and back again, weighing the offer.

"You want to pay for one night?"

Sadie gasps and steps closer to me, as though she can hide.

The drunk man nods. "I'll pay for whatever I can get. She's, mm, delicious."

The Tiger considers it for a minute, and then turns and moves towards Sadie.

She's frozen in fear, and I throw myself in his path. "You can't do this. What will Devon say?"

Instantly, a hand cracks across my cheek and throbbing pain blooms in my face, radiating down my neck.

"Devon isn't here," he spits. "Even if he was, he wouldn't care what I do with this bitch."

"No," Sadie whispers. "Please. No."

The Tiger smiles, his face morphing into a malicious mask. "She finally begs. Keep that up. I'm sure he'll enjoy that, too."

He grabs Sadie and pulls her towards the drunk man who is rifling through his pockets for whatever cash he can find. I reach out and grab Sadie's arm, desperate to do anything to stop this from happening. To help her.

"Let go!" the Tiger roars, wrenching Sadie out of my grip and throwing her past him towards the sailor, who eagerly grabs her and keeps her from falling on her face.

"Don't do this," I beg, though I know it's pointless.

"Enough," he says with finality. "Don't forget I know where your baby sleeps. It would be so easy to lose her over the railing."

My stomach plummets to my feet, and I turn to Sadie, mouth open in horror. She turns away from me, her face pale and shocked.

But the Tiger isn't done. He turns to Tati, who is peeking out from behind me, and smiles, all of his teeth bared. "And let's not forget this little bitch. You should be more careful if you want to keep her safe."

Having read his lips, Tati clings to me, and I can feel her shaking with sobs.

I want to help Sadie, but there is nothing I can do. Not without risking the safety of my girls. So, I turn and wrap my arms around Tati. I give comfort to the only person I can while my best friend is dragged away by a drunk, horny sailor.

God only knows what awaits her below deck.

"Too bad it wasn't the other sailor," Annika says later that night. "He was way better-looking than the one Sadie got."

None of us spoke for a while after we were returned to the shipping container. It had been cleaned and smelled considerably better, but the air feels stuffier than ever after having breathed fresh sea air.

An hour or so later, Tati finally stops crying long enough to show me something she grabbed from the deck while I was arguing with the Tiger: a jagged piece of metal.

*For protection*, she signs, placing it into my hand.

My heart is torn—between horror that my little girl is trying to find ways to protect us, and pride, that she could still be so tough after everything she has faced.

Now that she's asleep, I work the metal against a ragged edge of the container, sharpening it into a kind of shiv.

"I doubt Sadie cares much about how attractive the sailor is," I snarl.

"She will," Annika says quietly. "Trust me. After a while, you take what little comfort you can find. And you'd rather sleep with an attractive monster than an ugly one."

I don't want to talk about it anymore. I don't want to imagine that kind of life for myself. But after a few minutes, I can't help but ask, "What other sailor are you talking about?"

"You didn't see him?" she asks. "I guess you were a little busy, but there was a second man on the other side of the deck. Blond hair, blue eyes, and an ass that would not quit. The man knew how to fill out a uniform." She laughs hollowly, but dies down when she sees that I'm not laughing with her. Not at all.

I drop the shiv and turn to her, eyes wide. "How tall was he?"

Annika frowns. "I don't know. I was a bit distracted by all of the fighting and threats. Kinda tall, maybe six foot. He had a beard."

A beard. I've never seen Dmitry wear a beard. Could he be in disguise?

As soon as the thought appears, I shake my head.

I'm being ridiculous. As though there aren't a million men who could match that description.

"He kept staring at you," Annika continues. "I thought he might put up some money for you for the night, too. I'm still surprised he didn't."

A shiver moves through me. Regardless of what Annika said, there is no level of attractiveness that could make sleeping with anyone but my husband an experience I'm interested in having.

I have to keep a low profile. I have to do what I'm told and not fight back until I know I can win. Until I'm sure I can escape. Otherwise, I risk putting my girls in harm's way. More than they already are.

Suddenly, the latch on the door squeaks open, and Sadie is shoved through the door.

She falls on her knees in the middle of the container and immediately curls into a ball.

"Sadie," I gasp, laying the shiv aside and crawling towards her. I wrap an arm around her body, and she's shaking. "Are you okay?"

She lifts her face, and I can see her lip is swollen and there are bruises all over her face and neck.

I gasp again, but try to temper my reaction. I don't want to upset her more than she already is.

"What happened?" I ask.

Sadie shakes her head, and I can't blame her for not wanting to discuss it.

Eventually, I get her upright, and we sit against the side wall together. I hold her and try to offer what little comfort I can, but the longer we sit there, the angrier I become.

I silently vow to kill every single person who hurt her. I'll kill the Tiger for threatening my girls. I'll kill the sailor for hurting Sadie. I'll kill anyone who gets in the way of my freedom.

When Sadie falls asleep, I go back to work sharpening the shiv.

# 7

# DMITRY

*I saw them.*

*I saw Courtney and Tati.*

I remind myself of it every second. Every breath.

Every step I take down to the kitchen and every bowl of oatmeal I scoop, I remind myself that I saw them. They are alive. Though, not especially well.

Every spare second I've had has been spent looking for where the women could be held. The deck of the ship is littered with shipping containers and there are a thousand different doors below deck that could lead anywhere, so I hadn't had any luck. Then, I decided to go up for some fresh air.

My roommate came into the room late, stinking of alcohol and sweat, and I couldn't sleep anyway. So, I pulled on some clothes that barely fit and went for a walk. I heard the yelling before I saw anything and didn't think anything of it. The men in charge of the ship seem to always be yelling at someone. They haven't yet learned how to spark fear without raising their voices.

Then, I heard a female response.

*Please, no.*

I knew who it was before I turned the corner, but the sight of Courtney still almost knocked me over.

She had on a loose pair of pajama pants—the same ones she was wearing when I last saw her—but they were stained and dingy now. Her dark hair hung in limp curls around an obviously thinner face. And behind her stood Tati.

They both looked so frail, so terrified. I nearly ran across the deck and wrapped them in my arms, but then a man stepped forward and threatened them.

My vision went almost black with rage, so it took me a moment to recognize that the man was the same one from the poker night. The man with the tattoo of a tiger on his forearm. I couldn't see the tattoo, but I recognized him.

He knew where my girls were. He was the one in charge of them.

*Don't forget I know where your baby sleeps*, he said.

Those words stilled me. Olivia was on the ship, too. My entire family was under that man's control, and I couldn't act until I knew I could save them. Until I knew I wouldn't get them killed.

So, I hung back in the shadows while Sadie was led away by the sailor, and as much as I wanted to, I didn't follow the man with the tiger tattoo or the women back to where they were being held. I didn't draw any additional attention to myself. I walked stiffly, numbly, back to my cabin and tried uselessly to sleep.

Now, I can hardly keep my eyes open.

Lunch service is in full swing. Jake was right in saying the quality of the food would grow worse over time. The produce is all frozen now and most meals lean heavily on bland rice. I know Courtney and the girls can't be eating well, and I hope there will be enough left over that they might get some, too.

"We aren't rationing," the chef yells, grabbing a plate from the lineup and sliding it back towards me. I barely have time to save it from clattering to the floor.

He is a wide man with a soft chin, and I've never heard him say anything below a shout.

"Give them a full scoop or you won't eat tonight," he says, spit flying in every direction.

Truly, I don't want to eat the food. I only eat it now to keep up my strength, but his spittle is making me want to reconsider.

"What a shame that would be," I mumble, voice thick with sarcasm.

The chef cocks his head to the side, eyes narrowed and focused on my face. "Who are you?"

I want to send my clenched fist flying into the man's flabby face. I want to tell him exactly who I am and bring him to his knees with fear.

"Andrew," I say.

"Well," the chef says, taking a slow, purposeful step towards me. "That is strike one, Andrew."

He stares at me for a few seconds as though he expects me to grovel or shake with fear. Instead, I meet his gaze, refusing to even feign respect for such an unworthy man. Eventually, he stomps away to yell at another cook for plating the chicken wrong, but I feel his eyes on me the rest of the service.

"You've made an enemy," Jake says when the waiters finally take the food away to serve.

"Of the chef?"

He nods. "If you get fired, they'll drop you off wherever we make port in Europe, and you'll have to find your own way home. I've seen it happen before."

"I'll be fine." I have no intention of making it all the way to Europe, but Jake doesn't know that.

He hums, unconvinced. "You should come to poker again tonight. It would give me a little competition. I swept last night without you."

It seems the only thing to do on the ship is poker. I skipped last night to search the ship for Courtney. It was a success considering I actually seen her out on the deck. Now, however, I need more information. I need a way to get to her.

"Plus," he continues. "You might actually be fired, and I'd hate for you to be stranded in Russia with no money. You need the cash."

I nod, acting like he has convinced me. "Fine. I'll be there."

~

The Tiger is at the poker game.

The nickname is not very original, but it's what everyone calls him, and I don't care to know his real name anyway. If it's up to me, he'll be dead soon.

"Ready to lose, boys?" he asks, cracking his knuckles like a movie villain.

"I can't lose tonight," a scrawny man says, stacking his chips into a neat pile. "I need more money if I'm going to warm my bed again."

The Tiger hisses at him to be quiet, but I recognize the sailor as the man from the night before who paid for Sadie, and I can tell he's already half drunk. It is a wonder he managed to get it up last night.

"She was worth every penny," he slurs.

Jake perks up. "She?"

"Mind your own business," the Tiger says. "Just play."

"Come on, man. We all know there are women on this boat," Jake says. "We aren't stupid."

"Debatable."

Jake smiles and leans forward onto his elbows, unknowingly doing the hard work for me. "Are you the one in charge of them?"

I can see the Tiger wavering, trying to decide if he wants to stay discreet or brag about his power. Finally, he shrugs. "Depends who you ask."

"He's asking you," I say. "Are you?"

The Tiger turns to me, assessing me for a moment before he nods. "I am."

"Well, shit," Jake says, dropping his cards facedown on the table. "Why are we playing cards, then? There is clearly something else I'd rather be doing if you catch my drift."

The drunk sailor thrusts his hips lazily in front of him, his tongue sticking out between his half-rotted teeth.

"They aren't for you," the Tiger says.

"They aren't for anyone yet, right?" I ask. "They haven't been purchased by anyone?"

"Not yet, but they will be."

"So, why should they go to waste until we reach the next shore?" The words are vile in my mouth, but it's the only plan I can think of. If I can somehow pay for a night with Courtney, we can formulate a plan. I can figure out the best way to get her, Tati, and Olivia off this ship once I know what their routine looks like and once I can have her help on the inside.

The Tiger lifts his chin and shakes his head. “We’ve been out to sea for four days, and you are already out-of-your-mind horny.”

“Horny and willing to pay,” Jake says, pulling a wad of bills out of his pocket.

“No one else needs to know,” I say quietly. “I mean, if you’re nervous what your boss is going to think, it can just be between us.”

I see the jab land exactly as I hoped. The Tiger doesn’t want to look weak. He’s a second-in- command who wants to look like the first. He doesn’t like the suggestion that he’s afraid of being reprimanded.

“The women are under my charge,” he says sharply. He cracks his knuckles again and leans back in his chair. “Tonight, we play poker.”

The drunk sailor groans, but the Tiger reaches out to grab the man by the collar, sitting him upright. The sailor is too wasted to be afraid. He smiles.

“But tomorrow night,” the Tiger continues. “Come here with cash in your pockets and your dicks in your hand. We are going to have ourselves an auction.”

~

I make a cool three hundred from poker, but I still spend the night tossing and turning, wondering if I’ve made a mistake.

What if someone outbids me, and I end up selling my wife to a disease-riddled sailor? I went into this plan knowing that was a possibility, but the reality of it is just now hitting me.

I won’t be able to stand back and watch it happen. I’ll have to fight for her, and we will all end up dead.

After imagining the scenario thirty different ways, each one ending with me thrown overboard while Courtney is dragged roughly away by some drunk, faceless sailor, I finally get up and go for a walk.

Being on the ship has been a stressful experience from the start, but the nights are calm. The sky is filled with stars and without the sound of the chef barking orders, it can even be a little peaceful.

I'm sitting on a wooden bench and staring up at the stars when I hear muffled voices.

I almost walk away in search of a more secluded spot when I hear what sounds like crying. A woman's crying.

Quietly, I stand up and move further down the side deck. Just before the pathway opens into a larger area, I see a door cracked open a few inches, pale light pouring from it. When I stop and press my ear to the door, I can hear heavy breathing and shuffling footsteps.

"Stop, please," a woman pleads quietly.

I know it isn't Courtney, but that doesn't matter. It could be.

I press the door open a few more inches and immediately see the shadowy shape of two people in the back corner of a small storage space. The scrawny sailor from poker has a woman pinned against the wall and his pants are around his knees, giving me a full and very unwanted view of his bare ass.

Then, the woman turns away from him, and I immediately recognize Sadie.

I stand there, frozen for a second, unsure what to do.

Stepping in and stopping the sailor could blow my cover. It could ruin my plan to buy Courtney tomorrow night and plan her escape. It could ruin everything.

But walking away feels wrong.

Sadie and I have never been on the best of terms, but she's Courtney's best friend. And no one deserves to be treated like this.

I'm still standing in the doorway, torn, when Sadie suddenly lifts her arm. Something in her hand catches the light, and I realize it's a sharpened piece of metal.

The sailor shifts back to see what she's doing and just when Sadie should be bringing the shiv down, piercing between his ribs and driving up into his heart, she hesitates.

Her eyes go wide, her hand stills, and the sailor sees the makeshift knife.

"Bitch!" he shouts, wrapping his hand around her wrist.

He has little in the way of muscle, but he's still large enough to overpower Sadie. I can see her fighting, but her hand is turning back towards herself, the point of the blade moving shakily towards her chest.

I'm across the room with my hand around the sailor's forearm before I realize I've made my decision. I can't stand by and let an innocent woman be murdered. Courtney would never forgive me if she knew.

And I would never forgive myself.

His eyes are glassy and unfocused, but when he turns to look at me, I see recognition cross his face. It is quickly replaced by horror when I rip the weapon from his hand and plunge it into his chest.

I almost feel guilty taking out someone so obviously incapable of defending himself, but then I see Sadie stumble away from the man's limp body, hand pressed to her stomach, mouth open in a silent sob, and I don't feel bad at all.

Sadie doesn't seem to know whether she should be more shocked by the dead sailor or me. Her gaze flicks between the two of us before finally settling on my face.

"Dmitry?"

I nod, and then hold a finger to my lips. "No one can know I'm here."

"You're here for ... for Courtney?" she asks.

"Of course." Sadie is clearly more shaken up than I knew. "Why else?"

She holds a hand to her head and takes a deep breath before speaking again. "They said that you sold them. That you sold your family. I guess I thought ... I thought—"

When Sadie looks at me, there is shame on her face, and I know she bought the lie. She believed them. The only question now is: "Did Courtney believe that?"

"No," she says quickly. "Never."

A weight lifts off my shoulders, allowing me to focus on the situation at hand. I look down at the sailor lying at my feet. Blood is beginning to pool around him, and I need to get him overboard before someone finds us. I kick his shoulder with the toe of my shoe. "Can you help me toss him over?"

I could do it myself, but not without getting blood all over me and the ship. With Sadie's help, we could dump him over the side without drawing attention.

Sadie nods, and together, we carry the man out of the room and across the narrow side-deck to the railing. Luckily, the drop just across from the storage room is sheer, and the man plummets straight down into the water, floating for only a second before sinking beneath the dark waves.

"The Tiger is back at the container waiting for me," Sadie says, pressing the heels of her hands into her temples. "What am I going to do? Courtney handed me the shiv, and I didn't think about what would happen after I killed him. Though, I wouldn't have killed him at all if you hadn't shown up. He would have killed me."

She chokes on a sob, and I lay a hand on her back, mostly to keep her quiet. "Courtney gave you the shiv?"

"Tati found it on the deck, and Courtney sharpened it," she says flippantly, like isn't important.

"Tati found it?" Suddenly, I wish I could grab the sailor from the ocean's depths and stab him again. I wish I could make it more painful for him. It would be some small consolation for the horrors my family is going through.

My kind, innocent daughter is scavenging the ship for possible weapons to fight back against her captors. That kind of trauma can't be washed away. That can't be erased and written over. She will carry this experience with her for her entire life, and I want to kill every single person on this ship in vengeance.

"What am I going to do?" Sadie asks, ignoring my question. "The Tiger is standing guard, and I—"

"You're going to return and tell him the sailor was too wasted to walk you back," I finish for her. "The man is a sloppy drunk. The Tiger will believe you."

Sadie stares up at me and nods, understanding. I follow her to the back of the ship—the stern, I've learned—and through a maze of shipping containers and cargo to where the girls are being kept.

It's a nondescript container beneath a tall stack of others. I never would have found it on my own.

Just as Sadie said, the Tiger is standing guard outside of it, hidden in the shadows. I grab Sadie's arm for a minute, looking around to be certain I'll be able to find the women again on my own, and then send her on.

She's shaking and terrified, but that doesn't mean anything. The Tiger will assume she's shaken from her encounter with the sailor. As long as Sadie can pull off the lie, he won't suspect a thing.

I want to stay and make sure Sadie gets inside okay, but I'm not sure what I'll do if he opens the door, and I see my wife and daughter huddled inside like cattle en route to the slaughterhouse. There is no way to be sure I won't kill him right then and there.

So, I walk away and let Sadie go the rest of the way on her own.

## 8

# COURTNEY

The Tiger came for Sadie late. We were already asleep when the door squealed open, and he pulled her out without so much as an explanation.

I shoved the shiv into her hand before my brain had even fully grasped what was happening. And as time passed without her return, I wavered on whether or not I wanted her to use it.

If she killed the sailor, she would be punished. Harshly. Likely with death.

If she didn't kill him, and the Tiger found the shiv on her, it could be traced back to me or Tati. I didn't think Sadie would turn in a child, but torture could do strange things to a person. There was no way to know what she would or wouldn't do.

The longer I sit, waiting for Sadie to return, the more my worries grow.

So, when she finally returns, pale, shaking, and terrified, I'm relieved.

She's alive.

The Tiger isn't going to take Tati away.

Everything is horrible, but it's a type of horrible I'm accustomed to, which is a small kind of comfort.

As soon as the door to the container is sealed shut, Sadie throws herself at me, and I nearly fall backwards. "Are you okay?" I stutter, startled.

Sadie grabs my shirt with both fists. "He's here."

I saw the Tiger leave and no one else came inside with Sadie, but I still look around the container in an effort to understand what she's talking about. "What?"

"Dmitry," she says in a harsh whisper. "He's on the ship."

Time slows down, and I can't breathe. Can't think. Can't do anything but stare at Sadie, trying to decide if she has entirely lost her mind or if I can trust her.

"Courtney," she says, grabbing my shoulders and shaking me. "He is here. He is really here. He just saved my life."

I sit, shell-shocked, while Sadie relays the last few minutes for me, explaining how Dmitry appeared out of nowhere and saved her from being killed. She tells me that he killed the sailor and they both threw his body overboard. Then, she tells me he escorted her back to the container and left.

"Did he say anything else?" I ask when I can finally find the words. "About saving us?"

She shakes her head. "I know that's why he's here—I mean, he said he was here for you—but there wasn't time to talk about anything else. I had to get back before the Tiger came looking for the sailor."

I'm disappointed I don't know more—it still feels impossible Dmitry could actually be here on the ship—but Sadie seems coherent, so I believe her. And for now, the knowledge that Dmitry is nearby is enough.

"I was so wrong about him," Sadie says, wiping a tear from her eye and shaking her head. "I never should have doubted him."

"You didn't know," I say, grabbing her hand and squeezing. "We've both been through a lot, and you didn't know."

"You told me. That should have been enough."

"I've lied to you before," I say, recalling the beginning of my relationship with Dmitry. I lied to everyone about what I was doing in his house, about why I was with him. Sadie came through for me then. She involved herself with dangerous men to try and save me, even though I didn't actually need saving.

Now, it's my turn to save her.

"I'm still sorry," she says. "He is a good guy."

I wrap an arm around her shoulders and lean back against the metal wall. Tati is sleeping next to us. I want to tell her Dmitry is on the ship, but I'm not sure it's safe. No one can know, and I don't want a nine-year-old to be the keeper of that kind of secret.

"He is a good guy," I agree quietly. I squeeze her against my side. "And he's going to get us out of here."

~

When the container opens late the next day, I think it might be Dmitry.

I know he can't just barge into the container and free us. We're on a ship in the middle of the ocean. Our escape will have to be more nuanced than that. Still, logic does little to curb my hopes.

So, those hopes plummet to the depths when I see it's the Tiger, and he wants us to follow him.

"You three," he says, pointing to Sadie, Annika, and me. "Come with me."

I wrap my arm around Tati, and she clings to my side, her fists balled in my shirt. "Not without my daughter. I'm not leaving her here."

I've spent all day comforting Tati with vague promises. I stroked her sweaty forehead and told her we wouldn't be here for long, that we would get out. Before knowing Dmitry was on the ship, I avoided such things because I didn't want to lie to her. I told her I would keep her safe, but I couldn't promise anything beyond that. But now, her hopes are high, and I might be being ripped away from her forever.

The Tiger laughs, but his face is pulled back in a sneer. "Trust me, you don't want her going where you're going."

My heart hammers in my chest, fluttering so fast it's hard to breathe. I'm already separated from Olivia. What if they take Tati away, too? What if I leave and when I come back, she's gone?

"I'll watch her," another woman says, leaning forward to lay a hand on my arm.

It's the first time I've heard the woman talk since we've been locked in the container. I don't know who she is, but I see the sincerity in her eyes. It does little to make me feel better.

"Come on," Sadie says, grabbing my hand.

I hesitate, digging my feet into the slick metal floor, trying to hold my position. Tati grips my leg, and I can feel her trembling.

I drop Sadie's hand and turn to sign to Tati, to tell her to stay quiet and stay with the other women, but before I can, there is a flash of heat across my face. My head cracks to the side, and I gasp at the sharp bite of pain.

The Tiger's hand is still lifted in the air, ready to come back down on me. "Do you want me to do it again?"

"Come on," Sadie urges, eyes wide.

I shake my head and follow Sadie towards the door. Just before stepping out, I turn and hold up the sign for *I love you*. Tati returns it with a trembling lower lip. The woman wraps an arm around her shoulders, and I take in my precious girl's face, hoping I'll see it again.

We've been on a strict schedule since arriving on the ship. Meals come at the same time every day, and the nicer of the two guards changes the bathroom bucket three times a day. Every change in that schedule, like when the Tiger took us out on the deck and when Sadie was taken away last night, has been bad. So, I have no reason to believe this is any different.

We walk down the narrow hallway that leads towards the deck we visited a few days before, but instead of taking the stairs up, the Tiger goes down, further into the belly of the ship.

The lights along the hallway are dim, and the metal walls seem to be pressing in on us. I've never suffered from claustrophobia before, but panic creeps into my chest, and I'm having difficulty breathing.

Suddenly, I feel Sadie's hand slip into mine. She's walking in front of me, but she must have been able to hear my labored breathing.

After everything she has endured, I should be comforting her. Still, I squeeze her fingers back, trying to send her a silent message that I love her, no matter what happens in the next few minutes.

Suddenly, the Tiger stops walking, and Annika nearly runs into his back. He scowls at her and then addresses each of us, eyes narrowed. "I expect you ladies not to embarrass me, do you understand?"

Not at all, but he takes our silence as an agreement and opens the door to his right.

I'm not even in the room when the smell of alcohol and sweat hits me. It is like walking into the bathroom of a dive bar. I didn't think anything could repulse me more than the bathroom bucket in our shipping container, but my nose wrinkles as I step into the dimly lit room.

My eyes have to adjust to the darkness. The only light comes from a few neon lights hanging on the walls, and a poker table has been set up in the middle of the room, though the game seems to be forgotten now that the women have arrived.

There are only three men in the room aside from the Tiger, but the space is so small that it feels like there are more of them. For a second, I am too overwhelmed to really see anything. I'm skimming the surface of the space, trying to get my bearings, to understand on some level what is happening to us. Then, I skim over his face.

*His* face.

Seeing it feels like hearing a long-forgotten line from my favorite book.

I know it instantly, and my heart swells with relief.

He blinks at me, but otherwise, his face is stoic, unruffled.

He has a beard now, and I realize that the man Annika described that night we were on the deck was Dmitry after all. He's been here all along, ready to save me. Even when I didn't know it.

My eyes fill with tears, and I want to cry, but I can't. Not here. Not now.

I'm in Dmitry's presence, and even though he's clearly in disguise and in as much danger as I am, I feel safer with him around. I don't want to do anything that would make the Tiger want to send me away.

The other two men at the table all but lick their lips as we line up in front of them, and even with Dmitry sitting five feet away from me, my stomach drops when I realize what this is.

"Well, men," the Tiger says, shutting the door behind us. "Let the bidding begin."

I try not to stare at Dmitry, but it's difficult. I want to know if he has a plan. I want to know if he has enough to buy me, and what the plan is after that.

I don't have Tati or Olivia with me, so we can't just jump in a life raft and hope to hit land. Even if we do get to be alone together, what is the plan?

"Hey, where's the other one?" the Tiger asks, gesturing to an empty chair in the corner.

The other man.

The one Dmitry killed last night to save Sadie.

My eyes widen in understanding, but Dmitry stays calm. He looks completely unaffected. The two men next to him shrug, and Dmitry just lolls his head to the side, looking kind of bored.

"I saw him shooting up in the stacks. If he hasn't passed out from the heroin, he'll be drunk by now. I doubt he's going to make it."

The Tiger frowns and then shrugs. "That's fine. Three women for three men. It might not be as exciting, but this way, everyone will be happy."

Clearly, the Tiger is not taking the feelings of the women into account, because we certainly will not be happy. I pray that Dmitry will win the auction, and I, at least, will be happy. For a little while.

"Can we call dibs?" a man with a thick mustache asks. It's hard to tell in the dark, but he looks closer to my dad's age than to mine. His eyes are pinned on Sadie.

"That is what the money is for." The Tiger grabs Sadie's shoulders and jerks her forward violently. "The bidding will begin at—"

"Wait," the third sailor says. He's a large, round man with ruddy cheeks. "Don't we get to see what we're bidding on first?"

"Put your glasses on and maybe you'd be able to see something," the older sailor jokes. Dmitry laughs but it doesn't reach his eyes. His hands are folded tensely in his lap.

The third man rolls his eyes and stands up. Suddenly, his attention catches on me, and his mouth falls open slightly. "I just want a little touch."

The Tiger thinks about it for a second and then nods. "One minute."

In an instant, the man is standing in front of me. He is oily and unshowered, and when his hand slides down my waist, I cringe away from him.

The man is not dismayed, however, and he slides his hand down further, resting on my hip for a moment before sliding across the front of my pajama pants. Just before his palm can find my center, I lift my own palm and slap him.

It wasn't anything I planned to do. Simply an innate reaction to being sexually assaulted. I gasp as my hand connects with his face.

His entire face goes red. "You bitch."

He lifts his hand, but before he can bring it down, The Tiger stops him with a quick tsk tsk.

"You buy it, then you break it," he says sarcastically, gesturing for the man to back away. "No damaging the merchandise until it's yours."

The man's nostrils flare as he glares at me, and I pray I won't have to go anywhere with him. If I do, I'm not sure I'll ever make it back.

When the man finally backs away and returns to his seat, I see Dmitry sitting on the edge of his. His hands are clamped on his thighs, his knuckles white. When he looks at me, I can see the fire burning inside of him. I tip my head forward slowly, trying to show him I'm okay, but he tears his eyes away as the Tiger once again claps his hands on Sadie's shoulders.

"Enough delay," he says. "Money out, men. It's time to start."

# 9

# DMITRY

I make one starting bid on Sadie just to ease any suspicion that could arise, and then sit back and let Jake and the head chef bid on her.

I hope the chef will win. After the way he touched Courtney, there is no way I'll be able to sit back and let them leave together. I'll kill him and everyone else in the room before I let that happen.

He usually doesn't join us for poker, but apparently the Tiger reached out to him personally about the auction. Now, his eyes are trained on my wife, and this entire auction feels like a terrible idea. I can't believe I came up with it.

"Three hundred," the Tiger says, waving a hand in front of Sadie like she's the shiny new car on a game show. "Do I see three hundred?"

Jake raises his hand and wags his eyebrows in Sadie's direction. She turns away to look at the floor, and the chef groans.

"Have her, Jake," he says with a dismissive wave. "She isn't worth it."

I only have five hundred dollars in my pocket, so I hope the chef feels the same way about Courtney. Though, of course, he would be wrong. She's worth everything.

"One snarky bitch to the snarky bitch," the Tiger teases, pushing Sadie towards Jake.

Jake doesn't seem to mind the insult and claps for himself, reaching out to grab Sadie's hand and pull her into his lap. She sits stiffly, holding her head high even as Jake wraps his arms around her and curls his fingers up her thighs.

Sadie isn't my wife. She isn't really even my friend. And still, I want to break every single one of Jake's fingers.

How much worse will it be if I have to watch Courtney be touched by someone else?

I grit my teeth and block the possibility from my mind. I'll win. We'll leave together and have an entire night. Everything will be fine.

The Tiger moves behind Courtney and reaches over her shoulder to grab a handful of her dark hair. He pulls it behind her shoulder. "This one is a fireball, and you can only hope she's the same way in the bedroom. Let's start the bidding a little higher at one hundred and fifty."

"Here," the chef says immediately, sitting up in his chair.

"Two hundred."

I raise my hand.

Back and forth it goes, each of us increasing the bid by fifty without hesitation or pause.

"Five hundred," the chef says, winking at Courtney before turning to raise a brow at me. "Will you challenge me, boy?"

*Boy.*

I should kill him just for that. If this chef had any idea who he was really talking to, he'd cower in fear. He'd beg me for mercy.

"Five fifty," I say with a tip of my head.

I can find the money. Jake can spot me something. I'll give the Tiger my—or rather, Andrew's—next paycheck. I'll sell the clothes on my back to the other sailors to make up the difference. I'll figure it out.

"Five sixty," the chef says, wavering for the first time.

Courtney's eyes are wide, and I can see the fear in her face. I can't fail her.

"Six hundred." I lean forward, elbows on my knees, and wait for the chef to increase the bid. Wait for her to challenge me.

Instead, he growls in frustration and turns to look at the third woman standing in the row. She's noticeably thinner than Sadie and Courtney. Her hair is thin and stringy, eyes sunken in. It looks like the chef would break her in half the moment they tried to touch.

"Fine," he says, throwing up his hands and falling back in his chair. "The sickly one for cheap is better than the beautiful one for my entire savings. The way I do it, it won't matter what she looks like anyway."

The third girl shivers, and I don't blame her. I'm only sorry she and Sadie will have to suffer for me to be with Courtney.

The Tiger claps his hands once. "Great. Hand over the money and take your prizes."

Jake jumps up, his arm firmly around Sadie's waist, and hands over his cash. I casually pull mine from my pocket and hand it to him in a wad.

My hopes fall when he begins to count it.

"You're one hundred short," the Tiger says.

Courtney was moving towards me, but now the Tiger's arm is over her chest, holding her back.

"Then she's mine," the chef says immediately. "If he doesn't have the money to pay, then he doesn't get to play. I'll take both women."

"You wouldn't know what to do with two women," I snap. Then, I turn to the Tiger, my voice level. "I'll pay you when I get paid next."

He shakes his head.

"With interest," I add.

"This isn't a leasing program," the chef shouts. "It isn't rent-to-own. Either you have the money or you don't."

A hand claps on my shoulder, and I turn to see Jake looking at me, his mouth twisted in regret. "Sorry, man. But he's right. You lost."

The Tiger hands me my money and then pushes Courtney towards the chef, whose eyes are sparkling with excitement.

My heart is pounding in my chest, my fists clenched at my side, and my vision is going dark. I can't see anything, can't hear anything. Rage is flowing through me to the point I'm surprised smoke isn't coming out of my ears.

"Don't worry. I won't be too rough," the chef laughs.

Suddenly, I'm across the room with a fistful of the chef's shirt in my hand. "I'll fight you for her."

He is surprised by my sudden movement, and then one of his thin eyebrows arches up. "You're kidding."

"If I win, then I get to take her with me. If you win, you keep them both." I let go of his shirt and hold out my hand to shake. "Deal?"

He starts to shake his head, but before he can say anything, the Tiger barks out a laugh behind us. "I thought that auction was a bit too tame. This is exactly what we need. A little brawl to liven things up."

I can tell the chef wants to refuse, but no matter how superior he feels, he knows the Tiger outranks him. If the Tiger wants to see a fight, he'll see a fight.

His top lip pulls back in a sneer, and he holds his hands up in surrender. "Fine."

Courtney is standing with Sadie and Jake at the edge of the hold with the Tiger near the door, ensuring no one comes in to interrupt us. The third woman is leaning against a wooden crate, looking bored.

The room is small, which makes the chef look even larger. Standing across from me, he looks like a wild bear.

I assumed a lot of his girth was fat, but when he takes off his shirt to fight, I'm surprised by how solid he actually is. I still think I can beat him, but it may be tougher than I expected.

I peel my shirt off, too, and toss it to Courtney.

She catches it and the chef snorts like an angry bull. "She isn't yours yet."

"Yes, she is," I say with a cocky smile. Courtney is mine. In every sense of the word. The ring on her finger is one I put there. I don't need to pay for her affection, I already have it. If the chef knew who I was and who she is to me, he wouldn't be fighting right now. He'd be begging for mercy on his knees.

"The rules are that there are no rules," the Tiger says. He waves an arm. "Fight."

Chef knows he's larger than me, so he stands his ground, forcing me to approach him. I stay low, hands up and ready.

The room isn't large enough to outrun him or tire him out. I'm going to have to fight hard and dirty.

As solid as Chef looks, he stumbles when I first strike him, and I quickly follow with a few quick jabs, giving him no time to reset.

He stumbles again, falling back into the wall, and I think that perhaps this fight will be over even faster than I anticipated, when suddenly, his body is hurtling towards me.

He used the wall as leverage to push himself forward, and I fall back, head slamming against the metal floor of the ship before I can understand what is happening. Then, there is a blow to my cheek.

Light explodes across my vision, but I have enough wherewithal to lift my hands and protect my face.

Chef is too heavy for me to roll him off me, but he's balanced in a strange position, leaned slightly forward, and I see my opening. I pull my knee up hard and fast, catching him in the hamstring, and he has to stop hitting me long enough to catch himself before he falls. It gives me enough time to slam my hands into his chest and push him over.

He grumbles as he falls, and for the first time, his heft has given him the disadvantage. While he's still trying to get himself up off the floor, I'm on my feet.

I move around behind him and kick him in the spine. He arches his back and falls again, this time flat on his stomach.

As he lifts himself, I wrap an arm around his neck and squeeze, tightening my hold with my right arm, and spreading my legs to brace myself.

Immediately, his hands tug at my arms, and he tries to break free, but I keep a firm grip, gritting my teeth against his struggles.

His fighting becomes weaker and, slowly, he slumps forward and to the floor.

I know he's down, but I can't make myself let go.

He had his hands on my wife. He wanted to take her back to his room and do God knows what to her. He is a piece of scum who wants to buy and sell women, and he deserves to die. That is all I'm doing. Delivering justice.

"Hey, man." The Tiger tries to loosen my hold, but I don't respond. I know I should, but I'm so close. Just another minute, and he'll be dead. Sixty seconds. That's nothing.

"Let go," he warns, voice low and threatening. He kicks my leg, but I don't feel it.

"Andrew," Jake says. "Let him up."

I'm going to do it. I'm going to kill the chef.

Then, I hear a female gasp.

I look up, remembering Courtney is in the room, but see Sadie instead. Jake is holding onto her, his hand spread across her hip. Her hand is over her mouth, eyes wide.

When I see Courtney standing next to her, she shakes her head slightly, calling me off, and I let go.

I fall back, pushing myself away from the chef, so I'm not tempted to grab him again.

"Shit," the Tiger says, rolling the chef over onto his back. "I thought you were going to kill the poor bastard."

I laugh but it's humorless.

I want to kill them all.

The Tiger turns on me and lifts his foot as though he's going to plant it on my chest. Before he can, I shove it aside and stand up.

I should be meek, quiet. I need to fly under the radar.

But my adrenaline is pumping, and I can't remember the last time I was disrespected like this.

"Don't fucking kick me," I spit. "Don't you dare."

"You have no fucking idea—"

I catch sight of Courtney over the Tiger's shoulder. Her eyes are wide, and she's glaring at me, speaking volumes with no words at all.

"No fucking idea what?" the Tiger asks, puffing out his chest and getting in my face. "You may have taken down this fat sack of shit, but you don't want to fight me."

He is wrong. I do want to fight him. I want to kill him.

But I can't.

Not yet.

I press my lips together and breathe slowly out of my nose. I shake out my shoulders. "Adrenaline. Sorry."

The apology is like acid in my mouth, but the Tiger steps away, somewhat appeased. "Take your bitches and go. I'm done dealing with you all tonight. Have them back at the poker room by sunrise."

The Tiger grabs the third woman, who will no longer be going with the chef, and leads her out of the room without another word. Jake extends an elbow to Sadie, who does not accept and only goes with him when he grabs her arm. Then, Courtney and I are alone.

Despite the small size of the room, the distance between us seems insurmountable. She's steps, yards, miles away from me, and I can't fathom walking over and being able to touch her.

Then, a sob breaks out of her, and I'm across the room in an instant.

"I'm here," I whisper, rubbing a hand across her dirty cheek. "I'm here. I'm sorry."

She falls against me, and the feel of her body in my arms is familiar. She's thinner than I remember, but she's warm, and her cheek rests in the hollow of my neck perfectly.

"Come with me," I whisper into her hair. "Let me take care of you."

I walk her through a maze of hallways back to my room. Thankfully, my roommate is on duty for the night, so we have the place to ourselves. I pull Courtney into the small bathroom with me and begin to wash her.

Clearly, she hasn't bathed or been taken care of in days, so I strip her clothes off and push her into the lukewarm water of the shower. She stands in the flow, her tears mixing with the water, and lets me wash her hair and lather soap over her skin.

I move gently, almost as though she's a stranger.

How many days has it been since we've seen one another? I've lost track. It feels like years.

I dry Courtney off and help her dress in some of the clothes Andrew had packed.

"These aren't yours," she says, sniffing the shoulder of her shirt and frowning at me.

I love that she knows my smell.

I explain what happened after she was taken and how I got onto the ship. I tell her that I've been looking for her from the moment I arrived and that the auction was my idea.

"It was the only way I could think to get you alone," I say. "I'm sorry."

Her chin wobbles, and she shakes her head. "It isn't your fault. None of this is your fault."

I don't believe her, but I pull her close and kiss her temple.

Courtney tells me that she only sees Olivia occasionally. She doesn't know where she's being kept or by whom. She tells me that Tati is sick and growing worse. Her headaches are crippling, and the conditions they are living in aren't helping.

"She's the one who needs a bath, not me," Courtney says, pressing her hands against her face. "She should be here with you. She should be sleeping in a bed for the night. I don't deserve any of this."

I know Courtney would trade places with Tati in a second. So would I. I would trade my life to free all of them right now if it were possible.

I kiss her fingers and pull her hands away from her eyes. "You don't deserve what has happened to you, but you deserve this."

I bring her fingertips to my lips and then uncurl her fingers, kissing my way across her palms.

"You deserve to be cared for."

I wrap her arms around my waist and cradle her face. She tries to gently pull away, but I hold her steady, staring into her eyes.

"I love you," I whisper. "And you are going to get out of here."

Her chin wobbles again, tears welling in her eyes, and I can't bear it. I can't stand that she's here because of me and, right now, there is nothing I can do about it.

So, I tilt her face up to mine and kiss her. Because I've missed her, because I love her, and because there is nothing else I can do.

Courtney goes liquid in my arms. Her body arches against mine, and her lips open, allowing me into her mouth.

She tastes the same—mint with a hint of cinnamon—and I inhale her, trying to cherish every single detail about her I've missed.

When she pulls away, I keep my eyes closed, not wanting to give up on the moment.

"We can't. We have to make a plan. We have to get out of here. We have—"

"All night," I finish, bending to kiss the end of her nose. "We have all night."

I see the doubt in her eyes, but I can also see that she has missed me in all the same ways I've missed her. When I drag her arms up over my shoulders and plant my hands on her waist, her eyes flutter shut.

When I curve my hands around to her backside, pulling her against me, she sighs.

"I've missed you." Her voice breaks. "So much."

I kiss my way up her jawline and nibble on her earlobe. "You don't have to miss me now. I'm right here."

Courtney tangles her fingers in the longer hair at the base of my neck and then reaches around to pinch at my beard. "You have a beard now."

"Disguise," I mumble as I kiss her neck.

"I like it."

"I'm cutting it as soon as we get home."

I feel her tense, and I smooth calming lines down her back. "We are going to make it home. You and me and the girls."

She takes a deep breath, and I know there is nothing I can do about the trauma she has endured. There is nothing I can do about the horrible way she has been treated. But even though I can't take care of our daughters right now, I can take care of Courtney.

I press my lips to hers softly, walking her back towards the bed, and slide my hands under the hem of her too-large shirt.

She tenses when my hand brushes across her skin, as though she's nervous, but then she relaxes, easing into my touch. I pull her shirt over her head, tossing it to the side.

"We should plan," she whispers, tipping her head back as I trail kisses down her jaw and across her collarbone.

"After," I say against her skin. I'm too far gone to think about escaping, to think about anything other than her body. I'm a man who has been without water and suddenly, here is a tall, delicious glass. "I need you."

Courtney reaches for the button of my pants, and I fumble for hers. Clumsily, as though we've never done this before, we undress one another. When Courtney goes to lie down on the bed, I grab her arm and shake my head. "That's my roommate's. Top bunk."

She turns and climbs the ladder, and I can't stop myself from leaning forward and taking a bite out of her as she goes up. She pauses, surprised by my touch, and I keep going. Nipping and kissing my way to her upper thighs. Courtney clings to the ladder and spreads her legs slightly, and I almost black out from lust. I kneel on one of the lower rungs and position myself between her legs.

When I lick across her center, she jolts and repositions herself on the ladder. "This is dangerous."

"This is hot," I growl, wrapping my hands around her thighs for more support.

With every stroke and suck, her legs tremble in my hands, but I won't stop. Not until she releases, not until her body is filled with nothing but pleasure and warmth and bliss.

"Dmitry," she gasps when I circle my hand around the ladder and her body to rub circles against her sensitive skin.

"Come for me," I command, pressing my tongue into her. "Come."

Her entire body tenses, her back arches, and then her hips begin to circle, matching the rhythm of my mouth. A deep, guttural moan comes out of her that I've never heard before. By the end of it, she's dangling from the ladder with limp arms, and I have to give her a push from beneath to get her up onto the bed.

As soon as I climb up after her, she tries to push me to lie down, but I shake my head. "This is about you."

She opens her mouth to protest, but I capture her lips in a kiss and cover her body with mine. Courtney wraps her legs around my hips and it feels like coming home. It feels like the hole that opened in my chest when she was taken has closed slightly. The ache is momentarily gone, and I can't stop myself from seeking more relief in her.

I press myself to her opening and thrust inside.

Courtney gasps, her fingers digging into my shoulder blades. She rolls her body against mine, drawing me in deeper, her breathing coming in small huffs that match the speed of our meeting.

Her body is soft, and I massage my hands down her body, rolling my palms over her breasts.

"More," she says, looking directly into my eyes. She sits up and kisses my mouth. Then, she speaks against my lips. "Make me forget."

I've never had more motivation to pleasure a woman in my entire life.

I pin her to the mattress and kneel in front of her, wrapping her legs around my hips. Then, I grab her legs for leverage and pull her against me.

The connection is deeper than anything I've ever felt, and I groan as she slides away.

Again and again, our bodies slap together. Courtney closes her eyes, her arms thrown over her head as we shake the entire bunk bed, despite it being bolted into the wall. I thrust into her as fast as my body will allow, and when I smooth my hand down her stomach and across her center, her back arches.

"Yes," she moans, clapping a hand over mine, directing me towards her sensitive nub. "Yes, please."

"So polite," I tease, circling my thumb over her in time with my thrusts.

Her legs clench around my waist, squeezing me to her, and I can see the muscles in her flat stomach working as she gets closer.

Just when I think she's going to fall apart, she slaps my hand away, grabs my shoulders, and pulls herself up so she's sitting in my lap. Suddenly, she's the one in control, and I am not complaining.

Her breasts are swaying in front of my face, and I draw one into my mouth, swirling my tongue around her nipple while Courtney circles her body over me.

We are tangled in one another, as close and vulnerable as two people can be, and it still isn't enough. I still want more of her. Now and forever.

I grab her waist and draw her against me again and again. Courtney curls her fingers in my hair and kisses me, her tongue exploring my mouth until I can't think of anything but her. Until I don't remember where I am or who I am. All I know is I'm happy, and I love this woman.

I feel her body tense as her second orgasm rocks through her. The sensation of her pulsing is enough to bring me to the edge.

I grab her ass and crush her against me, begging for more, for everything.

Heat builds in my stomach, tight and coiling like a snake. When Courtney cries my name, it explodes.

I gasp and it feels like I'm breathing for the first time. I cling to her, circling my arms around her tiny waist until I'm afraid I might suffocate her. Courtney wraps her arms around my neck, and we cling to one another as the orgasm flows and begins to ebb away.

When we're done, Courtney curls against my chest, and I hold her. We cling to one another like the world is ending, and we're one another's shelter.

That's what Courtney is. My shelter.

She talks about the beach outside of our house. She dreams of making it back there with our girls, of the family trips we should take abroad.

I want all of that, too, but in the back of my mind, I wonder if I can ever be for Courtney what she is for me. Can I ever be that soft place to land? Can I save her the way she has saved me?

My life is messy and cruel, and she and the girls are experiencing that firsthand. They deserve safety and peace, and I don't know if I can give her that.

Courtney tells me about the conditions of the shipping container and the schedule of the Tiger's visits, as well as the visits of another man who helps take care of them.

"Another man?" I ask. "I didn't know there was anyone else."

"He is quiet," she says. "I don't know what his role is. He has dark hair and blue eyes, but he hasn't said anything about his name. He's nicer than the Tiger, but—"

"None of these men are nice." I clench my teeth and take a deep breath, trying to calm down. "They are all monsters, and I'm going to get you out of here. I'm working on it now."

"How?" Courtney asks.

I wish I could tell her, but I don't know yet. "I have to get to all three of you at the same time. Now that I know where you and Tati are, I have to find Olivia. Once I do that, I can formulate a plan."

"And you'll tell me what this plan is?" she asks, drawing a finger down my chest.

I nod. "Of course. As soon as I know, you'll know."

~

I'm not sure when we fall asleep or how long it has been when the knocking sounds at the door.

"Time is up," the Tiger yells from the other side of the door.

Courtney gasps and clutches me. Her entire body is trembling, and her face is pale.

"It's okay," I whisper, kissing her hair, wishing I could go with her. Wishing I could kill the Tiger and keep her with me. "I'll see you again. It will be okay."

I help her dress in the dirty clothes she came in, and when I open the door, I see the Tiger take in her new, cleaner appearance. His eyes narrow, and I know the look too well.

Desire.

"Someone got a bath."

Courtney glares at him, and he wraps his hand around the back of her neck. "Come with me."

It takes everything inside of me not to rip his hand off with my teeth. I watch until they reach the end of the hallway and turn the corner. I watch until she's gone and then wait a few minutes after that.

Then, I set about my day, all the while harnessing my rage and frustration into action. I have to get us all out of here.

## 10

# COURTNEY

Tati is sitting up in the middle of the container, letting Larissa braid her hair.

Seeing the two girls do something so normal feels bizarre under the circumstances. Though, for the moment, I'm relieved.

Tati is awake and well enough to play. Well enough to want to do something besides cling to me. At least temporarily, I can think about something other than her declining health.

Though, I'm not sure how much of a gift that is.

Coming back to the container after a night with Dmitry—a night with a shower, clean clothes, and his arms around me—is harder than I ever would have thought possible. It feels like starving inside a cage when there is a plate of steaming food just on the other side. It's torture of the harshest kind.

My husband is here on the ship, but I can't reach him.

My toddler is being cared for by people I don't know, but I can't see her.

The Tiger had brought Olivia to me once a day since we boarded the ship, but since my night with Dmitry, I haven't seen her. No contact, no word.

I tried to ask the Tiger about Olivia when he brought the stale bread that serves as our breakfast, but he just spat at me and left.

Sadie hasn't been responsive since the night of the auction. She just wants to sleep, and I can't blame her. I spent the evening with Dmitry; she spent the evening with an unknown sailor.

I have no idea what he did to her or what he made her do. I feel guilty that she suffered while I found a reprieve.

The nicer of the two guards slipped her a second helping of breakfast when he came for the bathroom bucket. He didn't say anything to her or draw any attention to himself, but he must have noticed she was behaving differently than normal and was trying to help her keep her strength.

Dmitry said no one on this ship can be trusted and that they are all monsters, but I have my doubts about the dark-haired guard. He might be swayed to help us when the time comes.

Suddenly, Tati is in front of me, her little hands on my shoulders.

*Can you tell Larissa that we live on the beach? She doesn't believe me.* Tati's blue eyes—so much like Dmitry's even though he's biologically her uncle—blink up at me, and I want to cry.

I've said nothing to give Tati undue hope, but clearly, she has it anyway. She still considers the beach house our home, and I want to cling to that small glimmer of wishful thinking.

"We live on the beach," I tell Larissa, bringing Tati's forehead to my lips. "Our dining room looks out on the water. It's very beautiful."

Larissa looks amazed and turns to tell Annika about our home. Annika is much less impressed—in fact, she looks more curious than anything, inspecting me with a raised brow—but she feigns wonder for Larissa's sake.

Tati and Larissa meet again in the middle of the container, this time with Tati braiding her friend's hair, and I lean back against the metal wall and try to imagine what it will be like to be home again.

I spoke with Dmitry about what it would be like to go home, but it was more for his sake than mine. He was there with me physically, but emotionally, he felt a million miles away. There was something off in his expression, something haunted that unsettled me. Even if I wasn't certain of it, I wanted him to believe that we would make it back to our old life one day. That we would get off this ship alive and be a family again.

Now, I try to cling to the hope I offered him. And when I can't find the hope, I grab hold of the vengeance instead. It's better than nothing.

~

The Tiger comes for me, Annika, and Larissa late in the evening.

He apparently determined it was too much of a risk to take us all out to the deck for air at once, so now he moves us in groups.

Tati, Sadie, and the other woman whose name I still don't know went out the night before, and now it's our turn.

I push Tati into Sadie's arms, and it seems to awaken something in Sadie. She still isn't as alert as I'd like to see, but she nods in understanding and hugs Tati to her chest.

The air is crisp, slicing through my thin pajamas, but I tip my head back until I see only sky. Until the ship around me is beyond my vision, and I can imagine I'm somewhere else. Somewhere beyond the confines of this emotional, physical prison.

When a finger brushes down my neck, I think for a second that I must be imagining it. But then I feel a body press against my back.

"You have a pretty neck."

The Tiger.

I jerk away, but a thick arm is around my middle before I can, holding me against him. He grinds his hips against my backside, breathing heavily.

"You better get used to being used," he whispers, his voice harsh and threatening. "You're facing a lifetime of it, and men pay more when they think you've enjoyed it."

When his mouth clamps down on my neck, I yelp and drive my elbow back and into his stomach. It doesn't hurt him, but it surprises him enough that his arm loosens, and I slip away from him.

Annika pulls Larissa away, directing her attention to the water beyond the railing, and I don't blame her. I would do the same thing if Tati was here. I don't want Annika to do anything to put herself or Larissa in danger. They need each other.

"What good do you think fighting is going to do?" he asks, tilting his head to the side like a predator examining its prey. "Where are you going to run to? I suppose you could jump overboard, but the cold would kill you. Do you want to die?"

If I didn't have Olivia and Tati to think about ...

If Dmitry wasn't aboard this ship ... .

Then yes, I would rather die.

I would throw myself over the railing without hesitation because death would be preferable to being touched by the Tiger. By his vile, disgusting hands.

But I have a family to think about. I have a little girl waiting for me in a shipping container, and I have to get back to her.

"I'm fighting because I want to live," I say. "The moment I give in to your touch is the moment my life is over."

The Tiger smiles and moves towards me, legs wide and arms spread like a goalie guarding the net. "Then you better say your final prayers."

I try to dart past him, but his arm catches me in the stomach, knocking the wind out of me.

"Go back to the container," he barks at Annika and Larissa. "If you don't, I'll find you and throw you each overboard myself."

Annika nods and rushes Larissa away. I'm glad. I don't want Larissa to see this.

The Tiger pushes me against the railing until the handrail bites into my spine, and I wince.

"This could be nice for you if you'd just give in," he says. "I'm a generous lover."

I could almost laugh. Nothing about the Tiger strikes me as generous, least of all his ability to love. Instead, I slam my fists into his chest.

It's like hitting a brick wall.

He grabs both of my hands, bundling them in one of his, and then begins to fumble with the drawstring of my pants. I try to wiggle my hips away from him, but there is nowhere to go. I'm pinned.

He spreads his legs around mine, pinning me in with his knees, and I want to scream. Instead, I see my last shot at rebellion. Even if it won't deter him, I know it will feel damn good.

I press off from the ground as hard as I can and arc my knee directly between his legs.

Solid contact.

The Tiger's eyes go wide, and he drops his hold on me, preferring, instead, to press a palm to his junk.

"You bitch," he groans, bending forward.

I try to sneak past him, but he recovers quickly and slams a hand into my stomach, pushing me back against the rail.

His knees are still pinched together in pain, but his face is going red, and I know that I've made a mistake. Whatever he had planned for me, I just made it ten times worse.

"You don't deserve my cock," he spits, looking down at me with flared nostrils. "You need to be punished."

I'm tempted to beg him—for my life, for safety, for mercy.

But I can't bring myself to do it.

I was not raised to be a woman who would get on her knees, to beg or otherwise. I won't let him see me weak and broken. I lift my chin and glare up at him. "Then do it."

Suddenly, the Tiger grabs my shoulders and begins pushing me backward, and I realize almost too late that he's trying to push me over the side.

There is a deck below us, so I wouldn't land in the water, but it would hurt. The fall might even kill me if I hit something on my way down.

"Hey!"

The shout comes from behind the Tiger, and he doesn't loosen his hold on me, but he turns. As he does, I can see over his shoulder to a figure standing behind him.

Dmitry.

He looks at me for only a second, but his face is a cold mask, and he quickly turns back to the Tiger.

"What is going on?"

"Mind your business," the Tiger barks. "I'll take care of her."

"Do you mean throw her overboard?"

The Tiger stares down at me, but he rolls his eyes, annoyed with Dmitry. "Why does it matter to you?"

If only he knew.

"It doesn't," Dmitry says with a shrug. "But it might matter to Devon. I'm sure he told you she's an important slave."

"How do you know anything about her?" the Tiger asks, gripping the front of my shirt and turning around to face Dmitry.

"We talked. The other night," Dmitry says. "Between fucking. I don't think you want to hurt her."

"Oh," the Tiger says, laughing to himself. "I really, really do."

Dmitry takes a step forward, but the Tiger must trust him now because he doesn't back away or move to block me. He lets Dmitry approach.

"Don't do something you'll regret," Dmitry says. "Why don't you let me take her off your hands?"

The Tiger frowns. "What the fuck does that mean?"

"It means that you can't hurt her, and I'm guessing you aren't in any condition to have any fun with her," he says, tipping his head in the direction of the Tiger's crotch. "So, let me."

The Tiger shifts uncomfortably at the mention of his injury and then snorts. "You just want another fuck."

"So what if I do?" Dmitry asks cruelly. "It won't make a difference to her. She won't enjoy it."

I'm thinking there is no way this is going to work. No way the Tiger will fall for Dmitry's plan. But the next thing I know, he's grabbing me by the collar of my shirt and dragging me across the deck.

"Here," the Tiger says, throwing me in Dmitry's direction. Dmitry nearly catches me but lets me fall at the last second, smiling as though he's amused. The Tiger smiles too, proud of himself. "Don't be gentle. This one needs to be broken in."

Dmitry bends down and grabs my arm, yanking me roughly to my feet. "I won't."

"Stay close by. I need to go make sure the other women went back to the container, but I'll be back later to collect her when you're finished." With that, the Tiger gives me a final sneer before turning and stalking away.

Dmitry grabs me just above the elbow and pulls me back into a corner between a wall and a stack of lifeboats.

"Fight," he says, voice low.

"What?"

"Fight me," he repeats. "Make it sound like this is a struggle. I'm supposed to be punishing you."

"But he's gone," I start to say.

Dmitry shakes his head. "He could be nearby. We aren't alone, so make it believable."

"What are you going to—"

His mouth is over mine, silencing my question before I can even ask it. I'm not complaining. I sink into his kiss, my hands curling over his shoulder and up his neck. Kissing him feels like taking a deep breath.

He pulls away sharply. "Fight back."

He jerks one of my shoulders and then pushes me back against the wall, the bang echoing across the deck.

I push against his chest, but Dmitry snorts. "That was weak."

"I'm sorry I don't know how to resist my husband."

He hushes me and glances around. "Pretend I'm not your husband then."

I raise a brow. "Like role-playing?"

Dmitry steps forward, shoving his knee between my legs and forcing me back against the wall. "Don't act like we haven't done it before."

I feel my pulse quicken, blood rushing into my face and warming my cheeks. "Pretending to be strangers is different than pretending you're an attacker."

He grabs my hand and jerks it above my head, adding my other before I can even think to fight him. "Who's pretending?" Dmitry leans forward and bites my neck hard.

"Ow," I say, trying to pull a hand free to slap him, but he holds tight.

He has the audacity to smile at me. "That's better. Get angry. Make it real."

He catches my mouth again, but this time I bite his lower lip. He yelps, but I feel him smile against my mouth, and I can't believe it, but I don't hate this.

His tongue swirls against mine, laying claim to my mouth, taking and conquering. It's different than the gentler side of him I usually get, and I squeeze my eyes shut, pretending he's someone else.

It's easy when his hold around my wrists hurts, when he kisses me with crushing force.

I arch my back like I want to get away, but he grinds his hips against mine, pushing me back down. I can feel his excitement through his jeans, and I can feel my own inside my panties.

This shouldn't be thrilling. It should be terrifying, yet with Dmitry's body pressed against mine, it's impossible to be truly terrified. Even though I have my doubts, I can't help but feel hope when we're together.

Maybe we'll get out of here after all.

Dmitry pulls away from me suddenly and grabs my face, his fingers digging into the soft flesh of my cheeks. His top lip pulls back in a snarl. "So, you think you can fight back and get away with it? You think you won't be punished? I'm going to make you wish you jumped."

I blink, confused, and then I hear the voices. Male voices. Amused voices.

"Why doesn't the Tiger let *me* punish the cargo for him?" one of the voices asks.

Dmitry blinks three times, almost like a secret code. Blink blink blink. *I love you.*

He grabs my face harder and kisses me again. I jerk my face away, gasping like my body wasn't made for his, like I don't want him.

Then, he turns me around, sandwiching my body between the wall and his body. He keeps my hands pinned above my head, but his other hand slips down into my pants and around to my front, his finger slipping into me without hesitation.

My body is ready for him.

Anyone listening in might not hear him, but he moans in my ear, excited by my body's response to him.

He presses two fingers into me, and I widen my legs to give him better access while I struggle to pull my arms from his iron grip.

There are no more voices, and I don't see anyone watching us, but Dmitry is right. We can't lower our guard while we're in the open. We can't risk giving away our secret.

"Get off me!" I yell while circling my hips, massaging myself against the bulge I can feel at my back.

"Never," Dmitry purrs in my ear.

His fingers curl inside of me, and I gasp. He is going to need to be worse at this if I'm supposed to pretend it doesn't feel incredible.

My thighs start to shake, which is always a tell-tale sign of my climax, and Dmitry knows this. So, when he massages his thumb over my center, pushing me closer to the edge, I think he's taking me there.

"Does that feel good?" he whispers.

I moan and nod my head, losing track of the charade, forgetting my role in this performance.

Suddenly, his hand is gone.

He is gone.

There is no warmth on my back, no hand between my legs, and his voice isn't at my ear.

I spin around, and he's glaring at me. His handsome face is twisted in annoyance. Eyes narrowed, lips flattened.

He blinks three times.

*I love you.*

"I thought so," he says. "And we can't have that."

I huff in frustration and try to push past him, but he grabs my arm and twirls me around. I hit the edge of one of the lifeboats, and Dmitry moves behind me, bending me over the ledge, pressing on my back to keep me from standing tall.

"What are you—"

His hand lands across my ass in a loud crack, and I yelp.

"You're spanking me?" I shout. I try to kick him, but he moves out of the way and spanks me again.

The pain is bright, blooming across my backside, but in the aftermath, it tingles. Dmitry runs his hand across the sensitive skin, and every sensation is heightened. Then, he spanks me again.

I grunt, absorbing the pain, and am rewarded with another caress.

"This is so fucking hot," Dmitry growls. His voice is harsh, but I sense the words are genuine.

I arch my back and shake my hips, inviting him to enjoy himself. Dmitry accepts.

He grabs the waistband of my pants and pulls them down around my thighs, taking my panties with them. When his hand smacks across me again, the pain is more acute, but the caress afterward is as well.

Dmitry smooths his palm over the sensitive skin, letting his hand dip between my legs, his fingers brushing against the very edge of my opening.

He is teasing me, taunting me with what I want, and no matter how much I arch my back and present myself to him, he refuses to budge.

I growl, and he chuckles spitefully. "The Tiger was right. You're a spitfire."

I look around and don't see anyone watching us. Even if they were, their view would be limited by the wall and the stacks of life vests and boats. So, I take a risk.

I reach behind me and grab at the obvious bulge in Dmitry's pants.

He freezes when I touch him and doesn't seem to wake up until I've unzipped his pants, my hand slipping inside.

"What are you doing?" he whispers.

I answer by gripping his length.

Dmitry must like the answer because he quickly slides his pants down and out of the way, allowing me more mobility. I use it to slide my hand down his length and back up again.

The next smack he delivers doesn't seem to hurt as badly as the others, but I yell anyway.

He slaps me again and again, alternating hands, and I stroke him to the rhythm.

“No, no, no. Stop.” Dmitry can decipher my meaning. *Yes, yes, yes. More.*

His breathing grows erratic, and just when I can feel him tensing up, I lower my hand.

He gasps, confused, and then growls when he realizes what I’ve done.

Dmitry’s weight falls over me, pressing my chest into the lip of the boat. His breath is hot on the back of my neck. “You’re bad.”

“Then punish me.”

He stands up, grips my hips, and is inside of me in an instant. There is no gentle easing or stretching, just our bodies fitted perfectly together. I moan and grab the ledge of the boat for stability.

Dmitry slams into me, pausing to deliver another smack occasionally, and I’m just focused on not crying out. Anyone nearby would definitely know I was not in any pain if they heard me.

This is bliss.

We are both already so close that it isn’t long before I feel him tense behind me, and I give in to the tether that has been pulling me closer to the ledge. I fall, groaning as my body grabs on to him as if it knows he’s going to have to leave, as if it wants to keep him close forever.

Dmitry lays his cheek against my back as the last waves of pleasure move through him, and my pleasure is already shifting into dread.

Despite the fact that we’re in the open, Dmitry presses a kiss to my spine and then pulls my pants up. I let him, desperate for any kind of closeness, for any brush of contact between us.

Too soon, however, he hands me over to the Tiger, and I’m taken away from him and back to the shipping container.

# 11

# DMITRY

It takes me hours to fall asleep after my encounter with Courtney and the Tiger, so when my alarm goes off at 5:00 a.m., I hit the snooze.

Breakfast is always the same, anyway. Some variation of oatmeal and pastries cooked from prepackaged mixes. Nothing Jake and the other cooks can't handle for a bit while I try to feel less dead.

When I do finally make it down to the kitchen, the normal hum of conversation has been replaced by silence. Everyone is going quietly about their work, and no one looks up or pays any attention to me.

"Morning." I nod to Jake, and he raises his brows at me accusingly. I hold up my hands. "Sorry I'm late. I slept like shit. Plus, you don't need my help making this slop."

"Andrew—" Jake starts.

"The chef sleeps in every morning, so why shouldn't we all get a turn?"

Jake's mouth presses into a tight line, and he turns back to his cutting board, chopping walnuts for garnish.

I'm confused about his reaction until I hear a throat clear behind me. I don't need to turn around to know the chef is standing directly behind me. Still, I do.

His arms are crossed over his broad chest, his white shirt straining over the belly beneath.

"Good morning, Chef."

"Outside." He hitches a thumb over his shoulder, pointing to the kitchen door. I follow him out and into the hallway.

I don't want to apologize. Everything I said was true. However, I need this job. I need a reason to be on this ship, to be near my family. If he fires me, I'm not sure what I'll do. I can't pretend to be another crew member on the ship, so my only option would be to hide in the cargo hold like a rat or try to launch an escape before they reach the next port and kick me off.

But I'm not ready. I still don't know where Olivia is being kept, and aside from putting my family in a tiny lifeboat and hoping we make it to shore before a storm hits or a ship runs us over in the darkness, I don't have any way to escape. I could call the Bratva for help, but I don't know where the ship is located or how they would get to us even if I could tell them.

I'm screwed.

"I'm sorry about that," I start, shaking my head. "It was unprofessional, and—"

"I want you out of my kitchen," the chef interrupts. "You aren't sorry, and I don't want you near me."

"I'll go in there and help. I'll be quiet and follow orders. You don't need to—"

The chef lifts his flabby chin and looks down his nose at me. "You said yourself the staff can handle meals without you. So, leave. That is an order."

I grit my teeth, resisting the urge to gouge his eyeballs out. "Are you firing me because I'm shit in the kitchen or because I beat your ass the other night?"

If possible, his ruddy cheeks flare an even brighter red. His arms tighten over his chest. "You don't respect me, and I don't want anyone working in my kitchen who might be a threat to me or others."

I snort. "Fuck off. You're firing me because I could have killed you. Remember, you agreed to the fight."

"I don't need to be reminded of anything," he barks. "You're the one who needs to be reminded of your place."

Oh, if only he knew my place. If only he knew how easy it would be for me to wipe him from the face of the world with no consequence.

The chef moves forward until he's only inches away. His entire face and neck are red now, tempting me like a shiny red button begging to be pressed. I think my fist would do the job nicely.

"So, I'm fired?" I ask, sucking on my lower lip.

The chef surprises me when he shakes his head. "I just want you the fuck out of my kitchen. I can't fire you because I didn't hire you, but keep testing me, and I'll appeal to upper management."

He couldn't fire me even if he wanted to, which I'm sure he does. I want to laugh in his face, though I suspect that wouldn't do much to earn me any favor with him. "What do you want me to do?"

"If you can keep that smart mouth of yours closed long enough, you can join the other servers in the captain's quarters."

Suddenly, I'm no longer amused.

I haven't seen Devon yet, but based on descriptions I've heard from the other sailors, he's on the ship. And if he's on the ship, certainly he'll be served with the captain.

Even with my beard, he'll recognize me. I can't go in there.

"I can't keep my mouth shut," I say quickly. "Reassign me somewhere else."

"That is your problem. If you smart off to the captain or his guests, you'll be fired, which solves everything for me. Either way, you are out of my life, so I'm happy."

"But—"

"Enough," the chef says with a final wave of his hand. "You don't want to argue with me, boy."

*Boy*. I snarl at him, and he raises his brows in surprise. He takes a small step backward like he finally recognizes he's in the presence of a dangerous man. That realization doesn't stop him from delivering his next piece of information, though.

"You know something? I checked the ship's logs after the auction the other night." He smiles when my eyes go wide. "I have good reason to believe you are not who you claim to be."

I freeze. "That's ridiculous."

He shrugs. "Maybe it is. Cross me again, and I'll start a formal investigation and expose your lying ass. Understood?"

I spin away without a word and march down the hall towards my room.

I lift the edge of my mattress and pull out the flip phone I stashed there. The screen flares to life immediately, but there is no service. Zero bars.

Getting in touch with the Bratva is my only option now. Devon will recognize me. The beard does a little to throw people off, but anyone who actually knows me won't be fooled. He will recognize me and have me killed, and my family will be sold into slavery. I have no other choice.

Except, it isn't a choice at all since we're too far out to see to get cell-phone reception.

I throw the useless piece of plastic back under the mattress and dig through Andrew's bags, hoping to find something that might help me get in touch with someone on land. As an experienced sailor, he was probably prepared to be at sea for a long period of time.

Buried in the bottom of his duffel bag, I find a satellite phone.

Thank God.

I try to punch in the number again, but there is nothing. No signal. No connection.

"Shit." I try it again, even though I know it won't do any good.

It looks to be in working order, so I'm not sure what is going on. Maybe I'm not using it right.

I open the door and poke my head into the hallway, half expecting to see Devon's guards coming for me because the chef changed his mind and alerted them to my unauthorized presence on the ship. Instead, I see my neighbor returning from his night shift. His eyes are bloodshot, and he rubs a hand in his eye socket as he unlocks his door.

"Hey."

He looks over, surprised to see me. "Oh, hey, man."

I hold up the satellite phone. "This isn't working."

"Correct." He nods.

"Why?"

His face screws up in confusion. "Weren't you at the orientation?" He shrugs as if he doesn't really care about my answer. "This is a shady-ass operation, man. The bosses put a jammer in. No calls in or out."

I curse under my breath.

"Yeah, I have a honey at home I'd like to talk to. But we should be there in a few days, and you can call whoever you need to call then."

I'm trapped.

My identity is about to be discovered, and I don't have access to anyone on the outside. No help, no assistance. Just me, my wife, and my daughter against an entire ship full of people who would gladly kill us all for a bonus in their next paycheck.

"If it's urgent, you can try to get into the comms station on the bridge, but good fucking luck with that," he says. "They don't let no one in there."

I give him a small wave of thanks and wait until he shuts his door before I dart down the hallway towards the bridge.

It is an insane idea, but it's truly my only hope.

There are always at least two guys manning the bridge. I can fight two guys at once. I've handled more than that.

The problem would be that once I fought them, help would need to arrive before they woke up if I wanted to get off this ship.

I could kill them, but I have to assume anyone working the bridge would be missed more than a perpetually drunk sailor. Rumors are already starting to spread that he stumbled and fell over a railing into the ocean one night.

When I get to the bridge, it feels like a miracle.

There is no one inside.

I lurk outside, peering through the windows to be certain because there is no way I can get this lucky. Not after the endless shit storm that has been the last few weeks.

I don't see any movement, so I stroll casually to the door, and to my disbelief, it opens.

I am just about to step inside when I hear boots behind me.

"There you are!" I turn and see one of the servers from the kitchen standing there, his chest heaving. "Jesus Christ. I've been looking everywhere for you. We have to go."

I shake my head. "Go where?"

"Service," he says, eyes wide like I'm out of my mind. "The chef sent me for you. If we're both not back in a few minutes, we lose our jobs."

I want to tell him the chef doesn't have the ability to fire anyone without express permission from his superiors, but I doubt that will do much to sway the very nervous waiter.

The easiest solution here is to push him over the railing. I could push him, make my call, and be gone before anyone knew I was even here. It would be a tragic accident. The man stumbled in his desperate attempt to find me before being fired.

I don't want to do it. I don't want to hurt another innocent man, but is anyone on this ship innocent? They all know something bad is happening here, but they don't care. Does that make them bad, too?

I take a step towards the man, and he waves his arm for me to hurry.

I take another step, and I'm going to do it. I'll push him over the edge and do what I have to do to save my family.

I've just reached the decision when another voice comes from further down the stairs. "Did you find him?"

The man in front of me yells back over his shoulder. "We're coming now!"

I look past him and see a second man with him—another server—waiting for us.

I can't kill them both. Not without one of them running to alert someone.

The comms room is still empty. Blissfully, magically empty, but I sigh and follow the two servers.

There is no other choice.

# 12

# DMITRY

I had imagined the food taken from the kitchen was taken directly into the captain's quarters, but I quickly learn that is not correct.

The two servers who stopped me from going into the comms room take me to a large prep room just off the dining area. There, I am given an itchy formal jacket that matches my black pants and a pair of gloves.

Waiters and waitresses rush around wiping food from the edges of the plates, filling pitchers with ice water and juice, and plating everything in a way that actually makes the food halfway appealing.

"Finally," a dark-haired man in a full suit says, scowling at me. "The chef said you'd be here half an hour ago. Being late on your first day isn't a good look."

I could respond with one million snappy comebacks, but honestly, I'm too nervous.

In all likelihood, Devon is on the other side of the large wooden door where all of the servers are lining up, and he's going to recognize me. When he does, will he kill me on the spot or draw it out? I can't imagine what information there could be to torture out of me. He would know I'm here to save my family, and I have no other plans. He could decide to torture me for pleasure, though. That doesn't seem too outrageous a thing to expect from the psychopathic mind of Devon.

"Button your damn jacket and get to work," the suited man says. Clearly, he's the person in charge. "Put covers on the food so they don't get cold."

The food is carried out of our kitchen on single large platters, but here each bowl is placed inside its own silver serving dish. As if the people in that room are royalty, rather than career criminals selling women and children for profit.

I do as I'm told without complaint, my mind racing with possibilities that all end with me being captured and killed.

For the first time, I don't see a way out.

How long will it take for Courtney to find out about my death? How long before she loses all hope?

My vision goes blurry when I think about never seeing Tati or Olivia again, and I look up at the ceiling to center myself. I've never cried openly in my life and now is not the time to start. I've made it this far; might as well hang in there for a few minutes longer.

All of the servers grab a tray or a pitcher and assemble in a short, neat line. The head server pushes and pulls us until we're in a perfect row. Then, he folds one hand behind his back and opens the large wooden door.

The room is simple like the rest of the ship, but the décor is lavish. A solid wood table sits in the middle of the room with ornately carved chairs around it. Greenery and glass décor litter the table from one end to the other, and when I reach the end of the table, I see Devon.

He is acting like a completely different person than the man I met a few times, whenever Sadie brought him around. Back then, he was still childish, still an asshole, but had some semblance of humanity to him. Enough to pass below my radar.

But now, he is a crumbling mess. Chaotic. Barely lucid. Barely holding it together.

He nods to the head server as he enters, but his movements are stuttered and awkward. His eyes dart around the room like he can't seem to focus on any one thing at a time. I wonder why no one around him seems bothered by this.

A man halfway down the table reaches for his glass, and Devon snaps his attention to him. "Wait for everyone to be served before beginning!" he shrieks.

The man pulls his hand back like a child caught reaching into the candy drawer, and everyone at the table sits a bit taller, backs straight.

They are afraid of him.

I see a man directly across the long table from Devon, who I assume has to be the captain. Even he seems uneasy around Devon. I can only see him in profile, but he avoids eye contact, preferring to keep his eyes low. In my experience, that means he either respects or fears Devon. My guess is the latter.

"Can someone draw the blinds?" Devon yells, gesturing wildly to the wall of windows. A few crew members rush over to pull the blinds closed, dousing the room in darkness that is interrupted only by the small lanterns along the length of the table.

Devon massages a finger down the center of his forehead and the length of his nose. He squeezes his eyes closed and rolls his neck like he has a headache.

"And play some music, for God's sake," he barks at a young woman standing in the corner. "I don't want to listen to the sound of everyone here gumming their food. It's disgusting."

The girl rushes to a set of speakers sitting inside a built-in shelf and quickly starts some soft instrumental music. Devon gestures rudely for her to turn it up, so she continues to do so until the music is almost too loud for me in the other room. It's blaring, and everyone seems uncomfortable, but nobody moves to cover their ears or protest in any way.

Even the captain wears an exasperated, slightly amused expression.

Suddenly, another door to the left opens, and a large beam of light cuts across the dark room. Devon spins around and squints into the light.

"Who the fuck is that? We're about to eat!"

A woman comes in carrying a bundle in her arms and it takes me a second to understand what I'm seeing.

She walks directly to Devon and, without hesitating, he reaches out and scoops the bundle away from her. A pink blanket falls, and I'm staring at a baby.

*My* baby.

The woman rushes away and leaves Olivia with Devon, and I feel as though my heart is being pulled from my chest. Like someone has attached a hook to it, yanking me forward like a truck stuck in the snow.

My little girl.

It has been so long since I've seen her that I'm not sure if I'm just imagining it or if her hair really does look longer. Her face less round. Her fingers longer.

She looks so much bigger, and I want to sprint across the room and pull her into my arms. I want to nuzzle my cheek against hers and listen to her giggle as my facial hair tickles her skin.

"I'm ready to eat!" Devon bellows.

Olivia flinches at the harsh sound and lets out a small cry of protest. Devon smiles down at her. "You heard the girl. Bring in the food."

Devon looks up at the door where I am standing with the other servers, and I swear his eyes land on mine. Just for a second.

I'm second in line from the door and in my position—leaning around the man in front of me to better my view—I'm easy to spot.

My heart stops.

My entire body freezes, and I'm unable to stand tall or pull back into line. All I can do is try to keep breathing and stare back at him, hoping he doesn't figure it out. Hoping he doesn't recognize me.

After what feels like a small eternity, Devon turns away and bounces Olivia on his knee a few times. She giggles, and my stomach flips.

How am I supposed to deliver food without stopping to see her? How am I supposed to walk into this room and pretend my heart isn't yearning for her? I'm not sure I can do it, but there isn't time to think about it any longer. The head server snaps his fingers to draw our attention and then waves for us to begin filing into the room.

I grip my silver serving platter and look down at the floor. I just need to keep my composure for a few minutes at most. I have to. For my family.

The first server steps into the room and through the door, and I follow close behind him. But after just two steps, I'm still standing in the doorway when a strange noise fills the room.

Everyone, including the server in front of me, turns towards the now-closed windows as the noise gets louder and louder.

It sounds like a roaring wind, lashing against the glass in waves.

Devon jumps from his seat and hands Olivia off to her caretaker, who is standing next to the door she entered through. Then, he runs for the windows and pulls back the curtains. He lets out an animalistic screech and then turns and runs from the room without another word.

The whole scene is so bizarre and the noise is so loud and disorienting that all I can do is look around with my mouth hanging open, bewildered.

The captain stands up with a shrug of his shoulders and shakes his head in a kind of unspoken apology. "Sorry, everyone. The meal will be delayed until Mr. Devon returns."

The other people relax back into their seats and the servers all trudge back into the prep room and lay their trays down. The head server leans against the wall and stares up at the ceiling.

"I need to use the restroom," I say loudly to no one in particular.

The head server waves a hand in my direction. "Do whatever you want. That psychopath won't be back for a while."

There is a chuckle of agreement throughout the rest of the waitstaff as I dart from the room.

I race down the hallway and through a door onto a narrow overlook. Below is a large deck with a helicopter pad, currently occupied by a helicopter whose blades are still spinning slowly.

That explains the noise.

Devon is waiting on the edge of the helipad, hands folded behind his back. He is facing away from me, but I still step back from the railing to do my best to blend in with the shadows.

Devon's body language is a one-hundred-and-eighty degree switch from what it was in the dining room. He is stretching up onto his toes and craning his neck in every direction to get a good look at whoever is coming out of the helicopter. He's excited. Antsy, almost.

Then, the helicopter passenger disembarks, and I understand why.

It's Elena.

She's in a dark skirt suit that gives her a kind of sturdy, boxy appearance. Her hair is pitch-black now, with none of the gray I saw threaded through it last time. She must have dyed it in the interim since our last meeting.

Since the meeting where she distracted me while my family was drugged and kidnapped.

I clench my fists, desperate to jump over the railing and snap her neck for what she did to me and my family. For what she's still doing to us.

Devon runs forward and greets his mother with a large bear hug that she does not return. Then, he places a hand on her back and leads her towards a door that is restricted for unauthorized crew members.

Even if I wanted to follow them into the room, I couldn't.

I don't want to. Because if I go now, I'll kill them. I'll end them both.

And it isn't the right time.

I know Olivia is being kept close to Devon, and I know where Tati and Courtney are being held, but I still don't have a way off this ship. No one on the outside knows where we are or how to get to us, so killing Devon and Elena would feel great, but it wouldn't do anything to get us away from the Yakuza.

I have to be patient.

The helicopter is quiet now except for the ticking sound of the engines cooling, and the pilot has walked around the back of the helicopter to the railing to enjoy the view and smoke a cigarette.

Then, an idea comes to me.

Devon and Elena are out of sight and the only other person around is the pilot, but he's all the way across the deck.

I've never flown a helicopter, but I've ridden in them before. Maybe there's a chance I could fly this one right off the ship with my family.

It's crazy, but I won't know until I get a look inside.

I move quietly down the stairs behind me to the deck below and then creep towards the helicopter, sticking to the shadows to avoid detection.

The pilot stubs out his cigarette and immediately lights another, so I know I have a few minutes.

I climb through the still-open door and haul myself into the pilot's seat. Immediately, I know there is no way in hell I could safely get my family off this boat.

The dash is a byzantine series of dials and knobs for altitude, knots, various types of pressure, and speed. There is a much higher chance I would crash us all into the ocean than be able to land anywhere safely. Plus, it would take me a long time to even figure out how to get off the ground, and as I learned in the dining room a few minutes ago, the helicopter is not a covert mode of transportation. As soon as it turns on, everyone will know.

I decide to abort the mission and get out, but as I step out of the seat, my leg knocks a metal key off a ledge and onto the floorboard. I bend down to pick it up and realize it's the key to the helicopter. Without thinking, I grab it and shove it into my pocket.

I glance through the side window to find the pilot smoking next to the railing, and realize with a start that he isn't there. Spinning my head in a quick circle, I look for him, only to see the man waiting for me on the deck.

"What in the hell are you doing in my helicopter?" he demands, eyes narrowed.

He is older than me for sure, but we're roughly the same size. He has on a pair of jeans with a tan windbreaker. I can tell he's a fit man.

"Oh, I've just always liked them, and I wanted to check it out." The lie is thin, and I can see he doesn't buy it.

"Bullshit." He steps back from the door and gestures for me to get out and follow him. "Come with me. I'm taking you to Elena."

I lower my head and nod, stepping down from the helicopter, pretending that I intend to follow his orders and come quietly.

As soon as my feet are on the deck, however, I lunge forward and wrap my arms around the man's neck.

He shouts in surprise, but the noise is muffled as my grip on his neck tightens. We both stumble backward and the man swats at me with his hammer-like fists. The blows are bearable, but they knock the wind from me, and I gasp for breath.

The pilot spins hard in one direction, shaking me loose from his neck. I'm back on him in an instant, but it's still enough time for him to reach into his pocket and pull out the knife he has there.

I feel the pressure of the blade tearing through my jacket before I feel the sear of pain across my ribs.

He stabbed me, but I can't think about that now. If I don't kill him, he'll tell Elena and Devon about the incident and it won't take long before they realize who they're looking for.

I ignore the burning in my side and grab the man's hand, squeezing his fingers to try and loosen his grip on the knife. He is fighting hard—we both know this will be a fight to the death—but the knife clatters to the deck, and I quickly kick it out of his reach.

The pilot is preoccupied with the knife, desperately fighting to get it back, and when he bends down to try and crawl towards the helicopter, I jerk my knee up hard into his chin.

I hear his teeth crack together and watch his eyes roll back in his head. I repeat the move a second time, and he slumps to the deck, limp and lifeless.

Dragging his body to the railing is more difficult than I imagined and it takes much longer than I'd like, but luckily, no one else makes a surprise appearance.

When I get to the railing, I drag him up by the armpits until he's half resting on my body. Then, I readjust my hold and haul him up until he's standing at his full height. From there, it's relatively easy to tip him over the railing and let gravity do the rest of the work.

His body falls into the ocean with a splash, and I jog down the side deck towards the opposite side of the ship as fast as I can.

I'm out of immediate danger, but the helicopter and the missing pilot are a ticking time bomb now. As soon as Elena and Devon realize the pilot is missing, it won't be long until they begin searching for the person responsible.

I need to find a way to get Courtney and the girls off this ship.

Now.

## 13

# COURTNEY

The door to the container opens so quietly I almost don't hear it. I sit up and see a dark shadow moving towards me. Only when it gets close do I realize who it is.

*Elena.*

This is the first time I've seen her in the flesh, though I've seen pictures of her before. Dmitry had a few of her and Rurik in his office before Rurik betrayed him.

Then, I see Olivia in her arms.

She turns towards me, her wide blue eyes blinking in the darkness. "Mama."

My heart breaks, and I try to reach for her, but Elena steps back and out of my reach. She wraps her arms around Olivia and pats her back, soothing my daughter to sleep on her shoulder.

"I'm sure that will fade over time," Elena says softly. "One day, she won't remember you at all."

My hands shake with unspent rage, but I can't do anything to her while she's holding my daughter. Or while my other daughter is lying asleep at my side.

"What do you want?"

"To see you," Elena says simply. "I wanted to see the woman at the center of it all."

She nods her head to Sadie. "I suspect this is the poor girl who got involved with my Devon."

"You're both monsters. Why would you hurt innocent people if you're angry with Dmitry?"

"Clearly, you were not born into this world, Courtney. If you were, you'd know that the best way to injure someone is to go after those they love." She looks down at Olivia and smiles. "That is why I've always limited the people I love. Kept them few and close. Rurik. Devon. But now Rurik is gone and Devon won't be long for this world."

I wrinkle my brow. "What does that mean?"

"You call him a monster," she says. "I call him a pet."

I shake my head. "He's your son."

"Yes, and he has served his purpose." Elena strokes a finger across Olivia's cheek. "The drugs are wearing on his mind. I haven't dosed him in almost two days, and yet, he's erratic."

I haven't seen Devon since before we got on the ship. I didn't notice anything special about his behavior then, though I've always found him to be compulsive and thoughtless. "Dosed him with what?"

Elena sighs like she's growing bored of talking to me. "This is a man's world. They want a woman to come home to and keep their bed warm, but they rarely respect your opinion. I didn't want my son to be that way. So, I helped ... awaken his senses to my persuasion."

"You drugged him?" The idea of drugging my own child feels unthinkable. I could never ... would never. "How could you do that?"

"To help him," she says sincerely. "Without it, he would have wanted to go out and explore the world, to leave his mother behind. He would have wanted to be part of *this* world that, as you are learning now, can be so very cruel. I protected him. I kept him with me, where he was safest."

"You broke him."

She smiles. "The world would have broken him long before now, so I think I've done him a favor. However, his time is running short, so I think it may be time for a replacement."

"Don't you dare hurt her," I growl, my voice deeper than I've ever heard before. I barely recognize it. "If you hurt a hair on her head, I will kill you."

Elena shrugs. "If given the chance, I think you'd kill me whether I hurt your daughter or not."

"True," I admit. "But if you hurt her, I will make it excruciating for you. You'll wish you were high on whatever you've got Devon on. You will beg for death and when you do, I'll keep you alive a little longer, drawing the torture out until death is a sweet reprieve."

Elena stares at me for a moment and then smiles, amused. "You're a real treat. I see why Dmitry settled down with you. Too bad things didn't work out for you crazy kids."

She shrugs again, as if there is nothing that could be done about the dissolution of our family, and turns to leave.

"Just end this now," I say, though I know it will do no good. "Let us go and be done with it."

She bobs her head from side to side like she's considering it and then wrinkles her nose. "No thanks. I think I'll see this plan through to the end. Sweet dreams."

~

Tati wakes just as the container door is closing, and I soothe her back to sleep. There is no rest for me, however, because the door is suddenly opening again.

Tati is no longer lying on my lap, so I roll onto my feet and crouch down, ready for whatever is to come. Or whoever.

If I've learned anything being stuck in this container on this ship, it's that anything can happen.

It could be the Tiger here to sell me to a horny sailor, Elena back to rub my face in the fact that she has my child, or Devon coming around to make his presence known. It has been a while since he has tormented anyone, so he might miss the taste of it.

The door opens only a crack, allowing in a sliver of the dark sky beyond, and a large shape slips into the container.

It isn't Elena, I know that.

The figure creeps forward slowly, taking slow, quiet steps. Whoever it is, they don't want anyone to know they're here.

My heart rate ratchets up. I don't know whether to raise the alarm or not.

"Courtney?"

I gasp and jump to my feet, throwing myself at him. I bury my face in his neck and take in deep, greedy breaths of him.

"Dmitry." I kiss his neck and circle my arms around him. "What are you doing here? Why are you here?"

He grabs my hips and holds me away from him, studying my face. "I'm here for you. I told you I'd tell you as soon as I had a plan. And well, I have one ... kind of."

"What is it?"

"Where's Tati?" he whispers. As soon as he sees her lying on the floor, he takes a step towards her, but I shake my head.

"She doesn't know you're here yet, and she's sleeping. She needs the rest."

"Is she still sick?" he asks.

"Better, but not much. I don't want to excite her before I know what we're doing." I grab his hand and pull him towards the door. "Is it safe to leave the container? Just for a little bit?"

Dmitry answers by pulling me outside and closing the door behind us. "I had a drink with the Tiger below deck and drugged his drink with some pills I stole from the infirmary. I don't know exact dosages, but I'd guess he'll be down for an hour at least."

"Is that enough time for your plan?" I ask. "What *is* your plan?"

"I know how to contact the Bratva, I know where you and Tati are being kept, and I know where Olivia is," he says. "I have all of the pieces, so all that's left is to put them together."

"Then let's do it," I say. "What are we waiting for? Where is Olivia?"

"We have to find her just before we leave," he says. "They're watching her more closely than anyone, so they'll know something is wrong if she goes missing."

"What if we can't? What if they have her too well hidden or she isn't where you expect her to be? We can't leave her for the last minute or everything could fall apart." Of course I want to escape. I want to get off this boat and back to my house and my life. But now that we're really talking about it, it's a huge risk. We could all end up dead. We could be putting our children in danger.

"We don't have another choice." Dmitry's words silence all of my doubts.

He is right. There is no other option.

"I just wish this was over," I say, laying my head on his chest. "I'm so tired."

Dmitry wraps his arms around me and smooths his hands down my back. "I know. It will be over soon."

No matter the outcome, it will be over soon. Either we'll escape and be on our way to freedom, or our plan will be thwarted and we will be killed. Honestly, if we're lucky, they will kill us.

The thought does little to give me comfort.

This could be the last time I see Dmitry. The last time I feel the warmth of him leaking into my skin. The last time I can look into his pale blue eyes and run my fingers across his tan skin.

I pull back and look into his face, my fingers brushing over his blond beard. "I love you."

He pushes my hair back from my face. "I love you, too."

When he leans down to kiss me, I fall into it with everything I have. I kiss him as if it's the last time—because it may very well be.

The thought encourages me to deepen the kiss. I run my hand around the back of his neck and tug at the collar of his shirt, bringing him closer to me.

Dmitry's hands slide from my hips under my shirt to my waist. His palms are broad and warm, and I want him everywhere.

"Now," I say against his lips, reaching down to unbutton his pants.

"Now what?" he asks, frowning as he watches me tug his jeans down.

I kiss him again and wrap my hand around his length. "Make love to me."

He groans as I stroke him. "Courtney, we—"

"Please," I beg, massaging my thumb over his tip. "I'm ready. It will be quick."

I need this. It's reckless and foolish, but I need him one last time. If my world is going to end, I want Dmitry to be my last memory.

His hands are already sliding under my shirt to cup my breasts even as he argues. "We have limited time."

I twist my hand down his length, making his body tense. "Then you better work quickly."

He hesitates for a moment, thinking about what he should do, but then he bends down and scoops me into his arms. Dmitry walks me backwards until my back is pressed against the railing, and I realize we're at the very back of the ship. The ocean laps against the metal sides of the ship, and it feels like we're a thousand miles away from danger, from anyone or anything that could hurt us.

It's just the two of us in the wide expanse of the ocean. Together.

He tugs my cotton pants down my legs and tosses them aside. Next, he peels down my panties. I lift my foot to step out of them, and he licks his lips as he watches me move.

"You're so fucking sexy."

I grab him in my hand and position him at my opening. "Show me."

With one thrust, Dmitry sinks into me to the hilt. I gasp and roll my body against his, desperate for even more. He grips my backside, holding us together as we both adjust to the sensation.

He slides out slowly before thrusting back in, and I'm already half wild.

Nothing should feel this good. It has the ability to turn my brain off, to turn me into an animal whose only desire is more. More of his body, more of his kisses, more of his touch.

More time.

But more is not guaranteed. This could be it, and I'm determined not to waste it. Not to let a single sensation slip away.

I grab his face and kiss him, swirling my tongue in his mouth, tasting him. His lips are soft and pliable against mine, his breath coming in soft huffs in time with his thrusting. Our bodies are connected in every way possible, and I'm full of him. Filled to the brim with Dmitry and my love for him.

I tangle my fingers in his hair and press my nose against his, staring into his eyes as our bodies find one another over and over again.

I want to believe that no matter what, we'll find each other. In this life or the next, he and I will always be together.

My vision goes blurry with tears, and Dmitry kisses the streaks on my face. His hand slips between us, finding my center, and his finger circles over me.

I've never been so out of control of my own emotions before. I'm crying while pleasure builds in my abdomen. Crying while I moan for him to go faster, to give me more. It's almost comical, but I'm far too turned on to laugh.

The orgasm stalks towards me like a skilled predator, creeping just out of sight. I know it's there, but I can't pinpoint where. Then, suddenly, it's on top of me.

I gasp and grab Dmitry's shoulders for stability as my legs go weak. My entire body is clenched, and all I can feel is warmth spreading to my limbs like molasses.

Dmitry groans with his next several thrusts and then slows, savoring each sensation as he finds his own bliss.

I cling to him when he's finished, not yet ready for him to slip out of me and away. Not ready to face whatever we will have to do over the next several hours.

I want to stay in this sensation with him.

Dmitry kisses my nose and then captures my mouth, sucking on my bottom lip.

"You're beautiful," he whispers, pressing his forehead to mine, his fingers brushing over my cheekbones. "I love you."

"I love you, too," I croak. The words don't want to come because I know, in a way, they are a form of goodbye.

I massage my hands down his chest and abs, feeling the strength stirring under his skin. As I do, however, he moans.

"What is it? Did I hurt you?" I ask.

Dmitry shakes his head and tries to pull away from me, but I grab the hem of his shirt and lift it up before he can stop me.

A raw, angry cut is open across his ribs, blood dripping from the wound.

"Jesus, Dmitry, what happened?"

He explains that he fought the pilot of Elena's helicopter and tries to diminish the severity of the wound, but I don't even let him finish before I pull on my clothes and go to the emergency box built into the hallway of the ship. I pull out the first aid kit and find the antiseptic and large bandages.

"We don't have time for this," he argues, trying to bat my hands away.

I narrow my eyes. "We just had sex on the bow of the ship. I think we can find a minute to patch up your wounds. I did go to school to be kind of a doctor, if you remember."

"We're at the stern," he says with a wink, his mouth pulled into a half smile. He spreads his arms wide, giving me free rein. "And I remember. Do what you must."

He tries to be tough, but he winces when I press a cotton ball of hydrogen peroxide to the cut. Then, I spread an antibacterial cream over the slice and press a large bandage to it. In total, the process takes less than a minute.

"Is it time?" I ask, grabbing his hand and walking back to the container.

He nods. "Get Tati, and we'll give this our best shot."

I lift the handle on the door, but before I pull it all the way open, I spin back around and throw my arms around Dmitry's neck, drawing him into a kiss.

He kisses me back tenderly, his hand smoothing down the length of my spine. "It will be okay, Courtney. We'll win. I know it."

I don't know it. I don't know anything at all. But I take solace in Dmitry's confidence and pray he's right.

I give him one last kiss and turn away to open the door, but it's already open.

Tati is standing there, eyes wide with shock and staring at Dmitry.

*Daddy?*

Dmitry kneels down, arms wide, and Tati runs into them.

*What are you doing out here?* I ask.

*I woke up and you were gone. I moved to sleep by the door so I'd know when you came back.*

I kiss her forehead. *Clever girl.*

Dmitry buries his face in Tati's neck, tickling her with his new beard, and she smiles, throwing her head back to get away from him, though she keeps her arms tightly around his neck.

I know we're nowhere close to freedom yet, but the dark cloud that has been hanging over me eases slightly at the sight of the two of them together.

As soon as we have Olivia, I'll feel even better.

"Come on, you two. We need to get going if—"

"Hello, Dmitry."

I gasp and spin around, putting myself between Tati and the man's voice.

It's the other guard. 'The nice one,' as I've referred to him with Sadie, though he doesn't look especially nice right now. His forehead is wrinkled and his mouth is pressed into a stern line.

"How does he know your name, Dmitry?" I ask. "Who is he?"

Dmitry stands up and moves in front of me, blocking me from the man. "An old friend," he says simply.

The man nods in agreement. "The oldest of friends."

# 14

# DMITRY

I almost can't believe he's standing in front of me, but then he tilts his head to the side slightly, his dark hair falling over his forehead, and I can see my old friend in there.

Sevastian.

"Sevastian?" Courtney asks in shock when I explain. "But he—"

"Died?" Sevastian finishes for her. "That's what everyone was supposed to think. I suppose the plan worked perfectly."

"It did," I assure him. "No one has any idea."

When Rurik came to me with the information that Sevastian had gone to the FBI, I knew he could no longer be my most trusted lieutenant. I knew I couldn't allow him to stay in the Bratva. It would make me look weak and everyone would question my loyalty to the organization.

However, I also couldn't kill my best friend since childhood.

"What plan?" Courtney asks, bending down to wrap her arm around Tati's shoulders and reassure her that everything is fine.

"The execution was staged," I explain quickly. "I pulled the shot. Went through his cheek instead. I didn't want to kill him, but I couldn't let him go unpunished lest other members of the Bratva find me weak."

"I still have that scar, too," Sevastian muses, rubbing the cheek in question thoughtfully. "He set me up with a new identity and some money. Dmitry let me live, and I've wanted to thank him ever since."

"What are you doing here?" I ask.

"Working." He shrugs. "I don't have many usable skills, but I can do security. So, I've been working for several different illegal trade routes ever since."

Courtney shifts to pull Tati closer to her side, and I know what she's thinking because I'm thinking it, too.

"How can you stomach it?"

Sevastian shoves his hands in his pockets. "Don't tell me you're soft now. I've always been the more emotional of our duo."

"Having kids changes you."

Sevastian looks at Tati. "Kids?"

"The baby on the ship is ours," Courtney says. "Olivia. They took her from us."

"I thought something was weird about this shipment," Sevastian says. "I didn't know who you were, but the way everyone talked about you and the little girl—"

"Tati," I remind him. "Her name is Tati."

"I know. I remember." Sevastian runs a hand through his hair and looks up at me beneath lowered brows. "Dmitry, really. You have to know that if I knew who they were, I would have gotten them out of here sooner. I wouldn't have let them get on this ship."

I nod. "That's good to know."

"But you were nice to us," Courtney says. "Nicer than the Tiger, anyway."

Sevastian chuckles. "That isn't hard to do. That man is a monster."

"You aren't."

"No," Sevastian agrees. "At least, I try not to be."

In the distance, lightning cracks across the sky, illuminating the deck, and we all turn to look at the sky.

"The water is getting choppy," Sevastian comments. "A storm is moving in."

Courtney grabs my hand. "What does that mean?"

I've never sailed a boat on calm waters, let alone in the middle of a storm. How will a tiny life raft survive in bad weather? I have no idea.

"It means our escape will have mood lighting," I say with a smile, hoping to lighten her spirits.

We can't delay. If we had more time, I'd push the escape back, but one of the servers mentioned that we were getting close to shore, and with the pilot missing and the key to the helicopter in my pocket, it won't be long before Elena and Devon are looking for the culprit.

It has to be now.

"Escape?" Sevastian asks. "Is that what you're doing right now?"

I nod. "As long as you don't plan to alert anyone to our plans."

He sighs. "I *lied* to the FBI, man."

"You talked to them." Talking to the FBI is more than any other member of my Bratva had ever done. The fact that he acknowledged his identity within my Bratva and spoke to a federal agent is reason enough not to trust him. I may not have wanted to kill Sevastian, but that doesn't mean I have to be best friends with him again.

"I talked to them to get them off your trail," he said. "If the video Rurik showed you had audio, you would have heard me lying through my ass to blame everything on the Yakuza and the Italians. I don't know if the FBI bought it, but they at least didn't get any useful information out of me."

The video didn't have sound, so I don't know if I should believe him or not. But I do anyway.

He seems genuine, and unless I want to really kill him this time, I don't have any other choice than to trust him right now.

"I'm not going to tell anyone you're here," he insists. "I'm going to help you."

I run my tongue over my top teeth and nod. "Fine. Do you know where Devon and Elena are right now?"

He shakes his head. "Elena just got to the ship today, so I don't know what her routine looks like. I'd guess she's in her cabin the same as everyone else."

"What about Olivia?" Courtney asks. "Where is she?"

"She has a separate nursery next to Devon's quarters, though he doesn't wake up for shit. I've been the person in charge of getting him out of bed before and good fucking luck is all I have to say. He is a heavy sleeper. Like his father, I suppose."

"Did they make a formal birth announcement?" I ask.

Sevastian snorts with laughter. "Yeah, almost thirty years too late. I can't believe Rurik had a secret son."

"I can't believe I let Rurik's secret son get the better of me."

"I don't know," Sevastian says. "I can believe you. You always were pretty gullible. Remember when I convinced you I had an alligator living in my bathtub?"

I smile despite everything. "You told me you let it walk around the bathroom while you took a shower and then put it back in when you were done."

"And you bought it hook, line, and sinker." Sevastian grins.

"So did you." I jab a finger towards him and, for a second, it feels like old times. It feels like he never left my side.

But he did. It's not old times. And we need to get moving before the shit hitting the fan begins to rain down over us.

As if to illustrate my point, thunder tears through the sky. I almost think I can see ripples in the water from the force of the rumble.

"We need to get out of here. Now," I urge. "We need to find Olivia."

Sevastian bites his lip. "They always have a nanny on her and a guard outside the door. I've taken the shift more than once. That is going to be tough."

"We also need to get into the comms room."

Sevastian sighs. "Shit. You never did like to make things easy on me."

"Do you still want to help?" I ask, wrapping an arm around Courtney and laying a hand on Tati's small shoulder.

Sevastian takes in all three of us and opens his mouth to say something, but just then, lightning rips across the sky, turning his skin a ghostly white.

He closes his eyes and takes another deep breath like he can't believe what he's saying. "God help me. Yes. Yes, I'll help. Whatever I can do."

## 15

# COURTNEY

Sevastian is going to help us, which is a huge relief. Having someone who knows the ship even better than Dmitry and knows the inner workings of the operation is going to be a huge asset.

Except, before our operation can even get off the ground, it's found out.

"What the fuck?"

We all turn to see the Tiger standing in a narrow hallway to the left. His eyes are still droopy from whatever Dmitry dosed him with, but he's coherent enough to know that Tati and I should not be out of the container talking to the likes of Sevastian and Dmitry. Though, I'm sure the Tiger doesn't know them by those names.

For several seconds, we stare at one another, no one moving or saying anything. Then, the Tiger comes to the realization that some kind of coup is going on, and he turns to run and raise the alarm, no doubt.

Without hesitating, I wrench myself out of Dmitry's hold and run after the Tiger.

I hear Dmitry's footsteps behind me and Tati whimpering for both of us, but I don't slow down.

The shiv Tati found on the deck—the same one I gave to Sadie to use against the sailor—is in the pocket of my pajama pants, and I pull it out and grip it in my hand. Then, when I'm within reach of the Tiger, I jump and plunge the sharp end into his back.

He yells and falls to the ground. Neither my weight nor the stab wound is enough to take him down, but the drugs are clearly still in his system, making him sluggish. Dmitry catches up to us in a second and presses his boot into the Tiger's back.

"Finish him," he urges.

The end of the shiv is covered in blood and small splatters of it dot my wrist and the sleeve of my shirt.

I know that, if anyone deserves to die, it's the Tiger. He is an evil man who locks women in containers and sells them for profit. Though, so does Sevastian, and he's ... helping us?

I want to say that he's an evil man with no soul, but I don't know that for sure. Plus, if I've learned anything being trapped on this boat, it's that life comes at you fast.

Annika is here because Dmitry killed her pimp in a shoot-out.

Actions have consequences, and I'm not sure I want to know what the consequences of killing the Tiger would be.

"Tie him up," I say. "Let's leave him in the container. No one will find him for a while."

"What? No." Dmitry falls down, driving his knee into the Tiger's back. He is fighting back, desperate to get away. "Give me the blade. I'll kill him."

"No." I spin around and see a storage closet not far away. I run to it and grab a length of rope. "We don't have to kill him. We'll leave him in the container the way he left us. It will be a fitting punishment."

"Death is fitting," Dmitry growls. "He needs to die."

I shake my head. "No. Please."

I can tell Dmitry doesn't understand my insistence, but he sees that I am serious. He grits his teeth before dropping his head down in a sigh. "Fine. Give me the rope."

We bind the Tiger's hands and feet and wrap a length of rope around his head and through his open mouth for good measure.

Dmitry and Sevastian carry him kicking and screaming to the container where the rest of the women are still being held.

As soon as we bring him in, they all wake up and back against the walls, ready for whatever horror the crew of the ship is about to unleash next.

"Is that ... ?" Annika asks, staring at the Tiger where he thrashes on the floor. Then, she looks up at me. "What the hell?"

Sadie rushes forward and says the same thing. "Where did you go? Where have you been? What is—"

Then, she sees Dmitry and Sevastian standing behind me. "Why isn't he tied up? Are we getting out of here?"

"He's on our side," I say to Sadie and everyone else, trying to silence the endless questions. "His name is Sevastian, and he's going to help us get out of here."

I feel a hand around my arm, and Dmitry pulls me back towards the corner of the container. His voice is low. "Us? Courtney, I'm only worried about you and the girls. I can't guarantee that everyone else will get out of here."

"No whispering," Annika says, pulling a sleeping Larissa to her feet and holding her against her chest.

I frown up at him. "Were you just planning to leave them here?"

He shrugs and nods. "I mean, yeah. Kind of."

"Tell us what is happening!" Annika shouts. Her voice is a hollow echo inside the container. I hold up a finger to try and buy us another second.

"We can't. What about Sadie, at least? Weren't you planning to save her?"

"I already saved her life once," he says. "The rest is on her."

"You can't be serious." I shake my head, not willing to believe Dmitry would be so cold. "Do you realize you are the reason some of these people are in here in the first place?"

Dmitry's mouth falls open like I've slapped him, and I reach out and grab his wrist. "I'm not talking about me and Tati. I'm talking about Annika."

He doesn't know who Annika is, but he turns to take in the rest of the woman in the container as I continue.

"You got into a shoot-out and killed her pimp. His brother sold her to the Yakuza."

Dmitry snorts. "Courtney, that hardly counts as my fault. She was already a prostitute. I didn't make her do that."

I hiss, "But you played a part in it. This is your opportunity to make it right. Help them."

He raises his brows, his blue eyes peering into mine. "Not if it means risking you or the girls."

I open my mouth to respond but Annika gasps. I turn and see that she's talking to Sevastian. His forehead is wrinkled in confusion, and Annika stumbles away, hand over her mouth. Her eyes are pinned on Dmitry like he's a ghost.

"You bastard."

"Annika, what is—?" I move towards her, but Dmitry grabs my wrist and pulls me back. I shake my hand free. "She's my friend."

"Friend?" Annika spits. "Well, friend, you failed to mention that your husband is the reason I'm in here. Perhaps that would have been a good piece of information to share between *friends*."

"Annika." Sadie steps forward and lays her hands on Annika's shoulders. "Courtney just didn't want to upset you. Telling you wouldn't have changed anything, so she—"

"Lied!" Annika spits. "She lied. Just like everyone fucking lies. All the time. This world is full of fucking liars, and I'm the only one who cares about the truth."

"Courtney," Dmitry whispers. "We have to go."

"See?" Annika balls her hand into a fist. "He isn't going to save us. He is here for her, not us. We aren't friends. We are obstacles. Fucking disposable."

"We're going to save all of you," I cry. "You just need to calm down so we can formulate a plan."

Annika steps forward, her eyes narrowed and hard as glass. "Fuck. That. And fuck you."

"What does that mean?" Sadie asks.

Annika turns on Sadie, and Sevastian steps between them, giving Annika a warning look. "This is going to be hard enough without everyone breaking rank."

She throws her head back and lets out a loud, sharp bark of laughter. "This is coming from the man responsible for keeping us in here."

"I didn't sell you," Sevastian says.

"No, you just carted our piss away and made sure to lock the door behind you when you left." Annika rolls her eyes. "You aren't innocent, and if you think I'm going to put my life in your hands or the hands of that fucking psychopath behind you, then you are insane."

"The only psychopaths here are Devon and Elena." I reach out to touch Annika's shoulder, but she shies away like a cornered animal, spinning towards the door and backing up.

Everyone clears a path for her, not wanting to get too close. I am the only one set on getting close to her, on breaking through her anger and betrayal, but with every step I take, she moves further away.

"Please, Annika. Let us help you."

She presses her dry lips together in a harsh line and then tugs on her worn, stained jeans with nervous fingers. Finally, she shakes her head. Her eyes are unfocused. "No, I don't think I will."

"Please, Annika, we—"

"No!" she screams, making everyone flinch. She pushes open the container door and steps outside. "You all do what you want, but I'm going to get myself off this ship. The only person I can trust is me."

She gives everyone one last look and then lifts her middle finger in a sick wave. "Fuck you all."

She sprints off to the right, and I lunge forward to chase after her, but Dmitry's arm wraps around my middle and stops me. "We can't follow her. We don't have time."

"But she's going to—"

"She's going to do whatever she wants," he finishes. "You can't make her go with us, and chasing after her will just be a distraction from the goal: find Olivia, call for help, get off this ship."

I know he's right, but I hate the idea that Annika will be left behind.

"We will save everyone else," he says, finally agreeing to my plan. "I will save every other person in this container, aside from this piece of shit," he says, kicking the Tiger in the back. "We can take them all with us, but you have to promise me you won't go after Annika."

I take a deep breath and nod. "I promise."

"Good," he says, grabbing me and planting a quick kiss on my forehead. Then, he turns to the rest of the container. "Let's get the fuck out of here."

Sevastian surprises us all by unlocking a second container of women only a few yards away from our container. Four of them—unwashed and terrified—come stumbling out and Dmitry curses under his breath.

"How many more are there?"

"This is it," Sevastian assures him.

Dmitry takes a deep breath and nods. "Everyone, follow me."

We do. Like ducklings trailing behind our mama, we follow Dmitry across the deck to where he "punished" me the other day. My face blushes when he touches the lifeboat I used for stability, and I'm worried everyone will see my handprints scorched into the side and know what we did.

They don't, of course, and there are much bigger issues to worry about, so I push the thought from my mind.

"Half of you need to go in this boat," he said. "Now."

"Wouldn't it be better to all go together?" I ask.

Dmitry shakes his head. "We can't walk around the ship with a group of twelve. It's too obvious. If we're going to remain covert, we need to get our number down. We have to split up."

Several of the women from the other container jump forward at once to be in the first boat, desperate to get out. Dmitry assists them one by one into the boat while Sevastian hands them each life jackets.

"Do you know how to get this thing into the water?" I ask Sevastian, looking at the rigging system holding the boat into the air.

He nods. "They did a run-through once, before we got on the boat. Hopefully, I paid enough attention."

"It will be fine," Dmitry says. Then, he turns to the women in the boat, which includes everyone except for me, Sadie, and Tati. "Head west away from the ship until you can't see it anymore and then turn north. You should hit land."

"And if we don't?" one of the women asks, a thin blonde with a tattoo of a butterfly across her chest.

"Stay put as long as you can and we'll try to find you when we land. From there, we'll contact the Bratva and arrange transport back home."

No one seems particularly comforted by this thin plan, but anything is better than being on this ship. Clearly, they are all willing to risk being lost at sea than being on this ship for another minute.

"There are provisions on the boat, but save them for as long as you can just in case," Sevastian advises. "You might need them."

Dmitry turns to me and holds out a hand. "Come on, Court."

I frown. "Excuse me?"

He tips his head to the boat. "Get in."

I laugh, though nothing about this is funny. "You're kidding, right? I'm not getting on this boat."

Dmitry grits his teeth. "Would you just listen to me? For once? Please. Get in."

I look into his eyes, giving him the same look he gave me back in the container. "No."

He pinches the bridge of his nose. "Take Tati and Sadie and get out of here. I and Sevastian and Olivia will meet you in another boat, and—"

"N. O. No. I'm not leaving this ship without my entire family," I say. "I won't do it. I'm going to help you find Olivia."

Dmitry opens his mouth to argue, but Sevastian steps forward. "We could use her help, Dmitry. You need to get to the comms room to reach the Bratva, so she and I can go find Olivia while you do that. Then, we will all meet up at the next rescue boat over."

Dmitry glares at his old friend, and then looks back to me, his anger shifting into obvious concern.

He is terrified.

I step forward and lay a palm on his cheek, drawing his face down to mine, pretending as if no one else is there. "It will be okay. We will all be okay."

Suddenly, his arm is around my waist and our bodies are flush together. He kisses me. It is a soft, hungry kiss that says more than words ever could.

When we pull away, I'm breathless. "We'll be okay," I say again.

Dmitry takes a deep breath, presses his forehead to mine, and then steps away. "Fine."

One of the women in the boat clears her throat. "Can we go now?"

Dmitry glares at her and then nods to Sevastian to help him get the boat in the water. They have to turn a crank to engage the boat in the lift, but once that happens, a series of gears and levers do their work and it only takes one person to turn the crank until the boat is high enough to make it over the side of the boat and then begin to drop down.

"How will we all get off the boat if one person has to stay behind to turn the crank?" Sadie asks.

"Weight will pull the boat down as soon as it's over the ledge," Sevastian says. "The last person will just have to jump over the side and into the boat before it gets too low."

Sadie seems relieved and gives him a soft smile. He returns it and continues turning the lever until the women disappear beneath the side of the ship. As soon as they do, Sevastian stops turning the lever, but the ropes continue to move anyway.

Within thirty seconds, they are in the water, and I look over the side and can see them detaching the boat from the ropes and moving away from the ship.

Hopefully soon, we'll be doing the same.

"Okay, time to move," Dmitry says. He points to Sadie, Tati, and Larissa. "You three, go to the next boat and hide. Don't make a sound. Stay low and quiet."

Sadie wraps her arms around the two girls protectively. Larissa has been crying since Annika ran off, but she wipes her tears and nods at Dmitry's order.

"We will," Sadie says.

Tati runs forward and wraps her arms around Dmitry's leg, and he bends down and kisses the top of her head. He presses her to him for one long second, and I can see his eyes going glassy. But quickly, he shoos her away with a smile and a promise to be back soon.

*We'll be back before you know it,* I tell her. *Be quiet and still. Be safe.*

*I will,* she says, wiping at her nose. There is blood on her sleeve.

She needs a doctor soon. I'm not sure what will happen if we can't get her off this boat.

I push the thought from my mind, instead focusing on the task at hand. I give her one final kiss and then push her into Sadie's arms.

"Be safe, you three," Sadie says, nodding to each of us. She gives Sevastian a slightly longer glance, and he looks away after a second, averting his gaze to the ground.

"You too," I tell her.

Then, she herds the girls into their hiding place, and I turn back to Dmitry.

"What now?"

"You go with Sevastian to the nursery," he says.

"But I want to go with you."

He shakes his head. "You need to find Olivia while I call for help."

"Why can't Sevastian call for help? We should both go find our daughter."

"They think I'm dead," Sevastian says. "The Bratva won't listen to anything I have to say. They'll think it's a trick or a trap. It has to be Dmitry."

I know he's right, but I don't want to separate from Dmitry. Not again.

Dmitry grabs my arm and pulls me into him. He strokes my hair away from my face while he speaks. "I will see you again soon. Go with Sevastian and get Olivia. Meet me back here, and we'll leave. All of us. Please."

Tears fill my eyes, and I nod. "Okay. Okay, I'll go."

He kisses me again, but it's just a quick peck. Then, he pulls away and leaves. Like that.

No goodbye, no parting words. Not even an "I love you."

And I understand why. Because that would be saying goodbye. And this isn't goodbye. I will see him again in a few minutes. We will get off this ship. Together.

At least, that is what I keep telling myself as Sevastian and I move through the ship towards the nursery.

~

Sevastian knows the ship well. Whenever we hear people coming towards us, he pushes me into small nooks and crannies, hiding me until they pass.

He doesn't need to hide because he's supposed to be here. He is wearing the uniform of the rest of the crew, and no one knows he has defected.

Sevastian talks to people when he has to, but he keeps the conversations short and brief, telling them he's on a task from the Tiger and can't delay. As soon as they pass, he pulls me from hiding and we keep moving, staying silent and low.

We move down the side deck, up a set of exterior stairs, and then down a long stairwell with metal walls on either side.

"How much farther?" I ask, hating every step I take further from Dmitry and the surface of the ship.

"Not much," he whispers. "It's just down the hall to the right."

"What about Devon and Elena?"

"They'll be in the meeting room upstairs. It should just be Olivia and the nanny inside."

"What about a guard on duty?"

He turns around and smiles, pointing to his own face. "You're looking at him."

That's a relief. Sevastian and I will be able to handle one nanny on our own without a problem.

The hallway is empty and quiet as we approach the door. Sevastian stops in front of it, and I press myself to the wall a few feet away, keeping out of sight. He gives me one last nervous look before knocking.

Immediately, a middle-aged woman with graying hair and a short, plump frame answers the door, looking confused.

"Yes?" she whispers in a thick Japanese accent.

"Elena wants to see Olivia. She told me to come get her."

The woman frowns, a deep line etching between her brows. "She's sleeping."

"I know," he says. "But she wants to see her. Please get her and bring her to me."

The woman shakes her head. "No one told me anything about this. I would rather hear it from Elena herself. I can call Devon and—"

"And anger them both?" Sevastian asks, pushing past the woman and moving into the dark room. I stay pressed to the wall, though I desperately want to be inside to see the conditions of the room, to know whether my daughter has been well cared for while I've been trapped in a shipping container.

"You can't be in here," she hisses. "Let me call to confirm, and then—"

Her words cut off with a gasp, and I know Sevastian has changed tactics. I follow him into the room, and see the woman cowering against the wall, hands raised in the face of Sevastian's knife.

I'm about to ask him how we're going to keep the woman quiet so she doesn't alert anyone when suddenly, a dark shadow separates from the opposite wall and launches towards Sevastian.

I have just enough time to yell his name before he's tackled to the ground.

The two figures roll around, and I can see the dark shadow is another guard. One we hadn't anticipated being there.

The caretaker runs for the door, but I pull out my own shiv, still red with the Tiger's blood, and wave it at her. I close the door, and she shrinks back against the wall.

"We're here for the baby," I explain to her, talking loudly over the sound of Sevastian and the other guard yelling. "She's my baby. I'm not going to hurt her or you if we can help it."

The woman's eyes are still wide and terrified, but she nods in understanding.

I can't move away from the door without risking the woman escaping and alerting everyone to our presence, but I want to help Sevastian.

He and the guard are still brawling on the floor, but Sevastian seems to be getting the upper hand. He is hunched over the guard, both of his arms around the man's neck and shoulders.

The room is bare except for a metal crib and a few shelves of books and toys, so I grab one of the hard plastic play cubes and launch it into the melee, hitting the second guard square in the back of the head.

The toy bounces off him, mercifully rolling back my way, and I grab it tightly in my hand and lunge forward, bringing it down again, harder, on the back of his head.

The skin opens at once, blood gushing from the wound, but I back up to guard the door again. Even in the half second it took for me to strike, the nanny made a beeline for the exit. I cut her off and wave the shiv at her again, herding her back into the far corner of the room.

The guard grasps at the back of his head, moaning as blood pours between his fingers, and Sevastian raises his knife in the air—handle down—and knocks the man in the head a third time with the wooden handle.

Immediately, he slumps to the floor in a heap.

Sevastian stands tall, arranges his clothes, and then grabs a length of rope I didn't see him pick up—it's from the same rope we used to tie up the Tiger. He ties the unconscious guard up and then moves to the nanny. He is gentle with the woman even as she spits curses at him in a language neither of us understands.

Only when they are both secured do I move to the crib. Olivia is awake, eyes wide and staring at the chaos just beyond the bars of her crib. As soon as she sees me, she stands up and reaches for me.

I crush her to my chest and kiss the back of her warm neck.

"Mama's got you, baby. Mama is here."

There is a sharp static noise, and Sevastian and I both look to the guard as the source of the noise.

"Lukas?" a deep voice says. "What's going on?"

"Shit." Sevastian bends down and unstraps a walkie-talkie from the guard's belt.

"Is something wrong?" the voice asks.

Sevastian clears his throat and grabs the walkie. "No," he answers. "Everything's fine."

There is a long pause before the other man responds. "We're sending someone down to check on things."

Sevastian immediately drops the walkie and grabs my hand, pulling me and Olivia behind him. "We have to go. Now."

I don't argue. We run down the hallway and up the stairs in the direction we came.

## 16

# DMITRY

Unlike last time I went to the comms room, the room isn't empty. There is a communications officer standing in front of the controls. He appears to be alone, which is lucky, but if we keep knocking people unconscious, eventually someone is bound to notice. Especially if that person is in the comms room. The second he doesn't respond to a call, someone will be sent to check things out.

Time really is beginning to run out.

I nabbed the Tiger's gun before leaving the shipping container, but I don't want to use it if I don't have to. It will be too loud and draw too much attention. Hand-to-hand combat is the better choice. Even if it does take longer.

I turn the doorknob silently, but the second I push the door inward, the hinge squeaks.

The comms officer spins around and frowns when he sees my server's uniform. "What are you doing here?"

I don't even bother to come up with an excuse. I step inside, shut the door behind me, and lunge for the officer.

The man shouts in surprise and fumbles at his waist, but I reach him before he can pull whatever weapon he was planning to.

I plow into the man, and we both hit the ground. Hard. The officer gasps as the wind is knocked out of me, and I have to blink stars from his vision.

Usually, this kind of tumble wouldn't affect me, but the wound to my ribs is sapping my energy more than thought. I am starting to feel a bit lightheaded.

The man grabs me by the shirt and tries to push me off him, but I pull back my fist and let it fly, my knuckles cracking across the man's face. A cut opens on his cheek, blood dripping down, as I hit him again and again.

The man lifts his arms to protect his face, and I spot the knife sheathed at the man's hip. I snatch it out and consider stabbing the man in the heart. It would be simple, effective, and ensure the man doesn't call for help the moment he wakes up.

However, Courtney's earlier mercy plays in my head. I didn't understand why she didn't want to kill the Tiger on sight after everything he had done to her, but then she explained Annika's story to me.

I killed Annika's pimp and now she's on this ship somewhere, refusing to go with us and threatening our escape at the same time. Killing this man could have unforeseen consequences.

In a split second, I spin the knife around and hit him with the metal handle. It takes two blows, but his eyes roll back in his head, and he's out cold.

The phone looks like a classic landline, and when I pick it up there is a dial tone. I say a silent prayer of thanks and tap in the number to Pasha's burner phone, which I memorized.

He answers on the third ring.

"Dmitry?"

"Pasha, I need help."

He sighs. "Shit. I'm so glad to hear from you."

"The ship is about to make port, and we're going to escape on lifeboats."

"We?" he asks. "You found Courtney and the girls?"

"And a lot of other women," I admit. "There will be two boatloads of people. I'm not sure where we will land, but I have my phone with me, and I'll be able to call you when we do."

"Spain," Pasha says. "The ship will make land in Spain. I checked around. I'm already there."

"In Spain?" I ask, not believing it.

"I got here yesterday. When you didn't send word sooner, we figured we'd have to meet the ship. You just tell us where to be, and we'll be there."

The weight on my chest eases, and I take a deep breath. "Damn, that is good news."

"How many people should we expect?"

I count them quickly in my head. "Fourteen, I think."

"Fourteen? Damn."

"Can you handle that?" I ask.

"We'll have to," he says before quickly adding, "It will be fine. Don't worry."

"I don't know where our boats will find shore."

"Based on the course of the ship, we can estimate. If we see you, we'll flash our lights three times. Once fast and twice slow."

Pasha really has thought of everything. I can't even begin to describe how thankful I am for his preparedness and his loyalty. After weeks of being on my own, it feels good to be part of a team again. "Thanks. We'll see you soon."

"That you will," he assures me. "It will be good to have you back, boss."

I smile and bid him a final farewell before hanging up.

The communications officer is still out cold on the floor, so I drag him under the desk and push the chair in, hiding him from view. If anyone comes into the room, they'll see him immediately, but he's hidden from passersby.

Just as I stand tall to leave, a loud siren blares over the intercom system.

It's late for this kind of message, so my stomach drops the moment I hear it.

The game is up.

"Passengers," Elena says, her voice clear and harsh over the intercom. "Our ship seems to have taken on a few unwanted pests before setting sail. Several key members of the crew are missing, as well as some important cargo. The culprit is believed to be Dmitry Tsezar, leader of the Tsezar Bratva. Dark hair, beard, blue eyes, and currently going by the name 'Andrew.' The person who brings him to me, dead or alive, will receive a reward. Happy hunting."

Fuck. I briefly wonder if the chef clued them in to my secret identity aboard the ship, but then realize it doesn't matter. Regardless of who figured it out, they are coming for me. I have to get out of here.

I pull the communications officer out from under the desk and strip off his top layer of clothing. His body is heavy and limp, which oddly works to my advantage. Gravity helps him slide out of the clothes as I pull them over his head. Then, I shrug out of my black server coat and pull on his tan button-down and white jacket. Lastly, I take his hat and pull it down as low over my hair as I can.

It doesn't fully disguise me, but if anything, it will keep eyes from landing on me. Crew members lower on the totem pole won't want to get in the way of an officer during a crisis.

I don't have much time, though. As soon as they radio the comms officer and he doesn't answer, they'll send someone to check on him and figure out my disguise. I have to move fast.

I run from the comms room and take the metal stairs down from the bridge to the main deck. Crew members are gathered in small huddles, discussing the ongoing search.

Most of them seem to be smiling, acting somewhat jovial about the whole thing. Clearly, they have no idea how serious Devon and Elena are. This is no normal stowaway situation.

It works to my advantage, though, because I'm able to walk directly past their group to the side deck, making my way back to where I'm supposed to meet Courtney and Sevastian with the girls.

If I can get to them without being stopped, we might be able to get in the boat and into the water before anyone realizes who I am. They'll be so busy searching the ship, they won't even realize we've left.

As soon as I turn the corner, though, and make it several doors down the length of the hallway, I see Devon and Elena rounding the corner on the opposite end. They are walking with a purpose, noses to the ground like hunting dogs. Unfortunately, they are also cutting me off from reaching Courtney and Sevastian.

"Officer," Devon calls, waving a meaty hand in the air for my attention.

As casually as I can, I turn and head back to the main deck, pretending I didn't hear him.

"Officer," Devon repeats. "Stop. We need to speak with you."

I adjust my hat and increase my speed. As soon as I'm back on the main deck and out of their sight, I take off into a sprint, running to the opposite side of the ship.

I've just ducked into the side deck, back pressed to the wall to stay out of view of the main deck, when Elena and Devon emerge.

All of the crew members nearby stand to attention at Elena's approach.

"Where did that officer go?" she asks the men.

They all look at one another, unsure. They weren't paying any attention.

She growls at them in frustration. "An officer just passed through here and none of you witnessed him? Clearly, you are not on high alert as I ordered."

"Apologies, ma'am," one of the men says, tipping his head in respect. "We were discussing how to split up the ship to search. We did see a captain move through just a moment ago. He came from the comms room, but I didn't see him come back through."

Elena looks up at the bridge and frowns, turning to Devon. "Who is in the bridge now?"

"Officer Ledletter," he says.

"Call him."

Devon pulls out his walkie and calls for the officer to answer, but of course he does not. "Do you think it could be him?"

Elena nods. "It could be. Do we have any word from the Tiger yet?"

Devon shakes his head, and Elena curses, "Damn it. We need to get another guard to the nursery, now."

"What about the women?" Devon asks. "They need protection, too."

Elena rolls her eyes. "The women are not our priority. The baby is."

"*Your* priority," Devon argues. "The women are mine."

Elena spins around to face her son, and I pull back closer to the wall, afraid she'll see me watching from around the corner. "I couldn't care less who you want to fuck. If Courtney is still on the ship after we find Dmitry, you can do whatever you want with her. Right now, the priority is Olivia and killing Dmitry. That's it."

Devon lowers his head and twitches like a druggie strung out, looking for his next fix. He curls his fingers into a fist at his side before barking for a guard to go up to the bridge and see where the comms officer is.

I don't stick around to see what he discovers because I already know. My disguise is about to put a huge fucking target on my back. As soon as they discover the officer half naked on the floor with my server's uniform next to him, they'll know I'm disguised as an officer. Another announcement will be made and the figurative noose around my neck will tighten further.

I run down the side deck towards the stern and throw the hat over the railing and into the water as I go. I don't need it anymore.

"Hey, stop!"

I don't need to turn around to see it's Devon talking. He must've doubled back.

"There he is," he yells. "Get him!"

I lower my head and pump my arms, running as fast as I can. I duck down a small interior hallway and then turn right again, moving towards the front of the ship. The hallway opens onto a small, open-air deck with a roof overhead to keep out the sun during the day. Directly in the center of the space stand four guards.

They are all huddled together, clearly planning something, and they turn as I enter.

One of the men, a guard I recognize as working in the dining room guarding Devon earlier that morning, narrows his eyes to study me. I take a deep breath to try and disguise my rapid breathing and nod my head as I pass through.

I feel their eyes on me as I turn to the left and walk out of the side door and onto the side deck I was going down earlier when I was first stopped by Devin and Elena. If I can keep going, I'll eventually run into where Sevastian and Courtney are hopefully hiding with the girls.

Then, I hear Devon yelling behind me. His voice is distant but clearly frantic.

"Stop him!"

I look back through one of the windows into the room as I walk by and see the guards looking back and forth between Devon's voice and me. One of them lifts a finger to point in my direction, and I don't wait for them to clue in. Once again, I take off at a sprint.

I want to keep going to where I know my family is waiting for me, but if I do, I'll lead the guards right to them and there won't be time to launch the lifeboat. I have to shake my pursuers before I can meet up with them.

So, I take a hard right and move up an exterior set of stairs to a higher deck. Then, I duck into the first door I find.

The room is thankfully empty. It's a lobby area just outside the formal dining room. I didn't see it this morning because I was taken up the servants' stairs.

The wooden double doors are cracked open an inch, and I step forward and peek through them. The room is dark, so I push the door open and step inside. There is a row of wooden shelves along one wall that could work if I want to hide. I could lay low and wait for my pursuers to move on before sneaking out and going to the meetup point.

Hiding would be nice considering the slice to my ribs is starting to ache from all of the running and exertion. I haven't checked, but I can feel warmth across my side that makes me think I might be bleeding again.

Just as I'm moving towards the shelves, I'm knocked forward by a blow to my back. I hit the floor and roll over just as a guard I hadn't noticed before kicks me in the side—the same side where I was stabbed earlier.

I groan in pain and roll to my left, jumping to my feet.

The guard is a young kid—no older than twenty. Probably not even legally able to drink the liquor on board. But his face is an angry mask.

"You aren't supposed to be here," he growls.

I hold up my hands. "Let me go, and I won't be for much longer. I'm trying to get off."

"I'll get a reward if I turn you over," he mutters. "I could use a reward."

"If you come for me right now, you won't get your reward," I say evenly. "You'll be dead."

I know Courtney wanted to try not to hurt anyone else, but I can't keep knocking people out. I can't leave a trail of witnesses behind me. If this kid comes for me, I'm going to kill him.

He smirks. "I'd like to see you try."

Before I can respond, he pulls out a gun and levels it at my chest. I duck and roll just as the first shot explodes into the wood behind me.

I hit his knees, overextending them both, and wrap my arms around his waist, pushing him backwards.

He yelps in surprise, but he doesn't have time to do anything before he hits the floor.

We both scramble for the gun, but he hasn't been properly trained. He doesn't understand how to handle a weapon, how to have control over it, or how to fight.

I pluck the gun from his hand as easily as if he'd handed it to me, and then turn it on him.

The kid falls back on the floor, his head hitting the tile, and he holds up his hands, eyes squinting in anticipation.

I need to kill this kid. I absolutely should.

Yet, once again, I hear Courtney's voice in my head.

*No. There has to be another way.*

I groan in annoyance, spin the gun around, and whip him with the back end. His eyes roll back in his head immediately, and I quickly drag him over to the wooden cabinets, shove him inside, and then wrap my leather belt around the handles to keep him inside. Someone will find him eventually, just hopefully not before my family and I are on our way to the Spanish shoreline.

If we can't get off this ship, I know I'll die, I know Olivia will be raised by a psychopath, and I know Courtney will become Devon's sex slave, at best. At worst, she'll be sold into slavery.

But no one has said anything about Tati.

She's too old for Elena to lie to. She's a risk.

What will happen to her if we're all captured?

I don't allow myself to think about it. Instead, I press a hand to my injured side and move on through the dining room. If I can get down the servants' stairwell and back to the side deck without running into another guard, I should be able to meet up with everyone before I lose too much blood.

If I don't, then it's likely I'll bleed out, even if Elena doesn't have me killed.

Still, there is hope. I just have to keep moving.

Our plan hasn't been foiled yet.

# 17

# COURTNEY

Sevastian is busy throwing extra supplies into the lifeboat and outfitting the girls in life jackets, but I can't seem to do anything. Once Elena's announcement came over the intercom system, my world stopped.

Is Dmitry alive?

I swat the thought away for the hundredth time and try to convince myself he's fine. Dmitry is resourceful. He's a fighter. He has fought his way out of stickier situations than this one. Any minute, he'll come running down the side deck to where we're waiting for him.

I stand next to the boat and wait for his figure to appear.

"Grab more blankets."

I turn and see Sevastian nodding towards a storage cupboard in the closet across the hall. "We want to keep the girls as dry and warm as possible once we're on the water."

I nod and stumble the ten steps to the shelf.

If Dmitry is dead, I have to be able to leave the ship without him. If he doesn't show up, I have to be able to say goodbye. Tati and Olivia are depending on me. I know that.

Still, the idea of climbing into the boat without him makes me sick.

I grab five thin, scratchy blankets and tuck them into a storage hold beneath one of the bench seats in the boat. Then, I bend down and check on where the girls are hiding beneath the boat. Olivia is asleep in Sadie's arms and Tati and Larissa are tucked in on either side of her. They are wide-eyed and terrified, but safe.

A few times, guards have run past, and I've had to hide while Sevastian busied himself. Word of his betrayal hasn't yet reached Devon and Elena, so he doesn't have to hide like the rest of us.

"Maybe you should go search for Dmitry," I suggest. "You could find him and then bring him here instead of to Devon and Elena. No one would suspect anything until it was too late."

He presses his lips together and shakes his head. "He would never forgive me if I left you all alone."

"He would too," I argue.

"I promised him I'd stay with you all and keep you safe, so that's what I will do. Dmitry can take care of himself."

I stand up tall, puffing my chest out. It feels silly to be declaring my dominance while wearing a dirty pajama outfit, but desperate times. "I am the wife of the Bratva leader. Doesn't my authority count for something?"

Sevastian's mouth quirks up in a half smile. "As I am no longer a member, my loyalty is to Dmitry, not the Bratva. Sorry, but I do not recognize your authority."

I slouch forward and sigh. "Dammit."

Sevastian lifts the boat slightly, engaging the lowering mechanism, and then turns to me, his eyes narrowed and sincere. "Dmitry will be fine. I have a feeling about these kinds of things, and I'm confident he'll meet us here."

I want to take comfort in Sevastian's words, but I've only known him a few weeks and most of that time was thinking of him as my captor. I'm sure no one would blame me for not having full trust in him.

Just as I'm about to admit as much to him, Sevastian's attention jerks up, his gaze cast over my shoulder. Then, he smiles. "What did I tell you?"

I spin around and see the sight I've been imagining for the last half hour. Dmitry is walking towards us. Towards the boat we've prepared. Toward escape.

I run forward to meet him, ecstatic that our plan is falling into place, when I suddenly notice he isn't walking so much as limping. And that isn't a smile on his face; it's a wince.

His arm is pressed to his ribs, his hand on top for added pressure, and there is blood soaking through his fingers.

Dmitry is injured. Gravely.

I wrap my arms around him just as he takes a stumbling step and nearly falls.

"What happened?"

He opens his mouth to answer and gasps in pain, doubling over to shield his side.

"Come on," I urge, trying to swallow back the panic threatening to creep up my throat. "There's a first aid kit. I can help."

Tati starts to crawl out from under the boat, but I shake my head and gesture for her to stay hidden, and she listens, though there is concern written all over her face.

"What in the hell happened to you?" Sevastian asks, spreading out one of the blankets on the deck for Dmitry to lie on.

"Get me a first aid kid," I instruct, not wanting to waste a single second. I lift Dmitry's shirt and see that the slice to his side is much worse than it was before. It seems to have opened further and the skin around it is red and shiny with bacteria.

"Not good," Sevastian whispers over my shoulder.

I turn around to shoot him a glare and then pat Dmitry's chest gently. "Nothing I can't handle. I am a doctor, remember?"

Dmitry smiles like he's going to tease me about being a brain doctor, not a body doctor, like he usually does, but he winces again and closes his eyes. "It's just a cut."

"An infected cut," I tell him. "And you need stitches."

The cut is so much deeper than it looked earlier in the dim light. Now, directly under one of the deck lights, I can see exactly how bad it is. He shouldn't have been walking around, let alone fighting anyone. It is a miracle he didn't collapse before making it back to the boat.

I press a balled-up blanket to his side to stanch the bleeding and dig through the first aid kit for antiseptic. I twist off the cap and upend the bottle over the cut. Dmitry lets out a string of curses, but I don't stop until the bottle is empty. He needs all of the help he can get.

Then, I find a box of emergency laceration closures. I pull out the largest one I can find, affix one side of the sticky tape to his skin, and then stretch the bandage over the cut to the other side. The wound pulls closed slightly, and Dmitry grits his teeth. I repeat the procedure several more times until the cut is a narrow strip of red across his side rather than an angry open wound.

"Will those be enough?" Sevastian asks.

"For now." *I hope.*

I grab Dmitry's hand and pull him gently to a seated position. He winces, but the color in his face is already better. When he looks at me, his blue eyes are clear, and I can see that he's pulling through the pain and rebounding.

"Get him something to eat." I hear Sevastian jump into action and root around in the supplies. He returns with a granola bar.

"That's for the trip," Dmitry says, trying to wave it away.

I peel back the foil and force it into his hand. "A trip you won't be conscious for if you don't eat something."

He sighs but does as I say. While he eats, I find a body-wrap bandage and begin winding it around his midsection tightly. I also use the scissors from the kit to cut a strip of blanket to wedge between the layers to try and contain any additional bleeding.

By the time I'm done, his entire midsection is wrapped and bandaged like a mummy, but he's able to stand up without stumbling, so I count it as a win.

"Enough about me," he says. "We have to go."

Sevastian and I help Dmitry into the boat, despite his protestations while Sadie loads the girls inside.

Tati runs to Dmitry the moment she's inside and wraps her arms around his midsection. I see the flash of pain in his eyes as she squeezes his wound, but he doesn't say anything. Instead, he hugs her close and rests his cheek on her head.

"You next," Sevastian says, holding out a hand to help me inside. I accept and join my family.

Sadie hands me Olivia, who is still fast asleep in a tangle of blankets. She looks more like a human burrito than a toddler.

"Do you need any help?" Sadie asks Sevastian, moving to the side of the boat.

He glances up at her and then away quickly, shaking his head. "I just need to start the process and then I'll be able to jump in."

She smiles and then sits down, hands folded in her lap patiently.

Overall, the entire process is very ... calm. I imagined we would be desperately trying to get the boat in the water while guards fired at us and tried to reel the boat back in. I imagined Elena and Devon would be running towards us just as we began to lower down the side of the ship.

Instead, the corner of the deck we're on is quiet and everyone seems at ease. Or at least, as much as they can be under the circumstances.

Then, there is a loud metallic crack.

"Fuck!"

We all turn to Sevastian who is holding a rusted metal gear, broken off in his hand. He drops to his knees and tries to fit the piece back into the machinery, but it clatters to the deck again. He stares at it helplessly for a moment before looking up at us.

"What the fuck was that for?" Dmitry asks.

"The lowering mechanism," he says. "It's what allows the boats to drop all the way into the water unmanned. Without it, someone will have to manually lower it down."

An obstacle. That's all this is. A small obstacle. We can overcome it.

"Then we'll take a different boat." I quickly start pulling the provisions we loaded out of the storage bins. "We can move all of the supplies and be out of here in a few minutes."

Dmitry looks disappointed, but there isn't another option, so he nods. "Everyone, grab something."

I start handing armfuls of things to everyone, including the girls, but before we can move anything, a person rounds the nearest corner and slams to a stop.

"Annika?" I blink, surprised to see her here. After she ran off earlier, I assumed she'd be caught and face the same fate as Larissa's mother.

Her eyes are wide as she takes in our crew. Larissa reaches out for the woman who has become her surrogate mother over the last few weeks, but Annika stares at her blankly like she doesn't even know her.

"Annika," I say more gently. "You can come with us. We're escaping. Come with us, please."

She shakes her head, and I drop the supplies I'm holding and climb out of the boat. Like a cornered animal, she begins to back away. I can see that she wants to run again.

"Courtney," Dmitry warns.

I wave him away over my shoulder. Annika is here in part because of him. I don't want to leave without her. I want to right the wrong if possible.

I draw closer to Annika, making up more ground than she's retreating. I just need to get close enough to grab her, to keep her from running.

Suddenly, Annika bolts to her left, headed for the side deck that runs the length of the ship. I bolt with her, cutting off her escape.

"I know you are upset with Dmitry," I say. "And I know that is an understatement. You blame him for you being here, but if you let us, we'll get you out."

"Ha!" she screams in my face. "You think you're going to escape? Please. You'll die in the open water."

I hear Larissa release a scared sob behind me and take another step towards Annika. She's too worked up to realize, so she doesn't back away. I take another step and grab her wrist, holding her as tightly as I can without alarming her.

"And you'll die on this ship," I say. "The people here will kill you or sell you. We are giving you the opportunity for freedom."

Annika stares at me, and I don't see the woman I spoke with in the crate. The cool gaze through which she usually viewed the world has been replaced with a kind of wide-eyed craziness. Something inside of her is broken, and I'm not sure anything I say will fix it.

"There is no freedom from what I've seen. From what I've been through." She looks over my shoulder at Dmitry, her eyes narrowing. "My life has been decided by men like him for way too long, and it's time for me to make my own decisions."

"Decide to come with us," I beg. "I know you don't like Dmitry. For good reason. But he's not an evil man. He did what he thought he had to do to save his family. You can be part of that family. You can come with us. We will help you start over. Please, Annika."

Annika tips her head to the side in contemplation and looks at me as though she's trying to decide. Then, she slowly slips her hand from my grip.

I think she's choosing to stay. I think she's choosing to go with us, but just as I let go, she throws back her head and screams.

"They are here. Right here. The trespassers are here. Get them."

Her shouts reverberate off the metal ship, echoing into the vast expanse of water and sky, but I know someone on the ship will hear her. Our quiet little corner of the ship will soon be overrun with guards. We have to get out of here.

Dmitry curses behind me and jumps up to try and quiet Annika, but before he can even get out of the boat, Annika runs to the edge and crawls over the railing, standing on the ledge.

I'm too horrified to move even though Sevastian is calling my name, beckoning for me to get in the boat. I stand perfectly still, watching Annika as she looks over her shoulder at me and smiles.

"I am starting over," she says.

Then, like a mirage, she disappears from view.

Sevastian grabs my arm and hauls me towards the boat, practically throwing me inside, and it isn't until I hear the faint splash below that I realize Annika jumped into the water.

Suddenly, the boat starts to move. It's a jerky crawl over the same railing Annika just jumped from.

"Sevastian, no," Dmitry says, grabbing his side and standing up. "You won't be able to get in. We have to move to a new boat."

Sevastian shakes his head just as loud voices grow closer. "There isn't time."

"They'll kill you," he says, a pained look on his face I've rarely seen before. "They'll kill you for helping us."

Sevastian shrugs and smiles sadly. "I've cheated death before. Maybe I'll get lucky again."

He won't. We all know that. Yet, unless we all want to stay and die, there isn't another choice. Someone has to stay on deck and lower us down. That's the only way.

Sevastian gives one final nod and then uses both hands to speed up the process. He groans as he exerts himself, turning the dial and lowering the boat of women, children, and an injured man into the water.

We move over the edge of the ship and begin rappelling down the side, two taut coils of rope snaking from our boat up to the ship.

Dmitry stands up as we lower down, trying to see what is happening on the deck. I ensure Olivia and Tati are safe with Sadie and do the same.

Just as I stand up, a crowd of guards enters the space. Led by the Tiger.

I don't know whether he escaped the bonds I tied on him or whether he was freed by someone, but he's loose and coming for us. I should have killed him.

Dmitry pulls out a gun he had stowed at his hip and begins firing. Sevastian jumps in surprise and then begins working even faster. He knows he doesn't have much time left. Dmitry will only be able to hold them off for a few seconds at most.

One of the guards goes down as he's shot, grabbing his shoulder and falling sideways, but the Tiger presses on, undeterred by the bullets flying. Then, we're out of sight.

As the boat gets lower, it begins moving faster. Sevastian needs to turn the handle, but gravity is doing a lot of the work. The ropes want to break free of the gears. They want to drop us into the water.

So rapidly, we move down the side of the ship. Then, when the boat is about ten feet from the water, we stop.

"Shit, shit, shit," Dmitry mumbles. He reaches out and grabs my hand, but doesn't take his eyes off the railing of the ship.

Then, suddenly, Sevastian is visible.

It looks like he's looking over the side at us, but I realize that he's being held there. The Tiger is just over his shoulder, pinning him to the railing.

He has been overtaken.

"What are we going to do?" The water is dark beneath us. It looks close, but I can't tell if that is an illusion or not.

Dmitry stares up at where Sevastian is fighting. He has broken free of the Tiger's hold, and we can just see the top of his head as he fights off the guards, but things don't look good.

For one horrified moment, I wonder whether he's going to jump over the railing the way Annika did.

If he does, we might be able to pull him into the boat and save him, though the fall might kill him. Even if it doesn't, I'm not sure we'll be able to get our own boat in the water. If Sevastian jumps to escape the guards, they will likely turn their attention to the rescue boat and begin reeling us in.

"We have to cut it free," I say, turning to dig through our supplies.

"We're too high." Dmitry looks over the railing, staring down into the water.

I pull open a leather pouch and realize it's Sevastian's personal weapon stash. Inside is a gun, a knife, and a switch blade. I pull out the knife and the blade and hand the blade to Dmitry.

"Let's hope you're wrong," I say, moving to the rope at the back of the boat.

"The boat could overturn," he says. At the same time, we both glance at our girls. Tati is shivering next to Sadie, and Olivia is still blissfully asleep. Though, I assume she won't be for long.

I kneel down and reach back into the supplies. Inside is an inflatable raft. A last-ditch rescue option in case everything else fails. It's a tightly bound rectangle with a cord on one side. The instructions say "Pull and stand back."

"I'll keep this," I say, holding it up. "If the boat overturns, we'll inflate this and make for shore."

"Will we all fit?" Sadie asks.

I shrug. "Do we have another option?"

A shot rings out above us followed by a scream of pain. I can't tell whether it's Sevastian or one of the guards, but either way, things are escalating on deck. We don't have time to argue anymore.

Dmitry realizes this, too.

He shakes his head. "We don't have another option. Let's do it."

I wrap the life-raft string around my life vest, making sure it's secure, and I won't lose it in the fall. Then, I turn to Sadie. "Do you have the girls?"

She checks all of their life vests and then hugs Olivia to her chest. "I have them. I'll keep them safe."

I know she means what she's saying, but I also know things could easily go wrong. The boat could flip over and send Sadie sinking to the bottom. She could lose hold of Olivia in the chaos, and she could be lost to the dark water. Same with Tati or Larissa.

There are a million ways for things to go wrong and only one way for them to go right. I cling to that one in a million and move to the rope at the back of the boat.

Dmitry positions himself at the front. He winks at me, and then we both begin to cut at the rope.

It's a blended, reinforced rope—strong enough to hold up a boat full of people—so it takes several slices before I see any tearing.

Another shot rings out on the deck above, and I begin cutting with renewed force.

"I'm halfway through," Dmitry calls.

I yelp and tell him to wait for me to catch up.

I grit my teeth and slice carefully across the strands. Slowly, they begin to unwind. As they do, my heart rate increases. I feel like my chest is filled with bees, like an entire angry colony is buzzing away inside my chest.

"Okay," I say. "Keep going."

Dmitry nods and we both start cutting again. After only a few seconds, the boat is wrenched upward in one shaky tug. I scream in surprise and grab the edge of the boat to keep from falling backward. When I look up, I see the Tiger looking down at us. The only light comes from the deck over his head, so he's mostly in shadow, but I would swear he's smiling.

"Faster," Dmitry instructs, turning back to his own rope. "They're reeling us in."

The boat shakes again, and I realize we're moving up in slow but steady inches. Two, four, six. Soon, we really will be too high to drop into the water safely.

I cut with renewed vigor, gritting my teeth until I'm sure I'll be left with nothing but gums. As I get through the rope it seems to cut easier. Like the strands are breaking willingly, ready to drop their heavy load.

"I'm almost through," I say. "Just one or two more cuts."

"Same," Dmitry says, looking over at me.

One or two more cuts until our fate is decided. Until we know whether this plan is a disaster or a success.

We stare at one another for a second, but then the boat is pulled upward yet again. Eight inches.

We don't have time to be scared.

I mouth *three, two* ... When I get to one, Dmitry and I both turn away and cut.

I'm surprised by how easily my knife cuts through the rope now. Like butter. Like it's nothing.

I'm looking at the rope holding us up and then, suddenly, I'm not.

There isn't time to understand what is happening or what it means as the side of the ship races past my face.

I'm still standing up when we hit the water, and the force of it buckles my knees and sends me falling to the floor of the boat. Water splashes over the side, filling the boat up to an inch. Sadie is screaming, Olivia is crying, and Dmitry is shouting to see if everyone is okay.

And that is when I realize ...

We are all okay.

The boat is in one piece. The guards are cursing and yelling above our heads, but we're no longer strapped to the ship.

We are in the water, floating away from the ship, and we survived.

Well, almost.

Sevastian is still on board, but he sacrificed himself for us. Without him, we'd all be dead.

Lying on the floor of the boat, cold and wet and shaken, I say a silent prayer of thanks to him for his sacrifice. Then, I turn and grab my girls, holding them close to my chest.

When Dmitry wraps his arms around us, I finally let myself truly believe we will make it home.

# 18

# DMITRY

I allow myself a moment to hug my family before I grab the oars at the front of the boat and begin to row.

"You'll hurt yourself," Courtney says, laying a hand on my shoulder. "You shouldn't be doing any physical labor."

But I can still hear the voices of the Tiger and the other guards on the ship above us. We don't know if they'll get in a boat and come after us or if they'll start shooting into the water. We need to get away as fast as possible.

"I'll be okay," I tell her, though I can already feel my side aching. "I'll only row for a little while. Then we can switch."

She opens her mouth to argue, but then Olivia's crying reaches new heights.

"Get Olivia," I say gently. "I'm okay."

Courtney sighs and grabs Olivia, laying her over her shoulder and patting her back. Sadie hugs Tati and Larissa, keeping them close, though Larissa appears to be in much worse shape than Tati. Tears and snot run down her face, and she's beside herself in fear.

Tati seems blank. Unaffected, though I know she isn't. I know this is just another layer of trauma over her already difficult life.

I did this to all of them.

The only person in the boat who isn't here because of me is Larissa. That I know of.

I row long enough that my body feels numb. My arms are moving on reflex only, and even the pain in my side is gone.

Courtney has pulled out blankets for all of the girls and has them bundled tightly. She and Sadie bailed out as much of the water as they could on the floor of the boat, but it's still damp, and the bottoms of everyone's pants and blankets are sopping up water. Still, they are managing to sleep, exhaustion having caught up with them after the adrenaline rush of our escape.

"Let me take over," Courtney says, wrapping her hand around the oar and tugging lightly.

I'm too tired to argue. We are far enough away from the ship now that we aren't in imminent danger of being followed. If they were going to come for us, they would have by now, and there is no sign of anyone following behind us.

As soon as I stop rowing and my body is able to relax, my arm around Tati, my mind takes over and begins to race. I realize that Sevastian is gone.

Dead.

It seems obvious. Of course he's dead. Still, I hadn't let myself dwell on it. In my mind, he was still somewhere on the ship fighting off the guards. Because I didn't see him die, I didn't let myself play out the rest of the story. The part where he was overpowered by the guards and executed for his role in our escape.

He sacrificed himself for me and my family. And I can't let that sacrifice be in vain.

I point Courtney in the direction of where shore should be and then lie down on the bench to rest before I take over the oars again. I will need to be rested by the time we reach shore if I'm going to lead my family to safety.

Tati tucks her knees up to her chin and sits next to me, her small hand lying on my forehead while I sleep. For the first time in weeks, I don't have a nightmare. It isn't the best sleep I've ever had, but it's the best I've had in a long time.

Still, I wake with a start.

I bolt upright and reach for Tati, holding onto her while the boat rocks hard to one side and then violently to the other.

Courtney is clinging to the oars, her knuckles white, teeth gritted in exertion.

"How long has this been going on?" I shout. The waves are roaring around us and the sky, which was previously a deep blue and dotted with stars, is a dark gray, like God has thrown a fleece blanket over our heads to smother us.

"It came on suddenly," Sadie shouts back. "We didn't want to wake you because it wasn't too bad, but we seem to have rowed right into the middle of something.

The boat rocks hard again, slamming us all into the right side of the boat, and I see Sadie take the brunt of the blow in her back, trying to protect Olivia, who is sitting in her lap.

Everyone has life vests on, but I'd prefer if we didn't have to use them.

"Sit on the floor," I say, moving Tati off the bench. *Stay low and hold on.*

They listen. Larissa is crying, but she curls up next to Tati, and Sadie clings to Olivia and tucks herself halfway underneath the storage compartment at the back of the boat.

Once I'm sure everyone is down, I move to the front of the boat, gripping the sides for support, and take one of the oars from Courtney.

"I can do it," she insists. "You're hurt."

"We will do it," I say. "You take one, I'll take the other."

The water is splashing against the sides of the boat and then sucking back, threatening to rip the oars right out of her hands.

I squeeze into the seat next to her and then hook my left leg around her right, wrapping our ankles for another layer of security. If she gets pulled out of the boat, I'll know.

Then, we row. There is no time for talking or planning. The only thing we can do is power through the water and the wind with our heads down and our jaws clenched.

I look back several times to check everyone else is still in the boat, and they are. Tati is huddled down next to Larissa, rubbing soothing circles on the other girl's back, and Sadie is singing softly to a terrified Olivia.

I hate that they are all going through this. That I can't protect them from evil people or nature or any of the bad things the world can offer. I hate that they deserve so much more than me and the life I've given them. More than anything, I hate that I can't give them up.

"I think the storm is letting up," Courtney calls over the roar of the wind.

She's right. It's getting easier to pull the oar through the water, and within ten minutes, things have quieted down to normal.

I turn back and can see the storm still ravaging the water behind us, but ahead of us is smooth sailing.

I untangle my leg from Courtney's, take her oar, and tell her to rest. I won't be able to sleep again, anyway.

After the chaos of the storm, it's strange to experience such peace. The girls are all asleep behind me and the only sound is the soft hush of the ocean and the gulping of my oar slipping through the dark water. The silence swallows me up until I'm not sure how long I've been rowing or what time it is. It is so disorienting that when I see a dark shadow in front of us, I'm not sure what it's.

It is too long to be a boat, but there is no way we could have already reached land.

But that is exactly what we've done.

Directly in front of us is the shore.

"Courtney," I call back, pushing deep to find the energy to get us all the way to land. "Courtney, we're here."

She's at my side in an instant. "Are you sure?"

I tip my head forward to the shadow in front of us that is slowly revealing treetops and a stretch of sand in the moonlight.

She sighs and then kisses my cheek. "Land."

She gets the girls ready, drying them off as best she can with the few blankets that aren't soaked from the storm. Then, she gathers our food and water supplies in a pull-string bag and prepares to set out into the unknown.

The Bratva said they would be waiting for us on the shore somewhere, but even knowing the path of the ship, they could be miles and miles away. I'll call them as soon as I know where we are and hopefully we won't have to spend too long wandering in the dark. The last thing we need is to be picked up by local authorities. Even if we tell them the truth of what happened with us, being this close to the shore where the ship planned to dock, they could be working for the Yakuza. We can't trust anyone.

As soon as the boat comes to a stop in the sand, I offer a hand to help everyone out one at a time and then pull the boat out of the water.

Courtney helps me drag it into the tree line, and then we cover it with leaves and branches. It will be found eventually, but I want to keep it hidden until we're far enough away that it doesn't matter if the Yakuza know where we landed.

The girls don't have shoes on, so Courtney and I cut strips of the last remaining blanket to wrap around their feet to protect them from the sand. Then, we begin to walk.

We stick close to the water, but every time there is a break in the tree line, I creep up to it to see if anyone is there waiting. We do that three times before we see something.

A small wooden hut is built in the middle of the fourth break in the trees. It looks like a kind of lifeguard shack, almost, but there is a light inside the window, despite the fact there is no one on the beach.

I move back to the group and shake my head, prepared to tell them to stay quiet and low as we move past so as not to be caught when Courtney gasps and points over my shoulder.

I spin around just as two slow flashes of light break through the darkness.

The signal.

"Was there another flash before that?" I ask.

"One quick one," Courtney says. "Is it the Bratva?"

It has to be. Who else would flash their lights in that pattern? Who else would be waiting by the shore in the middle of the night?

I'm still hesitating, trying to be certain when it happens again. One fast, two slow.

They don't know we're here. They are signaling out to the water, hoping to draw us to them. It has to be them.

"It's them," I say. "Let's go, but move slowly. We don't want them to be surprised and shoot."

The ground between us and the hut is a sandy uphill climb, so we're all out of breath when we reach the landing. I go first, arms raised in surrender. I suspect my men will recognize me, but with the beard, it's better to be safe than sorry.

"It's me," I call towards the flashing lights.

As soon as I speak, the lights go out, plunging everything into darkness.

"Hello?" I call again. "It's me?"

I hear a car door slam shut. And then another.

As my eyes adjust to the gloom, I see two shapes moving towards us, their silhouettes growing larger.

"Shit, I'm glad we found you. That was lucky," I say.

Then, one of the figures reaches into his pocket. "Yes, lucky indeed."

He pulls out a gun, and Sadie gasps behind me. She must have recognized the voice, too.

Devon.

There is no time to run or grab a weapon or fight. Devon and the Tiger are on us in a second. The Tiger grabs me and Devon grabs Tati, pulling her forward by the arm. He knows that is the way to make me and Courtney compliant. Sadie, too. None of us would do anything to hurt Tati. He is using my child against me.

"Don't fight," the Tiger says evenly in my ear. "Come with us."

~

The whiplash of being recaptured so soon after accepting we were free is jarring. So jarring that I can't speak as we're led towards the hut.

More figures move out of the light of the hut and wait for our approach. As we get close, I see Elena standing next to the truck, her short gray hair windblown and sticking up around her face.

How did they know the signal? That's the only thought in my mind. Maybe they overheard my conversation with Pasha through the comms room. Maybe it was monitored and they knew our plan the entire time. That would explain why they didn't chase after us immediately. They didn't need to get in a boat and fight with us on the water. Because they knew where we were going and how to capture us.

I feel like such an idiot. I should have known better than to use the ship's communication pathways to plot with Pasha.

"This was almost a good plan," Elena says as we're brought before her and pushed down onto the sand. "Unfortunately, my methods of torture are more efficient than your rowing."

Torture. I frown, not sure what she means until another person emerges from the shack.

He stumbles through the door and falls onto his knees. A guard emerges just behind him, a gun pressed to his back.

Sevastian.

At least, I think so. His face is swollen beyond recognition. His eye sockets are bulging out with fluid and bruising, and his lips are puffy and split. Blood drips down his face from several open wounds, and he's holding his arm strangely as though it's broken. His fingers also seem to be bleeding profusely, but I don't look closely enough to know for sure. I'm not sure I want to know what all they did.

"I'm sorry," he says, shaking his head and looking down at the ground. When I hear his voice I know for certain it's Sevastian. "I'm so sorry. I held out for as long as I could, but—"

"It's okay."

I'm surprised to find that I mean it. Sevastian told me he gave the FBI false information before, information that would send them away from the Bratva and my plans. He was loyal to me then, but he broke now.

Knowing what I know about Devon and Elena—how cruel they are—I can't even blame him. I don't know how I'd respond to torture. Even though it has meant our recapture, part of me is just glad he's still alive. Even if not for long.

"How sweet," Elena says sarcastically.

Sadie lets out a sob behind me, and Sevastian gives his best approximation of a smile. "I'm okay."

The guard behind him hits him in the side of the head with the weapon for speaking, knocking him sideways, and Sadie lunges forward as if to catch him, though she's too far away.

I didn't realize she cared about him so much.

"Stupid girl," Elena says. "He held you captive. Please tell me you don't fancy yourself in love with him."

Sadie doesn't answer, but watches as Sevastian struggles to sit upright. As soon as he does, he's kicked in the side again and falls, spitting blood into the sand.

Sadie gasps and then falls in the sand herself, unconscious.

"She fainted," Elena laughs. "I didn't realize anyone outside of Victorian novels fainted. How quaint."

"And she hasn't even seen the bodies," Devon says.

"Bodies?" Courtney says, her voice so low it's almost a whisper.

Devon laughs, the sound unhitched and wild. "I suppose they do blend in with the scenery a bit."

I narrow my eyes and scour the dark landscape around the hut. The sandy shore shifts to larger rocks and then to rocky ground with small shrubs sticking from the ground, desperately clinging to life in the untenable soil.

Then, I see them.

Not shrubs as I previously thought. Bodies.

Piles of them.

Devon laughs when my mouth falls open. “Your men were unprepared. Surprising, since we landed a helicopter not far from here. I thought they would have heard the blades.”

They thought Devon and Elena were still at sea. They wouldn’t have been expecting an ambush.

“Oh well,” Devon says with a casual shrug. “Better luck next time.”

He nods to the Tiger, and without warning, I’m hauled to my feet again. I try to pull my arm free, but Devon makes a warning sound behind me. I turn and see his hands wrapped around Tati’s neck.

“Careful, careful,” he warns. “We’ll begin to kill the spares.”

The spares.

That’s what Tati and Sadie and Larissa are to them. Innocent people who don’t matter. People they can use to control me. They’ll kill them all without remorse if Courtney or I make a wrong move.

Rage so hot it makes me sweat tears through my body, and I can barely stand up. I clench my fists and grit my teeth, but the anger inside of me is desperate to escape. If it doesn’t, I worry I’ll explode from it.

“Grab the child,” Elena says from the hut. Then, she clarifies, “The baby.”

A large guard with a tattoo across the side of his neck moves towards Courtney, but she backs away and shakes her head. “No.”

Devon still has his hand around Tati's arm, and he pulls her in front of him. "Remember?"

"No," Courtney repeats, glancing at me for only a second before looking back at Elena. "You can't take her."

Elena laughs. "Yes, we can."

Suddenly, Courtney turns and runs towards the water. I think she's making a break for it, and Elena must think the same thing because she shouts for her men not to shoot her. "She has the baby. You could hurt the baby."

I don't understand what Courtney is doing until she suddenly stops and holds Olivia at arm's length, dangling her over the ground.

That is when I realize she isn't dangling Olivia over the ground, but rather, a precipice. Olivia doesn't even really know what's going on, which is for the best. We walked up a sandy slope to reach the hut, but just twenty feet forward is a craggy rock face separating the beach from the ground above the hut. The fall is probably fifteen to twenty feet to the ground, and the ground is hard and cold from the evening chill.

There is a chance Olivia could survive the fall, but it would hurt. A lot.

Elena orders the men to stop and then narrows her eyes at Courtney. "You wouldn't harm your own child."

"I would if it meant keeping her away from you," she says. "And if the fall doesn't work, I have other methods. Her neck would break easily, I'm sure."

The thought makes me want to run forward and grab Olivia from Courtney because I truly can't tell whether she's serious or not. I can't tell whether she would actually hurt our daughter rather than hand her over to Elena.

Even more, I can't decide whether I agree with her or not.

As proven by Devon's insanity, living with Elena is not healthy. Olivia would be emotionally abused at the very least. She would grow up to be little more than Elena's minion, used for whatever nefarious deeds Elena needed accomplished. It would not be a good life.

"You wouldn't," Elena says again. "Besides, we have your other daughter. Devon will kill her right now."

Courtney takes a step forward, her toes at the very edge of the drop. "And if he does, I'll jump over the side with Olivia, killing us both. Then, neither of you get what you want."

Devon looks slightly panicked at this thought, and I see his grip on Tati loosen.

"Do you want to risk it?" Courtney asks.

They stare at one another for a long time, waiting for the other to break. Finally, Elena does.

"You can keep the girl for now," she says. "But I will get her eventually."

Courtney shrugs, looking smug. "Maybe you will, maybe you won't."

Our lives are once again in danger, and I don't know whether we'll survive until dawn, but I'm in awe of my wife. Of her strength, resilience, and cunning. I've underestimated her in every way possible. With her by my side, it's difficult to imagine a situation we can't overcome together. Even as we're loaded into the backs of vehicles, guards surrounding us and keeping us apart, there is a strange and undying hope in my chest flickering against all odds.

## 19

# COURTNEY

I cling to Olivia throughout the duration of the ride. My threat worked back at the hut, but they could snatch her at any second. I have to be ready.

I'm not sure whether it would be better to kill Olivia than have her taken by Elena. Holding her over the ledge was simply the first thing I could think to do. It was my only recourse; threatening her life and mine was the only leverage I had over Elena and Devon. Without it, they could kill Dmitry and Tati without a second thought.

When the truck stops moving, I wrap my arms protectively around Olivia, almost squishing her to me. She's usually desperate to leave my arms and run around, not one to be held and cuddled, but the time apart has made her long for my touch as much as I've longed for hers. She rests her chubby cheek on my shoulder while her fingers play in my ratty hair. I breathe her in and silently pray I'll be able to save us both.

A guard walks around the back and opens the truck, directing us out one by one.

Sadie was loaded into the truck unconscious, but she woke up mid-ride, and is once again conscious and mobile. She climbs out, her face still pale, and holds a hand out for Larissa. Next are Dmitry and Sevastian. Then, Devon once again grabs Tati, followed by me and Olivia.

Guards stand between us, making the two feet between me and Dmitry feel like miles.

"Where are we going?" he asks. "What is the plan?"

Elena appears, apparently having ridden in the front seat, and points to the large metal building in front of us. The guards begin to herd us inside.

I assumed we would be taken back to the ship and continue on with our journey to whatever buyers the Yakuza have lined up for us. So, I'm not sure what waits inside the building. Whatever it is, it can't be good.

"What is going on?" Dmitry asks, but just as the words are out of his mouth, a guard strikes him hard in the back with what looks like a baton. He drops to his knees and groans.

Sadie grabs Tati and turns her away, so she won't have to see, and I try to stay strong. I don't want to frighten the children more than they already are, and I also don't want to let Devon and Elena know how much Dmitry's pain hurts me. I don't want them to have any more power over me than they already do. If I fall apart, we will never get out of here alive.

The building is dark and cold. One of the guards goes ahead and turns on a light, but there is so much dust in the air that everything is visible only through a haze of yellow.

It looks like the building could be some kind of hangar for airplanes or helicopters, but I'm not sure. The floor is dirt with sand and some patches of grass around, and I realize it's so cold because large windows in the opposite wall are wide open, allowing the sea breeze to come inside.

"Take the girls to the holding cell," Elena says. Then, she turns to me, her eyes narrowed. "Except for this one."

I tighten my hold on Olivia, and she rolls her eyes. "And the baby."

I relax ever so slightly, but the tension returns the moment Elena has Dmitry moved to the middle of the room. A guard drops him directly underneath the only light, and it looks like an interrogation. I move forward to join him, to be close to him, but Elena shakes her head and two guards move to either side of me, ensuring I stay back.

So, I do.

Elena begins to pace around the edge of the light, her body half in shadow. The light cuts a harsh line across her face, and I think it's a fitting analogy. She has always been two-faced. Two different people.

On one hand, she was the loyal friend of Dmitry Tsezar and a Bratva wife. On the other, she kept lifelong secrets that would allow her to one day overthrow power.

She's a psychopath in the purest form, and I realize that I can't allow Olivia to go with her. I can't allow Olivia to be raised by a monster.

No matter what that means, I will keep her far from the hands of these monsters.

"You killed my husband." Elena speaks with little emotion. Her words are flat, though her face is pulled into a soft smile.

"He started it," Dmitry mocks.

Elena turns to the Tiger and nods. He takes two steps forward, balls his fist, and jams it into Dmitry's stomach.

Dmitry groans and doubles over. Just as he's recovering and sitting up, the Tiger hits him again. I can feel Elena's eyes on me, so I don't look away. I watch the horrific scene, trying my best to look unaffected.

"You never did get your hands dirty," Dmitry says, his voice strained from his harsh breathing. "You've always been more comfortable on the sidelines."

Dmitry can't see Elena's face, but I can. Her smile flickers down on the corners, and she nods again. The Tiger brings his knee up hard and fast.

I hear Dmitry's teeth crack together. His head snaps back, and I blink away the moisture gathering in my eyes. He'll be okay. They won't kill him.

Right?

I don't know what they want with Dmitry. Elena wants revenge for Rurik's death, I assume, so maybe that's what this is. Maybe she's going to kill him right in front of me while I stand by and watch.

"I've always been more comfortable in the leadership role," she corrects him coldly. "I've always had people loyal enough to me that they were willing to do whatever I asked. Though, you wouldn't know about that. Your best friend became an FBI informant, and your next trusted lieutenant had been planning to overthrow you."

Elena circles around Dmitry, keeping a safe distance from him, until she's standing in front of him. She looks proper—hands folded in front of her, head held high. If I didn't know her and saw her on the street, I'd think she was someone's grandmother. I'd imagine her gardening and meeting friends at coffee shops. Not running criminal rings and trafficking innocent women.

"You've always been alone." She tilts her head to the side like she's studying him. "Your father barely tolerated you. Your grandfather was more interested in his business than your family. Even your own brother started his own family and distanced himself from you."

Dmitry sneers up at her, but Elena only smiles. "I overheard your conversation with Rurik. When you drank too much and got too honest, I was there. I know you have a soft heart in your chest, and it will be my pleasure to rip it out."

"You mean tell one of your guards to rip it out," Dmitry snarks back.

Elena steps forward, and the Tiger repositions to put himself between Dmitry and Elena, protecting his boss. "No, I will have the pleasure of doing this myself. Because I'm going to let you live, Dmitry."

My cold demeanor is revealed as a façade because I can't help but gasp at the information.

They aren't going to kill him right now. I won't have to watch him die.

Relief fills my body, spreading warmth to my cold, cold limbs.

Elena glances over at me, annoyed at my interruption, and then continues. "I'm going to let you live so you can watch me sell your family. So you will have to experience every agonizing second of your family being ripped away from you, of your children being poisoned against you, of your wife being used by other men like a communal hand towel. I'm going to give you a fate worse than death until you are begging me to end it. Until you would rather I cut out your heart than live another second inside your own head."

The warmth in my body turns to ice. My heart stutters to a stop, and I feel like I'm going to be sick. I feel like I'm going to pass out.

I widen my stance and hold onto Olivia, breathing her in. Reminding myself that this fight isn't over yet. There is still a chance of escape.

Though, the image of it is becoming increasingly fuzzy in my head.

Dmitry shrugs his shoulders. "Good luck."

Elena snorts in surprise. "Excuse me?"

"Good. Luck," Dmitry repeats. "You'll need it. You and Rurik planned for decades to overthrow me, and you failed. I killed him in a hand-to-hand duel. I came out the better man. I'll do it again."

"You're not the better man," Devon spits. His eyes are wide and black, pupils dilated. "Your bitch of a wife helped you cheat."

"Only after your bitch of a father pulled out a switchblade."

Before Dmitry can brace himself, the Tiger kicks him in the side.

The same side where the pilot sliced him earlier. This time, I can't watch. I squeeze my eyes shut and turn away.

My body physically hurts with his.

I wish he would just stay quiet; not anger them any more than they already are. However, I know that isn't Dmitry. He will fight in whatever way he can until there is no breath left in his body to fight.

"You're a bitch, too," Dmitry groans, gripping his side. "You won't fight me, either. Afraid I'll kill you, too?"

Devon storms across the floor, giving Dmitry a little time to prepare, though it does nothing to soften the blows.

Devon kicks him in the stomach, knees him in the nose, and punches him in the eye. One by one, Devon and the Tiger take turns beating Dmitry. They laugh when he falls and spits blood; they revel in every groan and every cough, but still, Dmitry doesn't lie down. He keeps getting back up. He keeps looking them in the eyes. He is strong.

Until he isn't.

The last blow is a boot to the back of the head. Dmitry falls forward on his face, his cheek pressed into the dirt, and he doesn't get back up.

I hold my breath, praying he isn't dead.

When he groans in pain, it's the best sound I've ever heard.

He tries to lift himself up, but his arms give out, and he falls back into the dirt. Elena, who has been standing on the sidelines throughout the beating, steps forward.

"That's enough for today, I think," she says. "Take them to the cell, boys."

The Tiger and another guard grab Dmitry while Devon comes to take me and Olivia. He reaches out a hand to lay it on my back, but I shrink away from him.

"Don't be shy," he whispers. "You'll have to get used to me eventually."

Getting used to Devon would be like getting used to poison ivy.

In the end, he walks closely but doesn't touch as we're led to the same cell where Sadie, Sevastian, and the girls are waiting. Dmitry is carried in and laid in the middle of the floor. Sadie gasps when she sees him and turns Tati away, which is when I fully realize how badly he's injured.

"Will we be given any water?" I ask. "Or blankets?"

The cell is dark, cold, and thick with the smell of mildew and rot. Not only will I need some basic supplies to ensure Dmitry makes it through the night, I'll need things for the girls.

"For the children," I say, lowering my voice, trying to appeal to any single ounce of mercy that Devon may possibly possess.

He narrows his eyes at me as though it may be a trick and then turns to leave. I think he's going to ignore my plea, but a minute later, he returns with a bowl of water and a burlap tarp. It isn't much, but it's something. He snorts in disgust as he leaves.

I hand Olivia to Sadie and begin tending to Dmitry's wounds as best I can. Luckily, there are only a few places where his skin broke, though that does leave the question of how many of his wounds are internal.

I readjust the bindings over his ribs to stop the bleeding that has resumed and use pieces of the wrap around his midsection to bandage a cut high on his cheekbone. Then, I rip pieces of burlap and dip them in the cold water. They won't do much, but I hope they will slow some of the swelling around his eyes and face.

He hardly looks like himself.

I maintained an emotional distance while taking care of him, trying to focus on what needed to be done and how I could help. Now that I have done all I can, however, it's difficult to hold back the tears. I sniffle and look up at the ceiling, releasing a shaky breath.

I don't want to cry in front of Tati.

"It's okay."

His raspy voice surprises me. "Dmitry?" I ask, laying my hand gently across his cheek. "Are you okay?"

He manages to let out a small laugh. "I've been better."

Sevastian helps me prop Dmitry up against the wall, and I have to keep Tati from squeezing him too tightly. Even in this dank cell, we're all glad to be together again.

Dmitry signs to Tati, telling her how far away from home we are and how far he came to find us. He makes it sound like a wild adventure. Like a story that would be in one of her fairy-tale books. Even if we know our story may not have a happy ending, Tati doesn't need to know that.

Eventually, she drifts to sleep nestled between Dmitry and me. Olivia is content sleeping on Sadie, so I let her stay there. In our situation, sleep is a reprieve I don't want to steal from her. I wish I could sleep so easily.

"When we get out of here, I'm ordering a new mattress," Dmitry whispers, drawing me from my gloomy thoughts. He nods his head, brow furrowed, cementing the idea in his mind. "Life is too short for uncomfortable sleep."

"Compared to this, it will be like sleeping on a cloud. I'm sure we won't notice."

He shrugs. "Maybe, but I still want a new one. A fresh start. What's the first thing you are going to do when you get home?" he asks.

I want to play this little game with him, if only to distract him from his pain, but I can't seem to find the energy. How can he talk so casually about getting out of here? At one point, I clung to hope. Now, I have no choice but to see things clearly. We are fucked. Beyond fucked.

"Come on, Court."

When I turn to him, his blue eyes are serious. I feel like he's gazing into my soul. As much as I want to, I can't deny him.

I sigh. "I suppose I'll take the world's longest nap."

He chuckles. "I think we all will. And after that?"

I want to stuff my face with an entire carton of strawberries and drink a gallon of water. I want to lock myself in my dance studio and work out until I've sweated out the memory of these horrible few weeks. I want so many things, but saying them out loud is painful because I don't think I'll ever have them again.

Thinking about our house, the beach, and the routines of our old life hurts too much, and talking about it all feels like torture.

Dmitry lifts the arm he had around Tati's shoulders and brushes his fingers across my cheek. "We are going to go home, Court. We'll all make it together. I promise."

I give him a weak smile, but the wobble of my chin gives me away. He knows I don't believe him.

Dmitry turns away from me and presses his head back against the wall. "When we get home, I'm going to clean up my life. I'm going to make things safer for you girls."

"I thought you were already doing that. With the import/export business."

He wrinkles his nose. "Things weren't going very well."

I frown, and he winks at me, though his eye is so swollen I can barely tell. "I wasn't failing or anything, but I wasn't happy, either. I planned to talk to you about it soon. Plus, while it was less violent, it wasn't any more legal. I had to bribe a lot of people to get things off the ground.

"So, if not that business, then what?"

Dmitry turns to me, wincing at a pain in his neck. "What do you want to do?"

I think again about going back to our house, the life we had before; of going back as though nothing happened, and I can't fathom it.

I realize all at once that I want a fresh start. An entirely new beginning.

"What about California?" The words are out of my mouth before I can really think about them. Annika mentioned something about California in the container. She said that the weather would be good for her and there would be more opportunity for a woman of her skills—I didn't ask at the time what she meant, and I'm rather glad I didn't. But it sounds nice. A new coast. A new life.

It's clear Dmitry is taken aback. He wasn't expecting such a drastic move, and really, I'm not even sure I want that. So, I wave away his concern. "Don't answer now. Sleep. We'll talk about it later."

"When we're free," he says, lowering his head and looking up at me from below furrowed brows, wanting me to agree.

"Yes," I say, grabbing his hand and squeezing his fingers. "When we're free."

~

Devon and Elena come early the next morning. Without explanation, they send guards into the cell. I clutch Olivia and Tati to me, so I don't have a spare arm to reach for Dmitry as he's taken.

Sevastian, too, is pulled to his feet. Sadie lunges for him, but he shakes his head briskly to discourage her. She listens and leans back against the wall.

Just as fast as they barged in, they leave, decreasing our number by two.

The two men never scream. They don't beg or plead, but we can hear the beating they receive. The sound of flesh against flesh, of their bodies falling into the dirt again and again.

Sitting there listening to that while clutching my two girls to me, I can't visualize the future Dmitry tried to lay out for me last night. I can't imagine ever getting out of this cell.

And that is when I realize that we won't get out. Not if things keep going the way they are. Not unless we do something drastic.

Dmitry and Sevastian are going to be too weak to be of much help, which I'm sure is part of Elena's plans. She wants to make sure the men are too injured to fight back, but she's underestimating me.

I can fight. I can escape.

I have to.

Tati can't hear the beating, but she knows what is happening outside of our cell just as much as I do, and she buries her face in my side and cries. I smooth a circle over her back and try to imagine leaving her behind. And Olivia. And Dmitry.

I will have to leave all of them behind if there is any chance of success. I'll have to escape on my own, get help, and pray that I can make it back before Devon and Elena have a chance to punish them for my disobedience.

The thought of failing brings tears to my eyes. The idea that I could ever leave my family in an evil place like this, for any amount of time, makes me feel sick. But then I hear Dmitry groan. Just once. But it's enough.

None of us will survive unless I get out of here and find help.

There is no other choice.

Dmitry is brought back to the cell first.

He is thrown through the door like a bag of garbage, followed by a tray of bread, rotting meat, and water.

Sadie feeds the children while I tend to Dmitry.

He is in worse shape than last night. His face is bruised and swollen beyond recognition, and he isn't coherent. I try to talk to him, but his words come out in a mumbled slur.

So, I take care of him the best I can. I wrap his wounds with the now-soiled bandages, I rinse his cuts with the water, and I feed him tiny pieces of bread, pushing the bites between his broken lips.

I try to keep him awake, afraid he may have a concussion, but eventually he can't fight the pull of rest, and he dozes off. I lay the girls down next to him, hoping the warmth of their little bodies will keep him warm and remind him, in some unconscious part of his brain, that he has a family worth fighting for. That he shouldn't give in.

Hours later, the guards bring Sevastian in.

They throw him through the door, lock it behind him, and then the lights in the rest of the warehouse go out, plunging the entire place into unending darkness. I can't even see my own hand in front of my face.

Which is why I yelp in surprise when Sevastian says my name less than a foot from my ear.

"Sorry," he whispers. "But you have to listen to me."

"How are you even talking right now?" I ask. "Dmitry couldn't even keep his eyes open."

"They beat him worse than they did me," he said. "Elena still thinks I betrayed Dmitry when I went to the FBI. I think she's hoping that if she shows me special treatment, I'll betray him and side with her. I know they'll still kill me in the end, of course, but it would be another blow to Dmitry. She just wants to shove my disloyalty in his face."

That sounds exactly like something Elena would do. It was the same logic behind Devon trying to convince me that Dmitry had sold me and the girls to him. They want to weaken the bonds between us because if we're united as a group, we're more of a threat. They want to create rifts.

"Will you fall for it?" I ask.

He snorts. "Please. I've seen what these people are capable of."

"Which is why you might be at a higher risk," I say. "You know the kind of torture they can employ. I don't think anyone would blame you for saving yourself."

"I'd blame me," he says quietly. I can't see his face, but I can hear the conviction in his voice. We can trust Sevastian. I'm certain. "Besides, you are queen of the Bratva. I would never turn my back on you."

"I thought you were only loyal to Dmitry, remember? You aren't in the Bratva anymore, so you don't have to listen to me."

"That was before I knew you," he says. "Now that I do, I know you are one tough bitch. I also know that if there is any chance of all of us getting out of here, it's you."

I swallow, nervous about his faith in me. "I've recently come to the same conclusion."

"Good," he says. "Then I don't have to waste time convincing you. I know how you can get out of here."

"You do?" I have to remind myself to keep my voice low. "All of us?"

"Just you. The rest of us would slow you down. Even if we did get out, they'd catch up to us within an hour and bring us right back here. If we want to call for help, you'll have to go alone."

That is the same conclusion I've come to, but it's still hard to hear it confirmed. I don't want to leave my girls or Dmitry behind. I don't want to leave any of them behind.

"It's the only option," Sevastian says, speaking the words I most need to hear.

I sigh and then nod. Only when I remember he can't see me do I speak. "Okay. I'll do it. Tell me what needs to happen."

Sevastian chuckles under his breath. "God, if we survive this, Dmitry might kill me for risking your life."

"I won't let that happen. Don't forget, I'm the queen. And a good king always listens to his queen."

Sevastian lays a hand on my shoulder and squeezes once. "Let's hope Dmitry is a good king."

# 20

# COURTNEY

The night before, when Dmitry and I were resting, Sevastian stood at the door of the cell, watching the movement of the guards. Hearing him explain their comings and goings makes me realize that I should have been doing the same. I should have been paying attention to what's happening beyond the walls of our cell if I want to escape.

Thank God Sevastian has remained hopeful and vigilant.

"They don't have anyone standing guard outside the cell overnight," he whispers. "Overconfidence on their part, to be sure. They think that door is impenetrable, but Elena never was one for the details. The hinges are a big weakness."

"You think you can remove them?" I ask.

My eyes have adjusted to the darkness enough that I can see Sevastian check to make sure everyone else is sleeping and then move over to the door. There is a soft tapping noise, almost like a distant woodpecker, and then he crawls back towards me, hand extended.

I reach out my hand and feel something long and cool slide into my palm. It's one of the door hinges, I realize after a minute.

"They were recently installed and are still oiled up. If they were old and rusted, it would be a more difficult job."

I stare down at the pin in my hand in disbelief that it could be this easy. "So, I can get out of this room, but how do I get out of the building? They had guards all over the place earlier."

"During the day," Sevastian clarifies. "At night, they keep a few guards at the main exits, and they do laps around the perimeter every fifteen minutes or so."

I raise my eyebrows. "A few guards are still a huge problem. I can't fight one guard without waking the entire building, let alone two."

"And that is why you won't fight," he says. "While they were beating Dmitry earlier, I was mapping out the building. There is a door on the south side that—"

I raise my brows again, chin lowered, and Sevastian rolls his eyes. He lifts his hand and points to the right.

"A door on that side where a lot of guards were coming and going. Best I can tell, it's their quarters. At night, they should all be asleep. So, that is where you'll go."

"What if there is no exit on the other side?"

He nods. "There is. I saw the Tiger walk out the main door with a few guards and then a few minutes later, he came out of that southern door. There is an exterior exit there, and that is your best bet."

I haven't even moved yet, and my heart is already hammering in my chest. "You want me to walk through a room of sleeping guards to escape?"

"You can't use the front or back exits, so—"

"So, I have to walk past twenty sleeping guards to bypass two that are awake." I hope Sevastian can tell by the sound of my voice that my confidence in his plan is limited. It sounds like way too big of a risk. All it would take is for one guard to be awake for the entire house of cards to come falling down. I honestly think I'd have a better chance of fighting the guards and running away. Though, that would raise the alarm and put my family in danger for my disobedience.

"Yep," Sevastian says, acting like he doesn't notice my doubts at all. "They won't be expecting something so bold. As long as you keep your head down, even if someone wakes up, he won't be able to see well in the dark and will just assume you're a guard headed to bed. Besides, there are more like fifteen."

"You're right. Five less guards make this much more doable."

"That's the spirit," Sevastian says, patting me on the shoulder. I have to resist the urge to bite his hand.

I go through the plan several times in my mind before I realize the most obvious issue. I stand up and hold out my arms. "I can't leave in this."

My pajama bottoms, once a pale pink, are now a dingy light brown. However, they are still obviously pajama pants. They are cotton and thin, not too dissimilar from the gray shirt I have on. "Unless the guards think one of their own sleeps in women's pajama sets, I think they'll notice me."

Sevastian stands up, too. "Don't worry, I've got that covered."

Before I can ask what he means, he reaches behind his back and tugs on his shirt, pulling it over his head. The room is dark, but I still feel uncomfortable looking at him.

"You want me to wear your clothes?" I ask. "But what will you wear?"

He points at me. "Your clothes. Take them off."

I sputter as Sevastian throws his black shirt at me and then unzips his pants. The zipper sounds like a chainsaw in the otherwise silent room, and I check to make sure no one has woken up. Seeing the two of us half naked in the corner would probably lead to a lot of incorrect conclusions.

"You won't fit in these," I argue.

"They have an elastic waist. It will be fine."

"You're twice my size."

"Then I'll be naked," he hisses, gesturing for me to drop my pants as he throws me his. "Get dressed."

He mercifully turns around, and I quickly disrobe and slip into his clothes. Thank goodness there is a belt because the moment I pull the pants on, they drop to mid-thigh. The shirt is just as baggy, but I tuck it in and manage to not look entirely ridiculous.

At least, I think so until Sevastian turns around and snorts.

"You look like a kid wearing his dad's clothes to sneak into an R-rated movie," he says with a laugh. "I'd know because I used to do that all the time."

"Did it ever work?" I ask hopefully.

He shakes his head. "Not once."

He must see my face fall because he hastily adds, "Though, the ticket holders were always awake. If they'd been asleep, it would have worked like a charm. You'll be fine."

I look down at myself, feeling less and less confident by the second. "Okay, so what do I do if I make it outside?"

"When you make it outside, you'll hightail it for the woods and then make your way towards the city."

"The city?" I ask. "We're in the middle of nowhere."

"Didn't you see the glow of the lights?" Sevastian asks. "Over the treetops. We're close to some civilization. Get there, get a phone, and call for help."

"From who?" I shout whisper. "The Bratva is dead."

"Not all of them. I don't think." Sevastian shrugs. "From someone. Some of the Bratva allies. Get in touch and get them here."

I scan my brain for Bratva allies or any way to get in touch with them, but I'm not sure. What if I leave the warehouse only to realize I can't help? To realize I'm useless and now my family is trapped?

I look towards Dmitry, but Sevastian sees where my train of thought is headed.

"You can't," he whispers. "He'll never let you leave. If you wake him up, you aren't getting out of here. None of us are."

"You were right. He really will kill you for this," I admit.

Sevastian laughs. "My nine lives have to run out eventually. Better at the hand of my friend than fucking Devon."

"Why would Dmitry kill you?"

We both startle, and I turn to find Sadie looking up at us, eyes narrowed. She takes in my appearance and frowns. "And why are you wearing that?"

"It is definitely not what you're thinking," Sevastian says. "She's just—"

"Escaping?" Sadie asks, eyebrow raised, looking from me to Sevastian.

There is no point in denying it. She's awake now. She'll see me leave. I need Sadie on my side if this is going to work. So, I nod.

"Yes. But I'm not escaping for myself. I'm escaping to save all of us."

"Well, no shit," Sadie says, rolling her eyes. "Your family is here. You wouldn't leave them behind."

"Or you." I grab her hand with both of mine. Her fingers are cold and clammy. Sadie always had such warm hands. We have to get out of here. "I wouldn't leave you here, either. I'm going to get out of here, get help, and come back for all of you."

"Why aren't you going?" she asks, looking over my shoulder at Sevastian.

"Because he isn't the wife of the Bratva leader," I explain, drawing her attention back to me. "I am the only one here, aside from Dmitry—"

"Who is out of service at the moment," she says, looking back at the heap of my husband and wincing.

I nod, hating that it's true. From the moment I first met Dmitry, he has been strong. A fighter. He still is those things, but I'm the only one who knows it. He is battered and broken right now, and I have to fight for both of us now. Until he can be strong again.

"I'm the only one here, aside from Dmitry, who the Bratva or any of our allies will listen to. If we're going to get anyone to help us, I am our best shot."

Sadie nods. "I assume you two have a plan?"

A weak one that I'd rather not explain for fear that saying it out loud will reveal the many weak spots. "Yes, we have one."

Sadie holds up a hand. "That's all I need to know. The less I know, the less they can torture out of me later."

The urge to hug my best friend overwhelms me, and I wrap my arms around her and pull her close. Sadie and I have never been the kind of friends who show physical affection, but she sinks into the touch, laying her head on my shoulder.

"Be careful," she says.

"Take care of them," I whisper back. She knows who I mean. The girls. Before this experience, I never would have said Sadie would be the person I'd trust to take care of my girls, but I've seen how maternal she can be, how protective she is over them. I trust her with my life and theirs.

"Of course I will."

"And Dmitry," I say. "If he wakes up, lie to him. I know Sevastian won't because he's too loyal."

"And I'm not?" she teases.

"Not to him, but you are to me." I hold her at arm's length and smile. "And if I know anything at all about you, it's that you can lie better than anyone I've ever met."

"True," she says. Then, she pushes me away and reclaims her spot on the floor next to Tati and Larissa. The two girls have grown close, comforting one another, and now they are huddled together for warmth. I have to get us all out of here, for their sake. They both deserve better than this.

"Are you ready?" Sevastian asks.

No. Never. Not a chance.

I nod. "As ready as I'll ever be."

Sevastian moves to the door and begins prying the second hinge out of the door. Then, he looks through the metal bars in the center of the door to check for anyone nearby, and when he sees the coast is clear, he begins work on the third and final hinge. It gives him the most trouble, and for one second, I think this all may have been for nothing. We are trapped here and there is no escape. No way out.

Then, he gives one final bang—louder than the others—and the pin comes free. He quickly catches the door as it starts to tip towards him, and then slides it open, giving me a foot of space to fit between.

I stare at the gap with trepidation and more nerves than I've ever experienced.

I don't want to go.

All I've wanted since the moment Devon broke into our house and kidnapped me and the girls is to get away, but now the chance is staring me in the face, and I don't want to take it. I don't want to risk everything falling apart.

I know if I stay that we will all die, one way or another. But it won't be my fault. As soon as I walk through that door, though, a thousand more possible outcomes appear, many of them deadly, and all of them my fault.

Devon and Elena could catch me escaping and kill me and my family on the spot. They could torture Dmitry for allowing me to escape. They could kill Tati since they don't seem to have any use for her.

I could escape, and they could still kill my family.

I could even make it far enough to get help, and the help could be defeated by the guards Devon and Elena have amassed. Even if I technically succeed, this could end in disaster.

I don't want to go.

"Go," Sevastian says, nodding his head towards the door. "Now. While the coast is clear."

I take a deep breath and push aside the panic that grips my chest. I ignore the dread that has sunk like lead in my feet, holding them in place. I ignore the swirl of disastrous thoughts moving through my head like a washer on the spin cycle. I ignore it all and take one step forward and then another until I'm through the door and on the other side.

I turn around to take one last look at Dmitry and my family, but Sevastian is busy putting the door back on the hinges. There isn't anything he could say to make me feel better anyway, so I turn around and face the dark warehouse in front of me.

I can just barely see the front door we were escorted through the day before, but based on the soft voices I hear coming from that direction, Sevastian was right about the two guards standing watch. One of them just passed by the door five minutes before, so if his calculations are correct, I have ten minutes to clear the area before I'm discovered.

The room is dark, but moonlight filters through the open windows near the ceiling, giving me a small amount of pale light by which to navigate my way across the dirt floor.

Sevastian's clothes are large and the pant legs drag under my feet, making it difficult to walk smoothly and quietly, but I don't want to stop and adjust them now. That will have to wait until I'm away from the warehouse and hidden in the trees.

I can see the door that Sevastian indicated straight ahead. The one that will lead into the guards' sleeping quarters, and I force myself to keep moving towards it even when every part of me wants to find another way.

I didn't do any reconnaissance, so I have to trust his judgment.

When I reach the door, I expect it to be locked or for someone to open it and wait for a password on the other side, but there is no barrier. I turn the knob, and the door opens, revealing an empty hallway in front of me. On either side of the hallway are doorways with no doors in them, almost like horse stalls in a stable. As I pass, I can see the dark shapes of beds and figures lying in them.

Nothing looks like I expected. I imagined walking through a narrow opening between cots, sidestepping feet hanging over the small frames. Instead, I'm only visible to the guards in the half second it takes for me to pass their doorways. Unless someone grows suspicious and comes out of his room, I should be fine as long as I keep my head down. Just as Sevastian said.

So, I do just that. I stare down at my feet and walk quietly, but quickly, down the hallway. I don't see the exit straight ahead, but I can tell the hallway turns towards the right, which is where I hope there will be a door.

I'm three-fourths of the way down the hallway when I hear footsteps behind me.

"Hey, wait up."

My entire body stiffens in fear, and my next few steps are stilted and awkward. Still, I press on, not turning around.

"Man, wait," the voice behind me says, growing louder. "You headed out for a smoke?"

A chorus of harsh shushes rises up from the rooms down the hallway.

"Shut the fuck up!"

"We're trying to sleep."

The man behind me chuckles, and I hear his steps quicken. I move faster to match his pace.

He might be fooled from behind in the dim hallway, but as soon as we're in normal light—or as soon as he hears my voice—there will be no mistaking who I am. I can't let that happen.

When I reach the end of the hallway and follow the right turn, I almost cry with relief when I see the door there, just as Sevastian guessed. Because that is what it was, after all. A guess. I could have found myself at a dead end.

I say a silent prayer of thanks as I push the door open and step into the cold night.

My instincts tell me to run for the trees, but that would give me away. I have to disappear into the night without causing any alarm.

I keep moving at a brisk, but normal pace once the door closes behind me. Then, I hear it open again.

"Where are you going?" the voice asks. He sounds slightly more suspicious now. I have to calm his worries.

So, I bend forward, grip my stomach with one arm, and throw the other above my head in a backwards wave as I groan deeply. "Sick."

"Oh," the man says. "Gross."

The only crunch of gravel I can hear is coming from my own steps, so I assume my trick worked and the man has stopped following me. I stumble across the open space and into the trees.

I pause for one second, gripping a tree trunk and ducking my head behind it as though being sick. Then, I keep moving.

I don't turn around to see if the man bought my lie. I don't check to see if he's following me. As soon as I know I am out of sight, I run.

## 21

# COURTNEY

Sevastian was right again. Just beyond the crop of trees, there is a road. I follow the narrow sidewalk along a curved road until I reach an intersection. Most of the windows along the block are out, but there is one corner building with lights on and a few people inside.

As I approach, I see that it looks like a corner store. A young clerk stands in front of a wall of cigarettes and cardboard boxes of candy lighters, and scratch tickets clutter the counter. I pull the glass door open and step inside.

I feel the clerk's eyes on me, but I take a sharp left and duck behind the aisles of snacks and candy.

I don't have any money. No cell phone, no identification, nothing at all to barter with. But I need a telephone. Or change for a payphone. Do payphones even still exist? I'm not sure.

I round the corner and move to the next aisle, and glance up long enough to see the clerk frowning in my direction. If I spend too long here and then walk out with nothing, it will be suspicious. So, this time when I get to the end of the aisle, I walk straight back towards the counter.

The clerk is even younger than I thought. His facial hair is growing in thin and patchy, and he has blemishes clustered around his chin and temples. His eyes go wide when he sees me, and I'm not sure if it's because I'm a woman or because I'm a woman in baggy men's clothes.

Probably both.

"Hello," I say.

He smiles and looks for my items to ring up, but the counter is empty. I hold my hands up to signify that I don't want to buy anything.

"I need to use a phone," I say slowly, as though that will bridge the language gap between us. "To make a phone call."

"A phone?" he says slowly, his Spanish accent thick.

I nod. "Yes. Yes. Sí. A phone."

He smiles and pulls an ancient cordless phone up from behind the counter. I reach for it, but before I can, his hand cuts across my path and points to a small sign next to the register. It's written in Spanish, so I don't know what it says, but I do recognize the symbol for the Euro.

I need money.

I bite my lower lip and hold my hands out, palms up. "No money. No dinero."

Is "dinero" dinner or money? I'm not sure, but either way, the boy seems to understand what I'm trying to say.

"Lo siento," he says, pulling the phone towards him.

I reach out and lay my hand over his, stopping him from putting the phone back under the counter. "Por favor."

The only other Spanish word I know is baño, so I need him to help me.

"Por favor," I say again, giving him the biggest puppy-dog eyes I can.

The kid's shoulders sag, and he looks back towards a door in the far corner of the shop. A door through which, I presume, sits the owner.

Finally, he sighs and pushes the phone towards me, circling one finger in the air. "Rápido."

I nod like I know what he means and grab the phone. As soon as it's in my hand, I realize I don't know who to call. I didn't think that far ahead, and now I'm frozen in place with the phone in my hand, my mind blank.

The kid is tapping his foot on the ground, so I start dialing the first number I can think of. It rings three times.

"Hello?" My dad sounds out of breath, like he ran to the phone. It's very early in the morning there, so I'm surprised he's even still home.

"Dad? It's me."

Sobs. That's all I can hear on the other end of the phone. My dad is weeping.

"Listen to me," I say loudly, drawing the clerk's attention. He can't understand what I'm saying, but I'm sure he's taking note of how loudly I'm speaking. "I need your help."

"Where are you?" he asks, sniffling. "You've been gone for weeks. I had no idea what happened. The police don't know. You were just gone. They told me you ran away, but I didn't believe it. Not for a second. Now, here you are. I can't believe it."

"Dad," I say again more calmly this time. "Listen to me. I need help. I need you to put me in touch with ... someone."

"Anything," he says. Then, he adds, "Are you safe?"

I don't want to lie to him, but I also don't want to explain the truth. There isn't time. If all goes well, I'll see him again one day, and I'll explain it then. Now, I need to focus on the mission at hand.

"I will be," I say, trying to remain hopeful. "But I need your help to get there."

"Anything," he says, and I know he means it.

"I need you to get me the number for ..." A million different names and places and faces rush through my head, some friend, some foe. Who can help us? Who has the power or desire to help us? Dmitry may have started cleaning up his act, but that doesn't mean there aren't plenty of people back home who wouldn't be more than happy to see him wiped from the face of the earth.

"Giuseppe's Bar and Pub."

There is a long pause. "A bar?"

"Please."

Any doubts my dad may have, of which I'm sure there are many, are pushed aside as he types out the name on his ancient computer. The clerk motions once again with his finger, and I nod and smile, trying to assure him I'll be done soon.

"You have a pen and paper?" he asks.

I don't, but I grab the pen on the counter for customers to sign receipts and scribble the number he reads me on the palm of my hand.

"Thank you so much, Dad," I say. "Really. Thank you."

"Don't thank me. Just get yourself and those girls home," he says, voice thick. "I miss you."

"I miss you, too."

When we hang up, I quickly dial the number my dad gave me before the clerk can take the phone away. He frowns disapprovingly at me, and I mouth "sorry" at him and hold up one finger. Truly, I don't know how many fingers this conversation will take. But I will keep ahold of this phone for as long as it takes to ensure my family will be safe.

It rings eight times, and I can tell the clerk is growing nervous. He keeps glancing back towards the door in the back. I want to tell him that I've faced much worse over the last few weeks than a grumpy boss, but instead, I twirl the cord around my finger and turn away from him. If someone answers, I need to be focused.

On the tenth ring, someone answers.

"Hello?" The man sounds more confused than anything. Which makes sense. It's a bar at the crack of dawn. They probably don't get many phone calls until after noon.

"Hello, I need to speak with the boss."

"I'm the manager," the man says proudly.

I clear my throat. "Not the boss of the bar. The boss."

There is a pause. "Who the hell is this?"

I stand taller even though the man on the other end of the phone can't hear me. If I want to sound confident, I have to look confident. I press my shoulders back and lift my chin. "This is the wife of Dmitry Tsezar, head of the Tsezar Bratva, and I would like to be put in touch with your boss. Now."

I'm worried the man will hang up and block my number. I'm worried that I've just laid out all of my cards, and he's going to call my bluff.

But then, he sighs.

"I'll see what I can do."

I see the two men sitting in the park at the exact bench specified on the phone call. I know they are here to see me, but it doesn't make me any less nervous.

These men are not my friends. They are not on my side. This is a business arrangement and it could go south at any moment. I need to remember that.

I keep a wide berth as I round the bench and step onto the sidewalk. They turn towards me the moment my foot hits the pavement. They are on high alert; I can see it in the dilation of their eyes.

"Courtney Tsezar?" one of the men asks. He stands up and keeps his hands in his pockets. His hair is dark black, and his face is pockmarked with scars.

I nod. "No one told me your names."

"Good," the other man says. He is older, with salt and pepper in his hair, and he doesn't stand. I don't know if it's because he's unable or because he doesn't see me as a threat. "You don't need to know who we are. We need to know who you are. And that you are telling the truth."

"I am," I say with a bit too much urgency. I clear my throat and try again in a calm voice. "It's all true. Every word of it. My family is trapped in a dirt cell right now, and I am here to get them out. Whatever the cost."

"You discussed the cost on the phone," the dark-haired man says.

I nod. The clerk couldn't speak English, but I still worried he'd understand some part of the conversation and call the police. I was talking about some seriously illegal transactions in the middle of a store.

"Then tell us what we're dealing with."

"And then you'll help?" I ask.

The older man shrugs. "That remains to be seen."

If I was less desperate, I'd demand a firmer answer. I'd demand a promise, a vow on his life. But in my situation now, a vague shrug is the best I can ask for. There is no other option.

So, I describe the army Devon and Elena are working with. I drag a stick through the dirt to make a blueprint of the warehouse. The sun is just starting to come over the horizon, so they both squint at it, but it seems to get the point across.

"It's not a high-tech operation."

"Not at this location," I say. "But they were on a ship. Part of a trade route with the Yakuza. They have a helicopter and might have more people nearby."

"We know what they have nearby," the older man says. "More than you do, anyway."

He is clearly not accustomed to dealing with a woman. I can see his distaste in the narrowing of his eyes and the thin line of his mouth. I want to tell him where he can shove his sexism. I want to tell him that I can handle myself just as well as any man.

Instead, I decide I'll just have to show him.

"Then it sounds like you'll be a great resource for me," I say confidently. "Are you in?"

The dark-haired man opens his mouth to respond, but the older man clears his throat to silence him. He stands up for the first time and takes one hobbling step forward and then another, slowly standing tall as his hips straighten beneath him.

He moves towards me, but I stand my ground, refusing to back away. Refusing to show any fear in the face of his intimidation.

When he's less than two feet away, he narrows his eyes at me, his dark gray brows creasing in the center. Then, he holds out a hand.

"Honor the terms you set, and we won't have to hunt and kill you when this is over."

I reach out and grab his hand. "Save my family, and I'll give you everything I promised and more."

When I break through the trees, the sun is a quarter of the way across the sky. For the first time, I can see the warehouse in the light. It's rusted and abandoned and looks like it should be demolished. If I hadn't gone for help, no one ever would have found us.

I'm halfway across the gravel when I hear the first alarm bell.

"Who is that?" a deep voice shouts.

I don't respond. I just keep walking. Unlike the last time I was here, I'm not trying to move quietly. I want them to see me.

"It's her. It's her!"

I keep walking even as eight guards rush towards me, guns drawn. They command me to get on the ground and put my hands behind my back, but I refuse. I stay on my feet until one of the guards physically kicks my legs out from under me.

They haul me inside by my armpits, legs dragging behind me, but I keep my chin lifted. Head held high.

The guards drop me in the center of the room in the same circle of light where they beat Dmitry the first night. I see dark spots on the ground that must be dried blood, but I try not to look at them. That's easier when I hear Elena's voice approaching.

"What do you mean she surrendered?" she hisses.

"They mean I surrendered," I say, standing up and facing her. "I escaped, but I came back."

Her top lip pulls back in a snarl. "What did you do?"

"I tried to run," I say, looking down at my feet. "I tried to get away, but I couldn't leave them behind. I'd rather die with my children than live without them."

She studies me for a cool second and then tips her head to the side. "There really is no place for such sentimentality. It will only get you killed."

"Maybe," I shrug. "But I'd rather be sentimental than a cold bitch."

A hand cracks across my face and heat blossoms in my cheek, and my jaw twinges. The guard responded to Elena's silent command before I could prepare for it.

"Let's see what your insults are worth when you're dead."

Devon turns to his mother, mouth open, ready to argue, but she silences him with a raise of her hand. "She's a liability. We have to kill her and go. It's the only way."

Devon looks at me with his mouth pulled down in a frown, looking like a child whose favorite toy was just taken from him. Then, he sighs and follows behind his mother as she marches towards me. Elena stops only a few steps away.

"Take off those ridiculous clothes."

I hesitate, and she nods to the guard on my right. This time, I anticipate the blow, but it does little to ease the pain that radiates through my brain.

"Take them off," she growls.

I maintain eye contact with her as I slide my belt from my waist and drop it on the ground. Sevastian's pants don't need much convincing; they are nearly to my knees already. I hesitate with the shirt, but the guard raises his hand in a warning, and I continue, peeling it over my head until I'm left in nothing but my bra and panties, both of which are dingy.

"All of them," Elena says. "I want everyone to see you for exactly what you are. When you die, I want everyone to know what a coward you are. I mean, what kind of woman runs away from her own family?"

"What kind of woman drugs her own son until he can barely tie his shoes?" I spit.

The third blow is closed-fisted, and I go down hard. I take most of the fall in my elbow, but my hip scrapes across the cold ground as well. I wince at the burning cuts, and Elena just laughs.

"You really don't know when to give it up." Elena shakes her head and then gestures for a guard's attention. "Get everyone else. I want Courtney to perform for an audience."

I'm too disoriented to know what she means. The blow to my temple knocked me slightly off my foundations, and I'm still blinking the stars from my vision when I see a blurry group of people arrive.

Then, I hear his voice.

"You fucking bitch," Dmitry roars. He lunges forward, separating from the crowd, but before he can even take a step, a guard throws him backwards.

Usually, it would take a lot more than a single shove to knock Dmitry down, but he's still weak and healing.

I blink until he's in focus, and then I smile at him, trying to tell him that it will all be okay. Because it will be. I think.

If things go the way I hope, it will all be okay.

"Let her go," Dmitry shouts. "Kill me."

Elena laughs maniacally, silencing everyone in the warehouse. She sounds fully unhinged, almost as crazy as her son. When she's done, she looks at me while she talks to Dmitry.

"Killing you would not please me," she says. "I want to kill the one you love. In front of your face. I want you to watch her die, and then, maybe, I will kill you. If you're lucky."

Elena commands two guards to finish undressing me. They rip my underclothes off me until I'm naked in the center of the large space, but I can't even find the energy to be ashamed or embarrassed.

Even as Elena tells the guards to beat me. Even as I spit blood and fall to the floor, I feel strong. I feel more powerful than I've ever felt in my life.

Because like a true queen, I found a way out for my people.

No matter how badly Elena has me beaten, help is coming.

All I have to do is stay alive until they arrive.

# 22

## DMITRY

Every time Courtney lifts her head out of the dirt, she looks at me.

Somehow, amidst the dirt and blood and pain, she finds my eyes. Again and again. And I know it means something. I know she's trying to tell me something, but I don't know what.

My body hurts. My mind is fuzzy. I feel like I should be able to read her glances, but I can't decipher them. I can't understand why she isn't begging me for help. Why she isn't trying to save herself.

The Courtney I know is a fighter. She would be bartering with Elena, arguing for her life. She would be buying time, trying to give me an opening to save her. Instead, she's taking the pacifist's approach. She's turning her cheek with every blow, offering her beautiful face to the guards as a sacrifice which they gleefully slaughter.

Her eyes are puffy, her top lip is cracked, and there are bruises forming all over her knees and arms from the repeated falls.

I want to break through the guards and throw myself over her, but I can't. Because of her damned glances.

Is she telling me to stay with the girls? To protect them over her?

That's what I would tell her to do if our situations were reversed. I'd want her to take care of our children, to focus on saving herself. But I don't know if I can do that.

"What is this really about?" I ask.

I catch Devon's attention, but Elena keeps her eyes on Courtney, watching closely as the guard backhands her, sending her sideways on the ground. Her body hits with a solid thud, and I have to hold myself back from rushing forward to catch her.

"Is this because she escaped?" I ask. "Because she made you and your men look like idiots?"

"The only idiot here is her," Elena snaps, still not looking at me. "She came back for her family only to be murdered. She should have kept running. I would have found her eventually, of course, but she could have earned herself a few more months of living."

"Are you really this vindictive?" I ask. "Was your love for Rurik really strong enough to inspire this kind of vengeance? From what I could tell, you two didn't even like each other that much."

Finally, she spins around. Her eyes are wide and seething as she marches towards me, hands clenched at her sides. Two of her guards rush forward to wedge themselves between us, afraid their boss is about to get herself into more trouble than she can handle.

"You don't know anything about our relationship," she roars. "You didn't even really know Rurik. You trusted him for years while he was plotting your downfall. Do you really think you have any right to speak of my love for him?"

She's right, of course. I didn't know Rurik the way I thought I did. But I knew parts of him better than Elena ever could have.

"You weren't there when we went out together," I say softly, quirking the corner of my mouth up in a smile. "You didn't hear the way he talked. About other women. His experiences."

Her jaw ticks, and I see the angry color drain slightly from her face.

"Or was that an arrangement the two of you had?" I hold up my hands in mock surrender. "Like you said, I don't know anything about your relationship, so I won't pass judgment. An open marriage may work for some people. It certainly worked for Rurik."

Elena's teeth are gritted so hard I think they'll crack, and she lifts a hand to slap me. Then, just as she's about to bring it down, she stops herself.

I stare at her, daring her to hit me. Every second she spends taking out her anger on me is one less second she's hurting Courtney. Clearly, Courtney has some kind of plan, and whatever it is, I want to buy her some time.

Elena takes a deep breath and then smiles at me with all of her teeth. Without saying anything, she turns back towards Courtney and the guards flanking her.

"On her knees," she says.

Like automatons, they force Courtney to her knees, and Elena pulls a gun from a hidden holster at her hip.

My heartbeat ratchets up until it's basically vibrating in my chest. Until it's hard to find air. Sadie grabs Tati and turns her away, and oh my God, this is happening. This is really happening. They are going to kill Courtney.

There have been plenty of moments in my life where I've felt out of control, where my instincts have taken over, and I act without thinking. Very rarely, however, have I been numb. Just ... numb.

The only other time that comes to mind is when I woke up from being drugged to find my house empty. My family gone.

This is worse than that, though.

When I woke up in Olivia's nursery with no idea where my family had gone, I knew I had to find them. It was a goal. An objective. Something to propel me from the floor and keep me going. It was what led me to the ship, to the container where the girls were being held.

Now, however, there is nothing to be done.

Even if I break free of the guards in front of me and get to Courtney, I can't save her. There is nothing I can do. I can't overpower her. Even if Sevastian and I fight together, we can't take all of these guards. Not before Elena would pull the trigger, anyway.

The fight is over.

If Elena is ready to end this, it will be over.

And then what?

She told me she'd sell the girls. That she would force me to watch my family being ripped apart. So, is that what my future holds? I'll be forced to sit on the sidelines, useless and weak, while my family is shredded. While my life and purpose are set aflame in front of my eyes.

Numb.

The lack of sensation seeps from my chest and into my arms and legs slowly, like death, claiming my movement and action for itself.

I can't move, can't think of anything beyond how this is it. This is it. It's happening.

And amidst all of it, Courtney looks up at me and winks.

Her beautiful heart-shaped face. Paler than normal due to living inside a container for weeks on end, and bruised due to her beating, but still beautiful. Still Courtney.

Her brown eyes are liquid caramel, golden even in the rickety fluorescent lighting. And winking.

I shake my head in disbelief, trying to understand what she's telling me. What she could possibly be trying to convey to me with that wink in the last moments of her life.

Elena cocks the gun, and the sound echoes off the metal walls.

Then, I realize, the sound I hear isn't an echo. It's coming from the door behind me.

I don't turn to see what it is because my eyes are locked on Courtney, desperate to take her in for every precious second we have left. But everyone else looks.

First Sadie and Sevastian at my sides. Then, the guards in front of me. Then, the guards standing on either side of Courtney.

Then, Elena.

Her forehead wrinkles in confusion, and I see Courtney smiling.

That's when I turn and see an army approaching. Guns raised.

That's when I see the green, white, and red patches on their jackets.

The Italians are here, and for once, I think they're on our side.

My mobility returns, and I herd Sadie and the girls out of the line of fire just as the shots begin to ring out.

~

Elena and her guards are so distracted by the Italians' arrival—and fighting for their own lives—that they barely notice our group running back towards the cell.

I shove Sadie and Olivia inside, followed by Tati and Larissa, and then Sevastian and I follow in last.

"What in the hell is happening?" Sadie asks, clutching Olivia to her chest.

“I don’t know, but you and the girls need to stay in here,” I say.

“They’re on our side,” Sevastian says. “I know that much.”

“Is this about where Courtney went last night?” Sadie asks.

I turn to her, brow furrowed. “You two both knew about that?”

They have the decency to look guilty, and then nod. Sadie points a finger at Sevastian. “But he knew more than I did. He helped her escape.”

“Which explains the outfit,” I say, taking in the image of my oldest friend in my wife’s pajamas.

“Sorry, but she had to go for help,” he says. “I didn’t know who she’d get in touch with or how she’d pull it off, but clearly she did. They’re here to rescue us.”

There are shouts and shots echoing in the room behind us, and I can’t hide in here with the women and children. I have to go help.

“Stay in here,” I say again to Sadie. “Keep the girls down and away from the doors.”

“You can’t go out there. You don’t have a weapon.”

“Neither does Courtney,” I argue. “She’s in the thick of it, and I’m going to go protect her.”

“I’m coming, too.” Sevastian claps me on the back. Then, he turns to Sadie and opens his mouth to say something, but before he can, Sadie rushes forward.

In a second, she’s stretched onto her tiptoes, her lips pressed to his.

The kiss is quick and innocent, but there is an obvious fire behind it.

I turn away to give them a second and then Sevastian is at my side, ready to fight.

The room is in chaos. Elena’s guards are fighting with the Italians, bodies are littered across the floor from both sides, and in the middle of it, surrounded by fighting on all sides, is Courtney.

She's still naked, crouched down in a defensive position, trying to avoid the rain of bullets being fired.

Luckily, Elena is distracted shooting at Italians, but I don't know how long that will last. Eventually, the fighting may ease up enough for her to take care of Courtney once and for all.

I look around for a weapon, and find a shovel leaning against the wall. It's ancient and rusted, probably sitting there long before Devon and Elena claimed the place as temporary headquarters, but it's better than nothing.

Sevastian finds a pair of large shears, and like townsfolk chasing after Frankenstein's monster, we move into the melee.

I swing the shovel, knocking men to the ground, and Sevastian goes for their throats. We kill one guy that way, but the next is more difficult. He kicks the shears as Sevastian tries to cut, and he ends up wounding the man's shoulder. With his other hand, the guard pulls his gun and fires at me, but I drop to the ground to avoid his bullet.

On his second try, Sevastian does manage to slice his neck, but then another guard jumps on my back. I feel the circle of the gun's barrel at the back of my head, and squeeze my eyes closed to prepare for the end. Then, the weight is gone.

Sevastian bats the man off me with his shears like it's T-ball practice, and then uses the gun he took from the other guard he killed to shoot him in the head. As I get to my feet, he grabs another gun and hands it to me.

"Thanks." For a second, in all of the melee, we smile at one another. It feels good to work with my friend again.

Then, another shot rings out far too close for him, and I refocus on the matter at hand.

When I find Courtney in the mess again, she has a gun now, and there is a dead guard at her feet. I don't know if she killed him or not, but she's using his gun to fire into the crowd. She hits the guard closest to her in the thigh, and he drops to one knee, screaming in pain. I've heard a broken femur is more painful than childbirth. Based on the look of agony on the man's face, I wouldn't doubt it.

Courtney quickly puts him out of his misery. She takes a clean shot at the side of his head, and he slumps forward, lifeless.

I came out of the cell to save Courtney, but now I realize, she doesn't need saving.

Courtney was looking at me during her beating, trying to tell me that she had everything taken care of. While I was resting and recovering from my injuries, Courtney was plotting her escape. She snuck past guards, contacted some of our biggest rivals, and then somehow convinced them to come fight on our side.

Courtney managed to broker a deal in one night that would have taken me weeks of negotiating. And now, she's in the middle of a gunfight, naked, killing our enemies.

She's the strongest, sexiest woman I've ever seen.

Courtney spins and kills another guard, and when he falls, she meets my eyes across the crowd. The eye contact breaks me from my spell, and I run towards her. As soon as we meet, we go back to back and begin firing at enemies on both sides.

As the bodies around us begin to stack up, the gunshots become less frequent. It's becoming apparent that the Italians are overpowering Elena's men.

Elena stumbles out of the fight with her gun raised, ready to take aim at anyone in her path. She's so focused on the chaos in front of her that she doesn't see Courtney and me just behind her. I almost step forward to capture her, but then I nudge Courtney. Without a word, she steps around me and presses her gun to Elena's forehead.

"Drop your weapon."

Elena obeys without hesitation. The gun clatters to the ground, and she holds up her hands. "I surrender."

The few surviving guards closest to her follow suit, dropping their weapons. Each gun is claimed by an Italian, and within a minute, the room is plunged into silence while every guard and Devon and Elena are brought to their knees in the same way Courtney was forced to hers. It's cyclical, and it feels like justice.

~

Without any ounce of shame, Courtney grabs Sevastian's clothes and pulls them over her naked body, never once taking her eyes off Elena. They hang off her thin frame, but she still looks powerful all in black.

The lines of her heart-shaped face have crystallized, sharpening into a mask of control. Of dominance. She has been fiery since the moment I met her, but now, there is a new sense of control. She has harnessed the fire inside of her and turned it into a weapon.

Elena must see it, too, because her usual cockiness is gone. The smug smile she has worn for days has fallen into wide-eyed fear. Her skin is pale, and her hands shake.

"I wasn't going to kill you," she says. "I told Dmitry I wouldn't. Remember, Dmitry? I said I would let her live."

"To torture me by torturing her," I say. "That hardly counts as mercy."

"It is a kind of mercy, though."

"Desperation isn't a good look on you," Courtney says. She tucks the baggy shirt into the gathered waist of her pants and holds out her hand for her gun. I give it to her.

As much as I want to kill Elena, I know she's Courtney's to kill. Elena did all of this to get back at me for killing Rurik, but she did it to

Courtney. In a way, it feels right that I would kill Rurik and Courtney will now kill Elena. So, I'm happy to let her end this.

"Just let us go," Devon says.

It's the first thing I've really heard him say in days. As this plan dragged on and on, he became more and more a servant to Elena. Not her partner, but her underling. I can't believe I never saw before how weak he was.

"We won't come after you. We'll disappear. You'll never hear from us again."

I expect Elena to hiss for him to be quiet, but she nods in agreement. They truly are desperate.

"I'll never hear from you again," Courtney says. "But not because I'm going to let you go."

Devon whimpers and then looks around at the Italians surrounding him and his mother. "I thought you all were supposed to be on our side. You supported my father when he tried to overthrow Dmitry. Why would you turn on us now? We could fight together, and you could have everything you wanted."

"We have everything we want," one of the Italians says. "We are here in Spain because of your father. He left us with nothing, and we had to join with the Yakuza to scrape by. Now, Courtney has given us more than your father ever did. We might not be loyal, but we're smart. We know where our best chances lie."

The man winks at Courtney, and she turns to me, her lower lip between her teeth. I know she's nervous about taking the lead for me —about what I'll think about all of it. I wink at her, and she stands a bit taller.

We are a team. We survive together, and we lead together.

"No one owes you an explanation," Courtney says, silencing whatever response Devon was about to make. "You've stolen enough from me, and I won't let you take a second more."

"I'm smart, too," Elena says quickly. "Not very loyal, but I am smart. I know you're in control now. I'll follow you. Help you, even. I've been in this world longer than you have, sweetheart. I can be of use. I know more about your husband than you do, and I know a good deal about you. You'll need my help."

"What do you know about me?" Courtney asks.

Elena smirks, her confidence returning slightly. "I know you aren't a killer. I know you're a gentle woman, too kind for this cruel world. Let me handle the darker elements for you."

"I'm not a killer?" Courtney asks, head tilted to the side.

Elena smiles at her. "No, sweetie. But that's okay. Not everyone is cut out for this life—"

The shot is so surprising even I jump.

Elena stays upright for a moment before she sags into her bones and falls forward, face-first on the ground. Devon stares at his mother's lifeless body for a moment before he shrieks and throws himself over her body.

Courtney lowers the gun slowly and steps away. "Shows what you know."

I grab the gun from her hand and kiss her cheek. Courtney leans back into my chest for a second, and then spins around to stand behind me, letting me take the lead now.

I lift the gun to shoot Devon, to get it over with quickly. I've seen what vengeance can do to people, so I have no use for it right now. I don't want to drag out his torment. I just want to end this.

Then, I see movement to my left. I look over and see that Sadie has stepped out of the cell. She's staring at Devon, whose shrieks have turned to sobs now. There is no concern in her eyes, no compassion, just curiosity.

I can understand her desire to see it unfold. He was her boyfriend for eighteen months. They lived together. He betrayed her more than Rurik ever betrayed me. I can understand that she would want to see him die.

I hold the gun out to her and nod, and she considers taking it for a second before shaking her head.

Sadie isn't a killer. Even while the sailor attacked her on the ship, she hesitated. She couldn't stab him. She's the one who is unprepared for this world. I nod in understanding and then take aim at the back of Devon's head.

His shoulders are heaving with sobs, his tears soaking the back of Elena's shirt, and when I shoot him, he sinks into his mother's back, cradled against her like a child. It feels fitting.

The Italians have subdued the remaining guards, so there is nothing to be done. No one to fight or run from. It's over. We are free.

Courtney seems to realize this fact at the same time I do, and she wraps her arms around me. I spin in her arms and kiss the top of her head.

"You did it."

She laughs like she can't quite believe it and looks up at me. "I know it was a risk to call the Italians, and I probably gave them too much, but—"

"You saved our family," I whisper, resting my forehead against hers. "No price would ever be too much. I just want to know how you thought to do that."

She shrugs. "Honestly, it was luck. I didn't have a phone or money, so I had to borrow a phone and call my dad to get a number for me, and the only place I could think of was the Italian-owned pub in midtown. So, I called there, and luckily, someone answered and put me in touch with Stefano Rossi. And amazingly, he listened to me, and he wanted to make a deal. And by coincidence, he happened to have a group of men stationed near where the ship would have docked, and they were able to get to the warehouse to help us in time. It was all luck. Dumb luck."

"Skill," I correct. "You thought like a leader. Like a boss."

"The boss of nothing," she says, wincing. "I gave up most of the illegal territory you had left and a lot of your business contacts. I hope you like imports and exports because that is all you have left."

"*We* have left," I correct again. "If you think I'm going to let you sit on the sidelines and be my trophy wife after the way you just proved yourself, you're crazy. We're partners, Courtney Tsezar. Whether legal or illegal, you're going to be by my side while we figure out our next step."

Her eyes go glassy, and she stretches up on her toes to kiss me. We are both battered and bruised, our bodies aching, but we kiss tenderly, enjoying the reprieve of one another. When she pulls away, she drags her hand down my arm and twines our fingers together. "Let's go get our girls."

We walk hand in hand back to the cell to free our family once and for all.

# EPILOGUE

DMITRY

*Three Months Later*

The second I pull the door open, a shot of long blonde hair runs through the door and past me, headed up the stairs towards Tati's room.

"Good to see you, Larissa," I call sarcastically after her.

"Sorry," Sadie says, walking in with a store-bought birthday cake balanced in her hands. "She has been talking about playing with Tati's doll collection all morning. She can barely contain herself."

I grab the cake from her and take it into the kitchen. "She can have some as far as I'm concerned, I almost broke my neck stepping on Dr. Dolly at the top of the stairs this morning."

"Yeah, right," Courtney calls from the living room. "Tati would kill you before she'd let you get rid of Dr. Dolly."

Sadie laughs and grabs a bottle from the wine fridge like she lives here. Which she almost does. She and Larissa are in a two-bedroom apartment just below our penthouse, so we see them every day and eat most meals with them.

I called in every political favor my father had stored up over the years to get us all new identities and a fresh start in a new state. When we first moved to California, I thought I'd hate having Sadie so close, but I really don't mind. It feels nice to have a kind of small family around, and I can tell Courtney loves the company. Plus, having Larissa around so often might convince Courtney we don't need another kid right now.

I want to have so many babies with Courtney. As many as she wants. But it still feels too soon. After ... everything.

Courtney claims she's okay, but I hear her moaning in her sleep. I've caught her crying in the shower. She and Tati are both traumatized in different ways, and I want to try and deal with some of that before we introduce a new family dynamic.

Courtney pads into the kitchen and points to the wine. "Yes, please."

"Obviously," Sadie says, holding out a glass. "You can't have a birthday party without wine."

"Isn't this party for an eleven-year-old?" I tease.

Sadie rolls her eyes at me and Courtney pats her back. "You're doing a good thing for Larissa."

Sadie shrugs and tries to hide her smile. "She's doing a good thing for me, too, I think."

That is true. Sadie has become an entirely new person since the paperwork was drawn up to make her Larissa's adoptive parent. That and a whole lot of therapy has gone a long way toward helping her overcome the scars of what she went through on the ship.

A loud ring interrupts the nice moment, and Courtney jumps and pulls it out of her pocket. "Oh, it's Shiloh."

She holds up a finger and runs into the other room to take the call.

"Is she still trying to find everyone?" Sadie asks.

I nod. "She's determined. We got the letter just before leaving the old house that the boat landed safely and they all survived, but she wants to make sure all of the women are doing okay."

"She might never find them all. Some of them could still be in Spain."

"She knows that, but she still has to try. It's who she is."

"Too good for her own good," Sadie says fondly.

"Truly," I agree.

There is another knock on the door, and I jog into the entryway to answer it. On the other side of the door is a giant stuffed giraffe. Sevastian pulls the animal to one side to peek out from around the neck.

"Hello."

"Courtney told you to buy her something small. Unassuming," I say, eyebrows raised. "She told you not to try so hard."

"I know, but she likes giraffes," Sevastian argues. "I figure Larissa will love this giant giraffe, and then she'll remember that I gave it to her, and eventually, she'll love me, too."

I pat Sevastian on the shoulder and shake my head. "She'll come around."

He groans and drops the giraffe by the door, propping it up in the corner. "I hope so."

Larissa's mom was a prostitute, so she didn't have good experiences with men to begin with. Then, she was trapped in that container, which Sevastian helped guard. Larissa isn't nearly as forgiving as Tati, and she's not pleased that Sadie and Sevastian have started seeing one another.

When we make it back to the kitchen, Courtney is already done with her phone call and is explaining to Sadie how close she is to finding another woman from the boat when Tati and Larissa tear into the kitchen.

*Can we have cake now?* Tati signs.

Her eyes are locked on the cake like a laser beam. It has been three months, but it's still good to see her act like a child. It's good to see her focused on friends and cake. It's also good to see her healthy. A doctor prescribed her medication for her migraines that has taken care of ninety percent of her pain. She still gets a headache occasionally, but not at the same frequency as before.

*Please?* Larissa signs, checking with Tati to make sure she did it properly. Tati gives her a thumbs-up.

Courtney laughs and says as she signs, "You two are ganging up on me now. That isn't fair!"

*Please!* They both say again.

Courtney, no match for our daughter's puppy-dog eyes or a birthday girl's wish, cuts them two slices of cake and then dishes some out for the rest of us, as well.

It's a small party. Tati and Larissa spend every second of it together, huddled in a corner giggling, while the adults talk in the living room and Olivia throws her chunky toddler crayons around the room, but it feels perfect.

It feels like exactly where we're supposed to be.

~

The girls convince their moms that they need a sleepover, so the penthouse becomes a man-free zone. Which works out well considering Sevastian and I have plans, anyway.

"You're sure it's fine that we're just showing up?" I ask.

Sevastian parks the car along a metered curb downtown. "Fine. I asked around and there are walk-ins all the time. As long as you don't bring a weapon and you pay up, you're good."

I grudgingly stash my gun in the glove compartment while Sevastian feeds the meter, and then we walk down the alley between two brick buildings. I feel strangely naked without my weapon.

"They accept cash," I say just to clarify.

"If that's all you have to offer," he says. "But they prefer other things. More tangible things."

Only a criminal would say money isn't tangible.

Sevastian knocks on a metal door, and it opens up immediately. A boulder of a man stands guard at the door. He gruffly asks if we have any weapons to turn over, and when we say we don't, he takes us at our word and lets us inside.

"That doesn't inspire confidence. What if someone lied?"

"I guess we'll find out when they pull a gun on us," Sevastian teases.

We both go stone-faced as we approach the group of men clustered around the table. All of them sit with straight backs, arms crossed over their chests, identical masks of suspicion and power on their faces. These are the men who run this city.

"Who are you?" an elderly gentleman asks. He is easily the oldest in the group.

"Dmitry. Sevastian," I say. "We're here to play."

"You have something we want?" the man asks.

He means a stash house or business connections. Something that would be of use to the leader of a mob. Something that they wouldn't normally be able to obtain without starting a turf war.

I have nothing of the sort. All I have is one loyal lieutenant and a desire to start fresh. To build a family here in California that is far from the reputation my father left for me. I want to lay the groundwork for a new Bratva built on honesty, transparency, and loyalty.

To get started, I just have to win a few hands.

I shrug. "Perhaps, though that hardly matters."

The old man raises a curious brow. "How so?"

I pull back a chair and take a seat. Sevastian stands at my right shoulder. "Because I don't plan to lose. I'm here to win."

A red-haired man across the table who is shuffling the cards frowns at me. "What do you want?"

I tap the table for him to deal me in. "Everything."

When I walk into the penthouse after midnight, I know Courtney will be in bed alone.

Thinking the girls would still be having their party, Sevastian and I went to Sadie's apartment first, thinking we could crash there for the night. However, we opened the door to find Tati and Larissa sleeping in a blanket fort in the living room. Sadie met us at the door and snared Sevastian, dragging him back to her bedroom, though he hardly resisted.

I'm now hoping I'll get just as lucky with my own woman. It has been far too long since we've had an entire night where Tati didn't crawl into our bed at some point because of a nightmare.

I crack open Olivia's door as I pass. I used to walk by her room without stopping, taking for granted that she was sleeping peacefully on the other side. Now, after everything that has happened, I savor every moment. Every second I have with my family is precious.

Her tiny chest rises and falls in even movements, and I pull the door closed, turning the knob slowly until the latch settles into place. Then, I continue to our room.

I expect to find Courtney lying in bed, half asleep, but the bed is empty and still made. Confused, I pad back down the hallway, through the kitchen, and it's only when I'm halfway across the living room that I realize where Courtney is. I take a hard right into the dance studio.

The room was a fourth bedroom/office combo, but we renovated it the moment we moved in and turned it into a dance studio. Courtney will be able to teach classes there the way she did before, but more than that, it gives her a place to escape. A place to decompress. Something she needs more than ever after the kidnapping.

I open the door quietly, hoping she won't hear me. Of course, she sees my reflection in the wall-to-wall mirrors, and spins around, wiping her hair out of her face.

"You're home late."

"And you're up late," I say. "I figured you'd already be in bed."

"Olivia didn't fall asleep until an hour ago," she says. "Some of her molars are coming in, and she was too uncomfortable to sleep."

"I'm sorry. I would have come home if I'd known." I also would have come home if I'd known she was wearing her leggings with the sheer panels down the sides. Paired with her thin white tank top that shows off a tantalizing amount of her chest, I never would have left the house in the first place.

She rolls her eyes and smiles. "You were doing something slightly more important than dealing with a teething toddler."

I cross the room, my footsteps echoing off the reflective walls, and wrap my hands around her waist. "Nothing is more important than you girls."

She looks up at me, and her eyes go soft. The way they do when she swoons. The same way they do just before I convince her to strip out of her clothes and dance for me.

"I'm all sweaty," she says, pushing softly on my chest. "I stink."

I wrap my arms tighter around her and bury my nose in her neck. "You smell great to me. Pheromones."

"Ew," she laughs, half-heartedly trying to get out of my hold. "Let me shower first."

"No."

"Let me change."

"No."

She sighs. "You're incorrigible."

"And you, my dear wife," I say, gripping her hips and dragging them against mine, "are incredibly sexy. Even when you are sweaty and stinky."

She rolls her eyes again, but her bottom lip is pinched between her teeth, and I know I'm getting to her. I know all of her tells, and she wants this just as badly as I do.

I slip my hands under the hem of her shirt and walk my fingers across the flat plane of her stomach. Just before I can reach the bottom of her bra, she spins away from me and slides in her socks to the speakers. She turns them on, and a soft bass pounds through the floors and into my chest. Courtney sways with the beat, circling her hips and sliding her arms over her head, twirling her fingers in the air.

I sigh at her beauty and the beauty of the moment. The incredibly normalcy of it all. My wife is dancing for me.

We are two normal people. A normal couple, squeezing in time for one another while our daughter is at her friend's house and our baby is asleep. We are normal, which is something I didn't know if we'd ever be again.

Courtney moves towards me slowly, one foot in front of the other. Just when she gets within reach, she spins away again, moving past me to grab a wooden chair from the edge of the room. When she slides it across the floor and taps the back of it, gesturing for me to sit, I do not hesitate to follow instructions.

She walks around the chair in slow, sensual circles, darting out of reach as soon as I touch her, teasing me until I have no choice but to take what I want. I grab her shirt as she passes and pull her onto my lap. She yelps in surprise and narrows her eyes at me.

"Naughty," she whispers, biting the tip of my nose. "I'm trying to dance for you, but you can't keep your hands to yourself."

"Can you blame me?" I breathe, smoothing my palms up the soft curve of her body. Courtney arches into my touch, rolling her hips over my lap. I'm so beyond ready that the simple movement makes me groan. Liking my reaction, Courtney does it again. But when I cup my hands over her breasts, she swats me away and stands up.

"Tease," I whisper.

Courtney raises an eyebrow in a challenge and drops to her knees in front of me.

The accusation dies on my lips. I stare down at my wife with open-mouthed awe as she nestles herself between my thighs and slowly opens the front of my pants. I practically spring out the moment the zipper is down, and she chuckles to herself, but I'm too busy staring at her lips.

She drags her tongue over her bottom lip, sucking it into her mouth for a second. Then, her mouth is around me—warm and breathy—and I tip my head back and moan.

We've been together since the kidnapping. Obviously. But this is the first time it has felt normal. Where it hasn't felt like we're having sex to forget. Right now, we're having sex to remember. To remember this moment and how we feel in it.

I curl my hand around her ear, twisting my fingers in her hair, and let her take as much of me as she wants. She puckers her lips and swirls her tongue and pushes me to the far-most edge of oblivion before slowing down and bringing me back. Again and again she does this until I'm half mad. Until I can't think until I'm inside of her.

I pull her off me and push her down on the floor at the same time I drop to my knees and crawl over her.

"We can go to the bedroom," she says, tipping her head towards the door.

I grab her chin and bring her face to mine, crushing my lips against hers. I don't want her in a place as mundane as a bed. I want to take her right here on the hard floor.

"I can't wait," I moan, hooking my fingers in her waistband and pulling the elastic down her legs. She draws her legs up, helping me peel her clothes off.

I kiss my way up her smooth legs, swirling my tongue behind her knees and planting soft kisses up the insides of her thighs. Then, I realize her panties came off with the leggings, and I press a kiss to her very center.

Her hips lift off the floor, and I pin them down with my arm and kiss her again. I slip my tongue inside of her and flick the sensitive nub between her legs. I push her to her own oblivion until she grabs a fistful of my hair and pulls me up her body.

I slide my hands across the smooth plane of her stomach and under her bra to cup her breasts. I'm not entirely sure how, but the next thing I know, she's naked underneath me, and she's the most beautiful thing I've ever seen.

"You need to get out more," she says, and I realize I've said it out loud.

"How am I supposed to go anywhere when you look like this?" I lick a circle around her breast and nip at her. "I'm happy here."

"Me too."

I look down at her, and she's smiling down at me, her full lips pink and parted.

I am happy. Despite everything we've been through, despite our past and the trauma we've endured, I'm happy now. And for right now, that is all that matters.

When I slide inside of her, I'm not thinking about what a bad time it is for another baby. I'm not thinking of all the reasons I should say no. I'm just thinking that this moment is perfect, and no bad thing could ever come from it.

I slide into her, and Courtney's eyes widen. She opens her mouth like she wants to warn me, but she must see the surrender in my face. Her face splits into a wide grin, and then she drags her nails across my back, and rolls her body up and against mine.

She presses her fingers into my lower back, clinging to me with every thrust, drawing me in deeper and deeper until I can't hold back anymore.

I gasp and spill into her, and I feel Courtney tense and release, her body moving in rhythm with mine.

When we're done, we lie on the wooden floor, entwined in one another, sweaty and naked and spent. And happy.

**Thanks for reading! But don't stop now – there's more. Click the link below to receive the FREE extended epilogue to DAYBREAK.**

**So what are you waiting for? Click below!**
https://dl.bookfunnel.com/c8wn2cegou

# SNEAK PREVIEW (BROKEN VOWS)

Keep reading for a sneak preview of BROKEN VOWS by Nicole Fox!

**She's my fake wife, my property... and my last chance at redemption.**

She's beautiful. An angel.

I'm dangerous. A killer.

She's my fake bride for a single reason – so I can crush her father's resistance.

But marrying Eve brings me far more than I bargained for.

She's fiery. Feisty. Won't take no for an answer.

She makes me believe that I might be worth redemption.

Until I discover a past she's been hiding from me.

One that threatens everything.

Now, I know that our wedding vows are not enough.

I need to make sure she's mine for good.

A baby in her belly is the only way to seal the deal.

*In the end, the Bratva always gets what it wants.*

**Luka**

Their fear tingles against my skin like a whisper. As my leather-soled shoes tap against the concrete floor, I can sense it in the way their eyes dart towards and away from me. In the way they scurry around the production floor like mice, meek and unseen in the shadows. I enjoy it.

Even before I rose through the ranks of my family, I could inspire fear. Being a large man made that simple. But now, with brawn and power behind me, people cower. These people—the employees at the soda factory—don't even know why they fear me. Other than me being the owner's son, they have no real reason to be afraid of me, and yet, like prey in the grasslands, they sense the lion is near. I observe each of them as I weave my way around conveyors filled with plastic bottles and aluminum cans, carbonated soda being pumped into them, filling the room with a syrupy sweet smell.

I recognize their faces, though not their names. The people upstairs don't concern me. Or, at least, they shouldn't. The soda factory is a cover for the real operation downstairs, which must be protected at all costs. It's why I'm here on a Friday evening sniffing around for rats. For anyone who looks unfamiliar or out of place.

The floor manager—a Hispanic woman with a severe braid running down her back—calls out orders to the employees on the floor below in both English and Spanish, directing attention where necessary. She doesn't look at me once.

Noise permeates the metal shell of the building. The whirr of conveyor belts and grinding of gears makes the concrete floors feel like they are vibrating from the sheer power of the sound waves. A lot of people find the sights and smells overwhelming, but I've never minded. You don't become a mob underboss by shrinking in the face of chaos.

A group of employees in blue polos gather around a conveyor belt, smoothing out some kink in the production line. They pull a few aluminum cans from the line and drop them in a recycling bin, jockeying the rest of the cans back into a smooth line. The larger of the three men—a bald man with a doughy face and no obvious chin—flips a red switch. An alarm sounds and the cans begin moving again. He gives the floor manager a thumbs up and then turns to me, his hand flattening into a small wave. I raise an eyebrow in response. His face reddens, and he turns back to his work.

I don't recognize him, but he can't be in law enforcement. Undercover cops are more fit than he could ever dream to be. Plus, he wouldn't have drawn attention to himself. Likely, he is just a new hire, unaware of my position in the company. I resolve to go over new hires with the site manager and find out the man's name.

When I make it to the back of the production floor, the lights are dimmed—the back half of the factory not being utilized overnight—and I fumble with my keys for a moment before finding the right one to unlock the basement door. The stairway down is dark, and as soon as the metal door slams shut behind me, I'm left in blackness, my other senses heightening. The sounds of the production floor are but a whisper behind me, but the most pressing difference is the smell. Rather than the syrupy sweetness of the factory, there is an ether, chemical-like smell that makes my nose itch.

"That you, Luka?" Simon Oakley, the main chemist, doesn't wait for me to answer. "I've got a line here for you. We've perfected the chemistry. Best coke you'll ever try."

I pull back a thick curtain at the base of the stairs and step into the bright white light of the real production floor. I blink as my eyes adjust, and see Simon alone at the first metal table, three other men working in the back of the room. Like the employees upstairs, they don't look up as I enter. Simon, however, smiles and points to the line.

"I don't need to try it," I say flatly. "I'll know whether it's good or not when I see how much our profits increase."

"Well," Simon balks. "It can take time for word to spread. We may not see a rise in income until—"

"I'm not here to chat." I walk around the end of the table and stand next to Simon. He is an entire head shorter than me, his skin pale from spending so much time in the basement. "There have been nasty rumors going around among my men."

His bushy brows furrow in concern. "Rumors about what? You know we basement dwellers are often the last to hear just about everything." He tries to chuckle, but it dies as soon as he sees that I'm not here to fuck around.

"Disloyalty." I purse my lips and run my tongue over my top teeth. "The rumbling is that someone has turned their back on the family."

Fear dilates his pupils, and his fingers drum against the metal tabletop. "See? That is what I'm saying. I haven't heard a single thing about any of that."

"You haven't?" I hum in thought, taking a step closer. I can tell Simon wants to back away, but he stays put. I commend him for his bravery even as I loath him for it. "That is interesting."

His Adam's apple bobs in his throat. "Why is that interesting?"

Before he can even finish the sentence, my hand is around his neck. I strike like a snake, squeezing his windpipe in my hand and walking him back towards the stone wall. I hear the men in the back of the room jump and murmur, but they make no move to help their boss. Because I outrank Simon by a mile.

"It's interesting, Simon, because I have reliable information that says you met with members of the Furino mafia." I slam his head against the wall once, twice. "Is it true?"

His face is turning red, eyeballs beginning to bulge out, and he claws at my hand for air. I don't give him any.

"Why would you go behind my back and meet with another family? Have I not welcomed you into our fold? Have I not made your life here comfortable?"

Simon's eyes are rolling back in his head, his fingers becoming limp noodles on my wrist, weak and ineffective. Just before his body can sag into unconsciousness, I release him. He drops to the floor, falling onto his hands and knees and gasping for air. I let him get two breaths before I kick him in the ribs.

"I didn't meet with them," he rasps. When he looks up at me, I can already see the beginnings of bruises wrapping around his neck.

I kick him again. The force knocks the air out of him, and he collapses on his face, forehead pressed to the cement floor.

"Okay," he says, voice muffled. "I talked with them. Once."

I pressed the sole of my shoe into his ribs, rolling him onto his back. "Speak up."

"I met with them once," he admits, tears streaming down his face from the pain. "They reached out to me."

"Yet you did not tell me?"

"I didn't know what they wanted," he says, sitting up and leaning against the wall.

"All the more reason you should have told me." I reach down and grab his shirt, hauling him to his feet and pinning him against the wall. "Men who are loyal to me do not meet with my enemies."

"They offered me money," he says, wincing in preparation for the next blow. "They offered me a larger cut of the profits. I shouldn't have gone, but I have a family, and—"

I was raised to be an observer of people. To spot their weaknesses and know when I am being deceived. So, I know immediately Simon is not telling me the entire story. The Furinos would not reach out to our chemist and offer him more money unless there had been communication between them prior, unless they had some connection Simon is not telling me about. He thinks I am a fool. He thinks I will forgive him because of his wife and child, but he does not know the depths of my apathy. Simon thinks he can appeal to my humanity, but he does not realize I do not have any.

I press my hand into the bruises around his neck. Simon grabs my wrist, trying to pull me away, but I squeeze again, enjoying the feeling of his life in my hands. I like knowing that with one blow to the neck, I could break his trachea and watch him suffocate on the floor. I am in complete control.

"And your family will be dead before dawn unless you tell me why you met with the Furinos," I spit. I want nothing more than to kill Simon for being disloyal. I can figure out the truth without him. But it is not why I was sent here. Killing indiscriminately does not create the kind of controlled fear we need to keep our family standing. It only creates anarchy. So, reluctantly, I let Simon go. Once again, he falls to the floor, gasping, and I step away so I won't be tempted to beat him.

"I'll tell you," he says, his voice high-pitched, like the words are being released slowly from a balloon. "I'll tell you anything, just don't hurt my family."

I nod for him to continue. This is his only chance to come clean. If he lies to me again, I'll kill him.

Simon opens his mouth, but before he can say anything, I hear a loud bang upstairs and a scream. Just as I turn around, the door at the top of the stairs opens, and I know immediately something is wrong. Forgetting all about Simon, I grab the nearest table and tip it over, not worrying about the potential lost profits. Footsteps pound down the stairs and no sooner have I crouched down, the room erupts in bullets.

I see one of the men in the back of the room drop, clutching his stomach. The other two follow my lead and dive behind tables. Simon crawls over to lay on the floor next to me, his lips purple.

The room is filled with the pounding of footsteps, the ring of bullets, and the moans of the fallen man. It is chaos, but I am steady. My heart rate is even as I grab my phone, turn on the front facing camera, and lift it over the table. There are eight shoulders spread out around the room, guns at the ready. Two of them are at the base of the stairs, the other six are spread out in three-foot increments, forming a barrier in front of the stairs. No one here is supposed to get out alive.

But they do not know who is hiding behind the table. If they did, they'd be running.

I look over at one of the chemists. They are not our family's soldiers, but they are trained like anyone else. He has his gun at the ready, waiting for my order. I nod my head once, twice, and on three, we both turn and fire.

One man falls immediately, my bullet striking him in the neck, blood spraying against the wall like splattered paint. It is a kind of artwork, shooting a man. Years of training, placing the bullet just so. Art is meant to incite a reaction and a bullet certainly does that. The man drops his weapon, his hand flying to his neck. Before he can experience too much pain, I place another bullet in his forehead. He drops to his knees, but before he falls flat on his face, I shoot his friend.

The men expected this ambush to be simple, so they are still in shock, still scrambling to collect themselves. It makes it easy for my men to knock them off. Another two men drop as I chase my second target around the room, firing shot after shot at him. He ducks behind a table, and I wait, gun aimed. It is a deadly game of Whack-a-mole, and it requires patience. His gun pops up first, followed shortly by his head, which I blow off with one shot. His scream dies on his lips as he bleeds out, red seeping out from under the table and spreading across the floor.

There are three men left, and I'm out of bullets. I stash my gun in my pocket and pull out my KA-BAR knife. The blade feels like an old friend in my hand. I crawl past a shivering Simon, wishing I'd killed him just so I wouldn't have to see him looking so pathetic, and out from behind the table. I slide my feet under me, moving into a crouch. The remaining men are wounded, and they are focused on the back corner where shots are still coming from my men. They do not see me approaching from the side.

I lunge at the first man—a young kid with golden brown hair and a tattoo on his neck. It is half-hidden under the collar of his shirt, so I cannot make it out. When my knife cuts into his side, he spins to fight me off, but I knock his gun from his hand with my left arm and then drive the knife in under his ribs and upward. He freezes for a moment before blood leaks from his mouth.

The man next to him falls from multiple bullets in the chest and stomach. I kick his gun away from him as he falls to the floor, and advance on the last attacker. He is hiding behind a metal table, palm pressing into a wound on his shoulder. He scrambles to lift his gun as I approach, but I drop to my knees and slide next to him, knife pressed to his neck. His eyes go wide, and then they squeeze shut as he drops his weapon.

The blade of my knife is biting into his skin, and I see the same tattoo creeping up from beneath his collar. I slide the blade down, pushing his shirt aside, and I recognize it at once.

"You are with the Furinos?" I ask.

The man answers by squeezing his eyes shut even tighter.

"You should know who is in a room before you attack," I hiss. "I am Luka Volkov, and I could slit your throat right now."

His entire body is trembling, blood from his shoulder wound leaking through his clothes and onto the floor. Every ounce of me wants this kill. I feel like a dog who has not been fed, desperate for a hunk of flesh, but warfare is not endless bloodshed. It is tactical.

"But I will not," I say, pulling the blade back. The man blinks, unbelieving. "Get out of here and tell your boss what happened. Tell him this attack is a declaration of war, and the Volkov family will live up to our merciless reputation."

He hesitates, and I slash the blade across his cheek, drawing a thin line of blood from the corner of his mouth to his ear. "Go!" I roar.

The man scrambles to his feet and towards the stairs, blood dripping in his wake. As soon as he is gone, I clean my knife with the hem of my shirt and slide it back into place on my hip.

This will not end well.

**Eve**

I hold up a bag of raisins and a bag of prunes a few inches from the cook's face.

"Do you see the difference?" I ask. The question is rhetorical. Anyone with eyes could see the difference. And a cook—a properly trained cook—should be able to smell, feel, and sense the difference, as well.

Still, Felix wrinkles his forehead and studies the bags like it is a pop quiz.

"Raisins are small, Felix!" My shouting makes him jump, but I'm far too stressed out to care. "Prunes are huge. As big as a baby's fist. Raisins are tiny. They taste very different because they start out as different fruits. Do you see the problem?"

He stares at me blankly, and I wonder if being sous chef gives me the authority to fire someone. Because this man has got to go.

"You've ruined an entire roast duck, Felix." I drop the bags on the counter and run a hand down my sweaty face. I grab the towel from my back pocket and towel off. "Throw it out and start again, but use *prunes* this time."

He smiles and nods, and I wonder how many times he must have hit his head to be so slow. I motion for another cook to come talk to me. He moves quickly, hands folded behind his back, waiting for my order.

"Chop up the duck and make a confit salad. We can toss it with more raisins, fennel—that kind of thing—and make it work."

He nods and shuffles away, and I mop my forehead again.

At the start of my shift, I strode into the kitchen like I owned the place. I was finally sous chef to Cal Higgs, genius chef in charge at The Floating Crown. After graduating culinary school, I didn't know where I'd get a job or where I'd be on the totem pole, and I certainly never imagined I'd be a sous chef so soon, but here I am. And now that I'm here, I can't help but wonder if it wasn't some sort of trick. Did Cal give into my father's wishes easily and give me this job because he needed a break from the insanity?

I've been assured by several members of staff that the dishwasher, whose name I can't remember, has been working at the kitchen for over a year, but he seems to be stuck on slow motion tonight. He is washing and drying plates seconds before the cooks are plating them up and sending them back out to the dining room. And two of the cooks, who were apparently dating, decided that the middle of dinner rush would be the perfect time to discuss their relationship, and they broke up. Dylan stormed out without a word, and Sarah, who should be okay since she was the dumper, not the dumpee, is hiding in the bathroom bawling her eyes out. I've knocked on the door once every ten minutes for an hour, but she refuses to let me in. Cal has a key, but he has been shut away in his office all night, and I don't want to go explain what a shitshow the kitchen is, so we are making do. Barely.

"Sarah?" I knock on the door. "If you don't come out in five minutes, you're fired."

For the first time, there is a break in the crying. "You can't do that."

"Yes, I can," I lie. "You'll leave here tonight without your apron. Single and jobless. Just imagine that shame."

I feel bad rubbing salt in her wound, threatening her, but I'm out of options. I tried comforting her and offering her some of the dark chocolate from the dessert pantry, but she refused to budge. Threats are my last recourse.

There is a long pause, and I wonder if I'm going to have to admit that I actually can't fire her—I don't think—and tell the staff to start using the bathrooms on the customer side, when finally, Sarah emerges. Mascara is smeared down her cheeks, and her eyes are red and puffy from crying, but she is out of the bathroom. As soon as she steps through the doorway, one of the waitresses darts in after her and slams the door shut.

"I'm sorry, Eve," she blubbers, covering her face with her hands.

I grab her wrists and pry her palms from her eyes. When she looks up, her eyes are still closed, tears leaking from the corners.

"Go to the sinks and help with the dishes," I say firmly. "You're in no state to cook right now. Just focus on cleaning plates, okay?"

Sarah nods, her lower lip wobbling.

"Everything is fine," I say, speaking to her like she is a wild animal who might attack. "You won't lose your job. Cal never needs to know, okay? Just go wash dishes. Now."

She turns away from me in a daze and heads back to help the dishwasher whose name I can't for the life of me remember, and I take a deep breath. I've finally put out all the fires, and I lean against the counter and watch the kitchen move around me. It is like a living, breathing machine. Each person has to play their part or everything falls apart. And tonight, I'm barely holding them together.

When the kitchen door swings open, I hope it is Makayla. She has been a waitress at The Floating Crown for five years, and while she has no formal culinary training, she knows this kitchen better than anyone. I've asked her for help tonight more times than I'm comfortable with, but at this point, just seeing one, capable, smiling face would be enough to keep me from crying. But when I turn and instead see a man in a suit, the tie loose and askew around his neck, and his eyes glassy, I almost sag to the floor.

"You can't be back here, sir," I say, moving forward to block his access to the rest of the kitchen. "We have hot stoves and fire and sharp knives, and you are already unstable on your feet."

Makayla told me a businessman at the bar had been demanding macaroni and cheese all night between shots. Apparently, he would not take 'no' for an answer.

"Macaroni and cheese," he mutters, falling against my palms, his feet sliding out from underneath him. "I need macaroni and cheese to soak up the alcohol."

I turn to the nearest person for help, but Felix is still looking at the bags of raisins and prunes like he might seriously still be confused which is which, and I don't want to distract him lest he ruin another duck. I could call out for help from someone else or call the police, but I don't want to cause a scene. Cal is just in the next room. He may have hired me because my father is Don of the Furino family, but even my father can't be angry if Cal fires me for sheer incompetence. I have to prove that I'm capable.

"Sir, we don't have macaroni and cheese, but may I recommend our scoglio?"

"What is that?" he asks, top lip curled back.

"A delicious seafood pasta. Mussels, clams, shrimp, and scallops in a tomato sauce with herbs and spices. Truly delicious. One of my favorite meals on the menu."

"No cheese?"

I sigh. "No. No cheese."

He shakes his head and pushes past me, running his hands along the counters like he might stumble upon a prepared bowl of cheesy pasta.

"Sir, you can't be back here."

"I can be wherever I like," he shouts. "This is America, isn't it?"

"It is, but this is a private restaurant and our insurance does not cover diners being back in the kitchen, so I have to ask you—"

*"Oh, say can you see by the dawn's early light!"*

"Is that 'The Star-Spangled Banner'?" I ask, looking around to see whether anyone else can see this man or whether I'm having some sort of exhausted fever dream.

*"What so proudly we hailed at the twilight's last gleaming?"*

This is absurd. Truly absurd. Beyond calling the police, the easiest thing to do seems to be to give in to his demands, so I lay a hand on his shoulder and lead him to the corner of the kitchen. I pat the counter, and he jumps up like he is a child.

I listen to the National Anthem six times before I hand the man a bowl of whole grain linguini with a sharp cheddar cheese sauce on top. "Can you please take this back to the bar and leave me alone?"

He grabs the bowl from my hands, takes a bite, and then breaks into yet another rousing rendition of "The Star-Spangled Banner." This time in falsetto with accompanying dance moves.

I sigh and push him towards the door. "Come on, man."

The dining room is loud enough that no one pays the man too much attention. Plus, he has been drunk out here for an hour before ambushing the kitchen. A few guests shake their heads at the man and then smile at me, giving me the understanding and recognition I sought from the kitchen staff. I lead the man back to the bar, tell the bartender to get rid of him as soon as the pasta is gone, and then make my way back through the dining room.

"She isn't the chef," says a deep voice at normal volume. "Chefs don't look like *that*."

I don't turn towards the table because I don't want to give them the satisfaction of knowing I heard them, of knowing they had any kind of power over me.

"Whatever she makes, it can't taste half as good as her muffin," another man says to raucous laughter.

I roll my eyes and speed up. I'm used to the comments and the cat calls. I've been dealing with it since I sprouted boobs. Even my father's men would whisper things about me. It is part of the reason I chose a path outside the scope of the family business. I couldn't imagine working with the kind of men my father employed. They were crass and mean and treated women like possessions. Unfortunately, the more I learn of the world beyond the Bratva, the more I realize men everywhere are like that. It is the reason I'll never get married. I won't belong to anyone.

I hear the men's deep voices as I walk back towards the kitchen, but I don't listen. I let the words roll off of me like water on a windowpane and step back into the safe chaos of the kitchen.

The kitchen seems to calm down as dinner service goes on, and I'm able to take a step back from micro-managing everything to work on an order of chicken tikka masala. While letting the tomato puree and spices simmer, I realize my stomach is growling. I was too nervous before shift to eat anything, and now that things have finally settled into an easy rhythm, my body is about to absorb itself. So, I casually walk over to where two giant stock pots are simmering with the starter soups for the day and scoop myself out a hearty ladle of lobster and bacon soup. Cal doesn't like for anyone to eat while on service, but he has been in his office all evening, and based on the smell slipping out from under his door, he will be far too stoned to notice or care.

The soup is warm and filling, and I close my eyes as I eat, enjoying the blissful moment of peace before more chaos ensues.

The kitchen door opens, and this time it really is Makayla. I wave her over, eager to see how everyone is enjoying the food and whether the drunk patriot finally left the restaurant, but she doesn't see me and walks with purpose through the kitchen and straight to Cal's office door. She opens it and steps inside, and I wonder what she needed Cal for and why she couldn't come to me. Lord knows I've handled every other situation that arose all night.

I'm just finished the last bite of my soup when Cal's office door slams open, bouncing off the wall, and he stomps his way across the kitchen.

"Eve!"

I shove the bowl to the back of the counter, throwing a dish towel over top to hide the evidence, and then wipe my mouth quickly.

"Yes, chef?"

"Front and center," he barks like we are in the military rather than a kitchen.

Despite the offense I take with his tone—especially after everything I've done to keep the place running all night—I move quickly to follow his order. Because that is what a good sous chef does. I follow the chef's orders, no matter how demeaning.

Cal Higgs is a large man in every sense of the word. He is tall, round, and thick. His head sits on top of his shoulders with no neck in sight, and just walking across the room looks like a chore. I imagine being in his body would be like wearing a winter coat and scarf all the time.

"What is the problem, Chef?"

He hitches a thumb over his shoulder, and Makayla gives me an apologetic wince. "Someone complained about the food, and they want to see the chef."

I wrinkled my forehead. I'd personally tasted every dish that went out. Unless Felix managed to slide another dish past me with raisins in it instead of prunes, I'm not sure what the complaint could be. "Was there something wrong with the dish or did they simply not like it?"

"Does it matter?" he snaps. His eyes are bloodshot and glassy, yet his temper is as sharp as ever. "I don't like unhappy customers, and you need to fix it."

"But you're the chef," I say, realizing too late I should have stayed quiet.

Cal steps forward, and I swear I can feel the floor quake under his weight. "But you made the food. Should I go out there and apologize on your behalf? No, this is your mess, and you will take care of it."

"Of course," I say, looking down at the ground. "You're right. I'll go out there and make this right."

Before Cal can find another reason to yell at me, I retie my apron around my waist, straighten my white jacket, and march through the swinging kitchen doors.

The dining room is quieter than before. The drunk man is no longer singing the National Anthem at the bar and several of the tables are empty, the bussers clearing away empty plates. Happy plates, I might add. Clearly, they didn't have an issue with the food.

I didn't ask Makayla who complained about the food, but as soon as I walk into the main dining area, it is obvious. There is a small gathering at the corner booth, and a salt and pepper-haired man in his late fifties or early sixties raising a hand in the air and waves me over without looking directly at me. I haven't even spoken to the man yet, and I already hate him.

I'm standing at their table, staring at the man, but he doesn't speak to me until I announce my presence.

"I heard someone wanted to speak with the chef," I say.

He turns to me, one eyebrow raised. "You are the chef?"

I recognize a Russian accent when I hear one, and this man is Russian without a doubt. I wonder if I know him. Or if my father does. Would he be complaining to me if he knew my father was head of the Furino family? I would never throw my family name around in order to scare people, but for just a second, I have the inclination.

"Sous chef," I say with as much confidence as I can muster. "I ran the kitchen tonight, so I'll be hearing the complaints."

His eyes move down my body slowly like he is inspecting a cut of meat in a butcher shop. I cross my arms over my chest and spread my feet hip-width apart. "So, was there an issue with the food? I'd love to correct any problems."

"Soup was cold." He nudges his empty bowl to the center of the table with three fingers. "The portions were too small, and I ordered my steak medium-rare, not raw."

Every plate on the table is empty. Not a single crumb in sight. Apparently, the issues were not bad enough he couldn't finish his meal.

"Do you have any of the steak left?" I ask, making a show of looking around the table. "If one of my cooks undercooked the meat, I'd like to be able to inform them."

"If? I just told you the meet was undercooked. Are you doubting me?"

"Of course not," I say. *Yes, absolutely I am.* "It is just that if the meat was undercooked, I do not understand why you waited until you'd eaten everything to inform me of the problem?"

The man looks around the table at his companions. They are all smiling, and I can practically see them sharpening their teeth, preparing to rip me to shreds. When he turns back to me, his smile is acidic, deadly. "How did you get this position—sous chef? Surely not by skill. You are pretty, which I'm sure did you a favor. Did you sleep with the chef? Maybe—" he moves his hand in an obscene gesture —"'service' the boss to earn your place in the kitchen? Surely your 'talent' didn't get you the job, seeing as how you have none."

I physically bite my tongue and then take a deep breath. "If you'd like me to remake anything for you or bring out a complimentary dessert, I'm happy to do that. If not, I apologize for the issues and hope you will not hold it against us. We'd love to have you again."

Lies. Lies. Lies. I'm smiling and being friendly the way I was taught in culinary school. I actually took a class on dealing with customers, and this man is being even more outrageous than the overexaggerated angry customer played by my professor.

"Why would I want more food from you if the things you already sent out were terrible?" He snorts and shakes his head. "I see you do not have a ring on. That is no surprise. Men like a woman who can cook. Men don't care if you know your way around a professional kitchen if you don't know your way around a dinner plate."

The older gentleman is speaking, but I hear my father's words in my head. *You do not need to go to culinary school to find a husband, Eve. Your aunties can teach you to cook good food for your man.*

My entire life has been preparation for finding a husband. The validity of every hobby is judged by whether it will fetch me a suitor or not. My father wants me to be happy, but he mostly wants me to be married. Single, I'm a disappointment. Married, I'm a vessel for future Furino mafia members.

Years of anger and resentment begin to bubble and hiss inside of me until I'm boiling. My hands are shaking, and I can feel adrenaline pulsing through me, lighting every inch of me on fire. This time, I don't bite my tongue.

"I'd rather die alone than spent another minute near a man like you," I spit, stepping forward and laying my palms flat on the table. "The fact that you ate all of the food you apparently hated shows you are a pig in more ways than one."

In the back of my mind, I recognize that my voice is echoing around the restaurant and the chatter in the rest of the room has gone quiet, but blood is whirring in my ears, and I can't stop. I've stayed quiet and docile for too long. Now, it is my turn to speak my mind.

"You and your friends may be wealthy and respected, but I see you for what you are—spineless, cowardly assholes who are so insecure they have to take their rage out on everybody else."

I want to spin on my heel and storm away, making a grand exit, but in classic Eve fashion, my heel catches on the tablecloth, and I nearly trip. I fall sideways and throw an arm out to catch myself, knocking a nearly full bottle of wine on the table over. The glass shatters and red wine splashes across the tablecloth and onto the guests in the booth like a river of blood.

I pause long enough to note the old Russian man's shirt is splattered like he has been shot before I continue my exit and head straight for the doors.

I suck in the night air. The evening is warm and humid, summer strangling the city in its hold, and I want to rip off my clothes for some relief. I feel like I'm being strangled. Like there is a hand around my neck, squeezing the life out of me.

Breathing in and out slowly helps, but as the physical panic begins to ebb away, emotional panic flows in.

What have I done? Cal Higgs is going to find out about the altercation any minute, and then what? Will he fire me? And if he does, will I ever be able to get another chef position? I was only offered this position because of my father, and I doubt he will help me earn another kitchen position, especially since I'm no closer to finding a boyfriend (or husband) since I left for culinary school.

Despite it all, I want to call my dad. He has always made it clear he will move heaven and earth to take care of me, to make sure no one is mean to me, and I want his support right now. But the support he offered me when a girl tripped me during soccer practice and made me miss the net won't apply here. He will tell me to come home. To put down my apron and knife and focus on more meaningful pursuits. And that is the last thing I want to hear right now.

I pull out my phone and scroll through my contacts list, hoping to see a spark of hope amidst the names, but there is nothing. I've lost touch with everyone since I started culinary school. There hasn't been time for friends.

This is probably the kind of situation where most girls would turn to their moms, but she hasn't been in the picture since I was six years old. Even if I had her number, I wouldn't call her. Dad hasn't always been perfect, but at least he was there. At least he cared enough to stay.

I untie my apron and pull it over my head, leaning back against the brick side of the restaurant.

"Take it off, baby!"

I look up and see a man on a motorcycle with his hair in a bun parked along the curb. He is waggling his eyebrows at me like I'm supposed to fall in love with him for harassing me on the street, and the fire that filled my veins inside hasn't died out yet. The embers are still there, burning under the skin, and I step towards him, lips pulled back in a smile.

He looks surprised, and I'm sure he is. That move has probably never worked for him before. He smiles back at me, his tongue darting out to lick his lower lip.

"Is that your bike?" I purr.

He nods. "Want a ride?"

My voice is still sticky sweet as I respond, "So sweet of you to offer. I'd rather choke and die on that grease ball you call a man bun, but thanks anyway, hon."

It takes him a second to realize my words don't match the tone. When it hits him, he snarls, "Bitch."

"Asshole." I flip him the bird over my shoulder and start the long walk home.

***Click here*** *to keep reading BROKEN VOWS.*

# MAILING LIST

Sign up to my mailing list!
New subscribers receive a FREE steamy bad boy romance novel.

**Click the link below to join.**
https://readerlinks.com/l/1057996

## ALSO BY NICOLE FOX

**De Maggio Mafia Duet**

Devil in a Suit (Book 1)

Devil at the Altar (Book 2)

**Kornilov Bratva Duet**

Married to the Don (Book 1)

Til Death Do Us Part (Book 2)

**Volkov Bratva**

Broken Vows (Book 1)

Broken Hope (Book 2)

Broken Sins *(standalone)*

**Heirs to the Bratva Empire**

**Can be read in any order*

Kostya

Maksim

Andrei

**Tsezar Bratva**

Nightfall (Book 1)

Daybreak (Book 2)

**Russian Crime Brotherhood**

**Can be read in any order*

Owned by the Mob Boss

Unprotected with the Mob Boss

Knocked Up by the Mob Boss

Sold to the Mob Boss

Stolen by the Mob Boss

Trapped with the Mob Boss

**Other Standalones**

Vin: A Mafia Romance

**Box Sets**

Bratva Mob Bosses (Russian Crime Brotherhood Books 1-6)

Tsezar Bratva (Tsezar Bratva Duet Books 1-2)

Printed in Great Britain
by Amazon

22786687R00165